Two to Tango

NATALIA WILLIAMS

ISBN: 979-8-9887512-2-9 (ebook)

ISBN: 979-8-9887512-3-6 (print)

Book Cover by Lucy Murphy, Cover Ever After

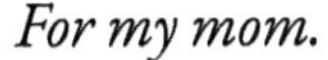

For my mom.

Also by Natalia Williams

Taking the Cake

Two to Tango

NATALIA WILLIAMS

Author's Note

When I set out to write this book, I wanted to share bits of my culture and my experiences as an immigrant kid. But these experiences are not one size fits all. Each journey is different, each childhood tells a different story, and Julieta's story is just one of many.

This dives into the pressures and struggles of being raised in a new country. Especially by immigrant parents that are trying to make sure their children don't lose their culture, while coming to terms with everything else they're losing. This story features discussions of immigration. There is Spanish dialogue, and I hope I have provided enough context clues for you to understand the conversation. This story also involves the passing of a beloved grandmother and subsequent themes of grief.

Thank you for reading.

Prologue

JULIETA

WHEN I WAS EIGHT years old, I got to watch my grandmother compete for the first time. She had traveled to the States for a tango competition —one that was local to us—and I sat there completely captivated.

Everybody will tell you that Celestina Rossi was captivating when she danced. That was the word. When she walked out onto that stage everybody knew they were in the presence of somebody great.

My mother insisted that we were all going to go see her. We got dressed up, and it felt like a rare special event. I got to wear my new outfit and lace-up canvas shoes. My brother was bored, of course, but he was only five.

I couldn't help but fall completely in love with what I was watching. It was like she glided on air. Her moves were swift but purposeful. She was strong but delicate.

Strong legs, graceful arms. Powerful, mesmerizing and so glamorous.

Her lips were painted a deep wine red —her signature—and she wore a dress that swayed every time she moved, almost as if it was dancing with her, trying to keep up. Facundo, my grandfather and her longtime dance partner, danced with her, too, leading her gracefully.

I watched them take perfect steps across the floor. I sat silently watching their bodies entwined as they moved forward and back, from one end of the dance floor to the other. She danced like she loved: with abandon, with passion, with feeling.

From the corner of my eye, I caught my mother looking at me curiously, but I was too hypnotized to look away. I felt frozen, trapped in the beauty of what I was witnessing, completely succumbed to the music.

And in that moment, at that table, in a tango championship watching my grandmother dance a beautiful dance, I thought, *I want to be her when I grow up.*

But I was eight. What did I know anyway?

I grew up to be a lawyer instead.

Chapter One
Julieta

"Yes, I'll get started on that first thing."

I haven't taken more than ten steps into the building before Barbara Prescott, my boss at Prescott and Associates, throws demands my way. She's in her office, huddled over her desk, elbow deep in paperwork already.

"I'm also going to need those appellate briefs, plus the summary judgment motion for the Warner case," she says in her no-nonsense tone.

I add it to my mental to-do list, walking briskly to my office.

"Morning, Jim," I call out as I pass by Jim Haskell's office, senior associate at the firm, his door wide open.

"Morning, Julie."

My office is towards the back of the building, the one where the air conditioner doesn't quite reach some days. The one where I can at least do my work in peace.

The stark white walls keep in theme with how I've managed to decorate. Functional and efficient and just enough of *something* to give this room a little indication that it's mine. A couple of family pictures, a plant that my mother gave me that I've had to research to learn the best watering practices, a stock framed photo I found at TJMaxx once. Not like, say, Larissa's with a bowl of candy and big vases with flowers and a bright painting and pictures of her sisters. Figurines and little knickknacks and an abundance of joy.

Larissa Post, paralegal at the firm, comes in shortly after. "Morning," she calls out. Her vibrant curls match the vibrant office she's so perfectly curated. Tight, gorgeous ringlets in a lush strawberry blonde.

"Hey, Larissa," I say from behind my desk. "How's it going?"

"Had a shit date," she replies, dejected. "How are you?"

"Oh no. Again?" I boot up my computer as we chat.

"It's fucking brutal out there. No wonder you don't want to date."

"Who said I don't want to date?" I brush my long brown hair off my shoulder.

"Oh, please." She laughs.

"So, who was this date with again?"

"Paul, the dentist?"

"Oh right." I nod. "The one with the cute dog."

"Maybe that's my problem. I need to stop swiping right on guys with cute dogs. I want to befriend the dog, not them."

"Maybe you just need to get a dog?"

"With these ridiculous hours I work? I couldn't do that to a pet. But if there were two of us..." she sighs. "It's rough out there is all I'm saying."

"I believe it. And you're right, our work doesn't help. Speaking of, Barbara is going to have my ass if I don't get these briefs to her, so I'll talk to you later."

"Need any help with it?" she offers.

"No, I've got it."

"Alright." She waves and leaves me to my work.

My office line rings shortly after. "Julie," I answer quickly.

"Hey, Julie." It's Jim again. "I've got a prospective client in need of translation on line two. Can you take it?"

"Of course." I answer and switch over to line two. "Julieta Martí."

"Buenos días, Señora Martí. Busco un abogado."

Larissa usually fields these calls, but since I'm the Spanish speaker, I'm handling this one. As the man on the line starts speaking, stating his case, I write down the information quickly. We discuss details and I ask questions as we chat.

When I first applied to law firms fresh out of law school, they were always taken aback by my background and the fact that I could speak Spanish.

"You don't even look Hispanic!" they would proclaim.

"Where are you from?" they would pry, as if perhaps they didn't believe me.

I was born in Argentina, I would tell them. I moved here with my family when I was five and was practically raised here.

"Oh, Argentina," they would brush off, with a tone that seemed to mean, "So, you don't *really* fit into the Hispanic stereotype society has mapped out. So, you don't check the boxes."

It was a rough road when we moved here, a jump in the dark that my family took to get a better life. All of them wanted the promise of a country where they could raise their children, find work, and get better pay.

But this country, with its space for opportunity and a better life, can be so unforgiving.

My parents did everything they could for my younger brother and me and in return, I made it my goal to make sure their sacrifices weren't in vain. It was drilled in me to go to college. Get a degree. Get a good job. Make good money. Buy a house. Lay a foundation down for a solid life. Go through all the steps and go through them properly. Follow the path and do so with pride. We were given this chance, and we should remember to be grateful.

So, I went to college, and I went to law school, and I got a good job. I bought a condo, which was close enough. I went down the checklist fervently. I am successful—at least in their eyes.

I finish the conversation with the man on the line, Ramón Lorenzo, looking for a lawyer to take on his worker's comp case, and head to the break room for my second coffee of the day.

The coffee area is a mess. Empty sugar packets and stirrers are littered about the counter. The creamer wasn't put back in the fridge. I clean up as I go, throwing away the garbage and organizing the contents of the fridge, muttering to myself, *Why can't anybody clean up after themselves?*

I walk back to my office briskly, mug in hand, and sit back down to work on more cases.

***

"Hey, Julie. I set up your appointment for tomorrow morning at nine." Larissa's voice breaks me from my work as I'm typing away at the computer.

"Great. Thank you."

"Lunch in a minute?"

I look at the time. "Yeah, sounds good." I step away from my desk to stretch my arms out and grab my lunch bag before we walk outside together.

Our two-story building backs up to a small pond with lush green grass surrounding it. Somebody had the foresight to put some picnic tables around it, and Larissa and I have taken to eating lunch out here whenever the time and weather allow. Right now, we're still dealing with end of summer heat that precedes rainy evenings brought on by hurricane season. A deceptively long stretch that lasts through summer into November.

"So, Paul showed up twenty minutes late," Larissa tells me as she unpacks her lunch, huffing in annoyance. She leans in like she's bursting at the seams, her curls bouncing in tandem, ready to vent to anybody about this awful date. "He told me as he sat down that he's not a big fan of tacos. Tacos! He kept getting annoyed that I was asking about his dog, and then he ended the night by talking about how gummies ruin your teeth. I *know* they ruin my teeth. I don't need you to be holier than thou right now, Paul."

"He sounds terrible."

"Terrible," she agrees.

Larissa is my age, near mid-thirties and constantly dating. She's highly sociable and friendly, and while I've always appreciated her work ethic, I've never been comfortable enough to get closer than colleagues. But sometimes I wonder if I should just try.

She sighs, stabbing at her salad. "This job is taking up too much of my time. There is no work-life balance here, you know?"

"Yeah. That's law for you." I shrug. "By the way, I need motions filed for the Hernandez case," I add, bringing the attention back to work.

"Of course." She nods, as if she understands that she's veered the conversation elsewhere. "You've got an appointment set up tomorrow at eleven."

"Did you figure out that issue with your password?"

"Yes, I did."

"Perfect. Thank you." I look at my watch, then take another bite of my own lunch in silence.

"Doing anything fun tonight?" she asks.

I huff out a laugh. "No. I'll probably be here late tonight."

She sighs again, "We are mercilessly bound to this job, to our paychecks. To the hope that we're helping somebody. But are we really at the end of the day?"

I don't expect perpetually happy Larissa to feel this way. Maybe she's having a hard day. Maybe her date with Paul the dentist took it out of her.

Or maybe, more realistically, she's right.

We work in employment law. I got into it for the hope of helping others, too. But it's become long hours and high emotions and a shitty boss to deal with.

"It's a tough job, that's for sure," I agree. "Is there anything you need?" I can carry this weight for her if I need to.

"I don't know." She shakes her head and smiles weakly. "I'm okay."

And with that, we finish up our lunch and stand to get back to work. The walk inside is quiet, but Larissa and I both turn our game faces on, ready to get on with the day. And I make it a point to take on more of the workload to give her a break.

I power off and head to the door sometime close to eight, blindly walking to my car and getting in. At this time, the rush hour traffic has died down. A perk of working so late, I guess.

By the time I'm at my apartment, parking in my designated spot, I realize that I don't know how I even got here. Well, yes, I know I drove here. But *really* how I got here. Because I got in my car, and the next thing I knew, I couldn't remember anything—my walk, my drive. I'd been too busy, too zoned out. Probably staring at my phone at red lights. Following up with more emails, texts. A constant loop of constant communication. Of somebody needing something, or somebody else demanding my attention, and me, willing to give it. All of my time, all of my energy. Scrolling from the morning I wake up, answering early phone calls and messages, right up until I close my eyes, letting the blue light accompany me to sleep. My phone sits on my nightstand right next to me every night, within arm's reach, easy to access. I'm ready to respond to anybody at any time.

Larissa had a point when she said there is no work-life balance. But some days I wonder why I would need it when I aim to fit my life around my job instead of the other way around.

I walk into my building and pass by the nighttime security at the desk, scrolling on his phone barely giving me a glance. He looks relatively young, always working the night shift, always bored.

I hop into the elevator and take it up to the seventh floor. I bought this place for its proximity to work, a quiet building in midtown that is a comfortable distance from the rest of my family.

Once home, I kick off my shoes, jump in for a shower, and step into comfortable pajamas. I grab a handful of nuts for a snack, having already eaten a quick dinner at the office. I bring my case folders to my bed, my phone nearby. And I go over notes and pieces of information, working on yet another checklist for the following day.

I brush my teeth, I wash my face, I apply my nighttime skin creams. This, too, is a checklist. One that I go down every night. One that I can follow with my eyes closed.

I make lists and I cross them off and I wake up and I work and I come home and I work and I follow every list like a robot.

And then I wake up and do it all again.

Is this the successful life my parents wished for me? Some days I can't help but wonder.

CHAPTER TWO

Julieta

"Hola," I call out, walking right into the house without knocking. I'm right on time for our weekly Sunday family dinner.

My brother, Dario, is already on the couch, channel surfing. I lean down to give him a kiss on the cheek in greeting.

The walls I walk by are covered with Argentinian relics and family photos in mismatched frames. I make it to the kitchen where I find my mom battling trays of empanadas. She fills a dough round, folds it over, and expertly twists the ends into a decorative shape, the kind I could never figure out how to do.

"Hola, ma," I say, peeking into the pot of empanada filling dreamily. My cousin Agostina bursts in shortly after me, calling out, "Hola!"

When she makes her way to the kitchen, she doesn't think twice as she grabs a spoon from the drawer, digs right into the pot, and stuffs her mouth full of the meat and olive mixture.

"Agostina!" my mom cries out.

I try to hide my laugh on the walk back into the living room. "She's going to ban you from eating empanadas," I tell her over my shoulder.

Agostina loves to eat the filling right out of the pan every time my mom makes it, not that I can blame her. Always little spoonfuls that don't really make a dent in the amount. At least, it never appears that way. But those spoonfuls add up. One time, she ate so much of it there was one dough round left, but no more filling for it. My mom was so upset, she didn't stop talking about it for six months.

"No, she won't," she responds, matter of fact.

She's probably right. My mother loves to feed her family, finds immense joy in it, no matter how pissed she is at them.

I'm about to sit down on the couch next to my brother when my mom calls me back into the kitchen to help. My other cousin Delfina is already in there dressing thickly sliced tomatoes with olive oil, salt, and dried oregano.

"Hey," I greet her.

"Hey, what's up?" She answers without looking up, her light brown hair pulled back in a ponytail.

Soon enough, the house is bursting with sound from my aunts getting everything ready for dinner. Tía Silvia is throwing a tablecloth over the dining table, tía Ana is in the corner of the kitchen pouring glasses of red wine, and tía Cecilia, back home after a quick trip to Argentina, is talking loudly over soft music playing in the background.

My dad was outside tending to the asado, but he steps in quickly to grab a couple of beers.

"Hola, pa."

He kisses my cheek, the smell of smoke and charred meats lingering as he greets me, and then heads back out just as fast.

Grabbing the silverware, I decide to head to the dining room. I start setting the table quietly, enjoying the ritual in this warm, loving home. The table gets pieced together with mismatched chairs, the leaf extended to fit all of us. The center is adorned with wine glasses, a bowl of baguette slices, and the tomatoes that Delfina has just set down.

This house is lived in and loved in. It's not new, built in 1960. I've always loved that fact though. This house was built the same year my mother was born. I love to think that when she came into this world in one country, bricks were being laid in another. A foundation was being set for a place that she would—in thirty-six years' time—call her own.

I remember when we immigrated to the States when I was little. My mother and father came first, accompanying my grandparents to a competition they were attending. My parents fell in love with it here, and started daydreaming about all of the possibilities for them, for the family. A whimsical, elaborate daydream that took flight when my father decided, almost too quickly, that he wanted to move. It involved a lot of conversations, weighing the risks, and then, once it was decided, we packed our belongings into large luggage and made the trek to a new world.

My father Julio, along with my mother Maria, and Dario—who was almost three at the time—moved to build a new life in a new place with a new language. I often wonder how they did it. How they got the courage to uproot their lives, everything that they had ever known, and move it to the unknown. They were filled with hope and bravery, the kind I can only dream about.

The rest of the family soon followed. My tía Ana—my mother's sister—and her husband Fernando packed up and moved with Agostina and her older brother Leo. My tío Luis, his wife Silvia, and Delfina joined us after that. And then my tía Cecilia came over last.

Maybe having all of us together helped the process. My cousins and I grew up together and learned to navigate this new country, learning the language and the customs together, too. We've all been close since birth.

And even as we've all grown up and fallen into our adult lives, one thing still stands, and that is Sunday night family dinner. Always hosted by my mom, who cooks enough to feed fifty, and sends us all home with a mountain of leftovers.

Dario, Leo, and my uncles walk into the dining room, ready to feast now that most of the work has been handled.

"Che, y las empanadas?" Dario asks, eyeing the dishes on the table.

"Ya vienen," my mom responds sternly from the kitchen. As if she always needs to remind him to be patient.

I love this ritual almost as much as I love my family. As much as I love my culture. And I do love it. It's a deep-seated love that I still struggle to figure out. My family likes to joke that I've become too Americanized. "She's an American now," they tease. "She's forgotten where she came from."

I haven't, but it's been a hard balance. I don't dare tell them that it's a struggle most days, though. A struggle of being born into one culture and being raised in another. A push and a pull, a divide over which direction to go in. Over how to split myself up to make it work out for everybody. My job needs me to be American with the commodity of being able to translate. My family wants me to be Argentinian with a successful, American job.

I can't tell them how tiring it's become. I could never.

Meanwhile, I meet once a month with a Latina networking group run by loud and proud Yuli, a Cuban woman who loves her heritage so much, she embraces it bravely. I, in turn, always feel out of place. Too Hispanic for some, not Hispanic enough for others.

Maybe it was growing up in a country that just wanted me out. So, I hid myself instead of being proud. I hid myself so that nobody could ask too many questions or pry too much. Instead of leaning into my culture, showing others who I was, I felt ashamed.

As older cousins, Leo and I took on a lot of the high emotions that came with the move and the immigration hardship. The others were too young to realize or understand it. They didn't have to deal with the worry and the struggle. Instead, they had the luxury of being free of it and just getting to be kids.

Delfina and Agostina watched telenovelas well into middle school. Leo and I got into American music by watching MTV. We spoke Spanish when we needed to, but rarely conversationally outside of our families. And we never cared for mate, the drink that's a staple in Argentinian culture.

And even though Leo was the oldest, I was the girl, and so much more was expected of me. Leo really got out. He went away to college then opted to move to a city over an hour away. I could never dream of doing that. The condo I bought, with my family's approval, was loved more so because of its location than any other reason.

"Julieta, mi amor, cómo estás?"

The greeting pulls me out of a stupor. We've got a special guest at dinner tonight.

"Hola abuelo." I give him my biggest smile.

Facundo Rossi is a soft-spoken man. Kind brown eyes, neatly brushed thin hair, and a genuine smile that always feels like a warm hug. He hugs me now when he sees me, giving me kisses on both cheeks.

My grandparents didn't make the move with us, opting to stay in their home country with their friends and their lives. They traveled a lot for shows, but I know my grandmother loved the feeling of going back to Argentina once the competitions were done. Going back to her community, her neighborhood, her home.

They would visit occasionally, and we took some trips to see them, but we all built our respective lives where we were. My mother made new friends, a group of women from church, and found her and Ana jobs working in a factory to make home furnishings: curtains, pillows, upholstery. My father became a custodian and handyman in a large apartment building.

My parents built this incredible life for us out of nothing, and I can't look at that and not want to be my best self. It's a crippling need to be successful for them, my immigrant parents that sacrificed so much for us.

"Bueno, a comer," my mother states, waiting for everybody else to sit down before she can get comfortable. My father and tío Luis are already digging in, filling up their plates while my mother encourages them to eat. The spread on the table is a gorgeous display of celebration. There is a tray of grilled steaks and sausages, those glistening, bright red tomatoes, the baguettes. There is a platter of my mother's practically famous empanadas, and glasses of red wine—some with ice cubes floating in them. And there's my loud, loving family surrounding the table.

"Y Diego cómo está?" tía Cecilia asks Agostina in reference to a guy she dated for all of five minutes.

"I thought it was Brett," Delfina says, filling up her plate, recalling another guy she dated.

"First of all, I would never date somebody named Brett. I have some standards."

Tía Ana just huffs in response to this. "When are you going to get serious, Agostina?"

"Déjala," Cecilia chides. Let her be. Let her have her fun.

Tía Ana just stares at Cecilia, something probably meant to intimidate. Shit, it's working on me. I make it a point to just keep my head down so I don't have to deal with her wrath, but Cecilia just laughs it off.

"Qué ganas de joder tenes," she says, in a teasing tone that clearly states *you're in the mood to be a pain in the ass.*

Agostina just keeps filling up a plate, not bothering to respond to any of it.

Cecilia has been on our side since we were born, but she was really a help when we were boisterous, curious teenagers.

When I was in the fifth grade, we had sex ed. We learned about periods and body parts and were shown too many pictures of STIs. My mother was appalled.

My Catholic upbringing was one where sex was never discussed. Periods were barely discussed. I was, in turn, terrified of boys and dating, not knowing what to even do. There were no open conversations. Sex was shameful. Cecilia allowed us to come to her with questions, welcoming every out of the box topic, and answered them in earnest while hiding it from our parents to our request. Delfina and I would spend nights reveling in the shit Agostina would get into, the mess of boys she would get involved with. Instead of retreating because she didn't have the answers, she went barreling headfirst into it anyway. Because she wanted it, because she wanted to. And Delfina … well, she romanticized everyone. And I just focused on my studies, too nervous around boys as it was, not even allowed to date until I was seventeen.

And tía Cecilia is no stranger to dating either. She's brought plenty of her own dates to these dinners and holidays. She dated a painter once, a beautiful woman with long red curls and gorgeous porcelain skin. I was always fascinated by her, by how they both talked about art and life. How they both seemed so otherworldly. But when that ended, she decided she needed some stability and routine in her life— *not the whimsy of an artist!* she'd said. So, she dated a tax accountant, and Mitchell was fine. I liked him, he was nice enough. But he gifted her a planner for her birthday once. And let me tell you what Cecilia doesn't like: planning and somebody telling her she needs to plan. So, she kicked him to the curb, too. These days she says she's dating herself. But I see a lot of Agostina in her. I think Cecilia does too, which is probably why she's always going up to bat for her.

That, and her and Ana don't always get along. Sisters, I guess.

"We're still waiting for Julieta to find somebody, too," my mom chimes in. From anyone else, this might seem insulting, but it's just par for the course from my family.

"How's work?" Cecilia asks me instead.

"Busy."

"Yeah? You look a little tired."

I *am* tired. A bone-deep exhaustion that I can't shake. The words from Larissa pop into my head again, unwelcome.

"She works so hard," my mom says. "But what a wonderful job she has. And how great it is to have work, especially in these times. Gracias a Dios." I know she's proud of me and all the work I've put into my career, but right now, with my grandfather present at dinner, it feels more like an act.

"Mi hija abogada," she says to the table, showing me off. She looks like she might cry. My mother has always been proud of my success as a lawyer, and she has always made sure to let me know just how happy it makes her.

"Si," I nod. "I am lucky to have this job." It's true, and I am very grateful.

"That doesn't change the fact that she's tired," Agostina adds in, speaking to my mother.

"Ya sé, Agostina," my mom responds, eyeing her. She turns to me. "Come más, Julieta."

She adds more steak to my plate, even though I didn't want it, and the conversation continues.

An hour later, most of us have finished eating, and dinner is starting to wind down. We're still sitting around the table, talking, when mother brings over a box of alfajores that abuelo brought for us.

Tío Luis grabs one first, unwrapping the gold foil wrapper and biting into the cookies sandwiched with dulce de leche, enrobed in chocolate. I reach over to grab one, but my abuelo calls me over instead. I notice he's holding a box as I walk to him and sit down.

"I was cleaning some things out last month and I found this," he starts. "I didn't even know it was in the closet, and I feel terrible that I found it so late, but I'm glad I can deliver it to you in person."

"This is for me?" I ask.

He gently places the box on my lap, nodding.

I glance around the room at everybody who has stopped conversations to look over at us.

It's a shoebox, still in good condition, with minor bends on the corners. Even though that should tip me off, it still comes as a shock when I take off the lid and come face to face with the contents.

"Holy shit," I hear Delfi whisper.

Agostina gasps. "No fucking way."

My mother places a hand over her mouth, while tía Cecilia just sits there smiling wide.

In the box, perfectly worn and loved, are my grandmother's dancing shoes.

"No entiendo," I furrow my brow, looking up at my abuelo.

"La tarjeta." He points, signaling to a note tucked on the side.

I open it up to find my grandmother's delicate loopy script on white sturdy stationery: *Para Julieta.*

"She left these for me? I still don't understand."

"Oh my God, this makes so much sense," I hear Delfi mutter to Agostina.

My mother's pursed lips are speaking volumes right now and my father has taken to eating another alfajor, unaware of the emotional turmoil about to erupt inside of me.

My grandmother passed away two years ago, a long road of health struggles coupled with old age. I still remember the phone call from my mother: early morning, I almost ignored it thinking it was Barbara calling. I spent the next week tending to everything, making arrangements, making space for whatever anybody needed. I don't even think I slept.

Why would she leave me her shoes? Me, of all people? Agostina would make better use of these. She does everything. Even Delfi, ever the romantic, would love them and give them a happy home. But me? They're just going to continue to collect dust in a closet.

And yet, I'm clutching them close to me. I couldn't bear to give them away to anybody else. Not now, probably not ever.

"Gracias, abuelo," I whisper and feel the sudden urge to cry.

I excuse myself to the bathroom to get it together.

I hear the murmurs as I walk out of the dining room and into the guest bathroom. My mother asks *what was that all about* and Agostina answers back just as abrasively, *you know exactly what*. All I can do is splash water on my face and take a deep breath to hold back the tears. To hold back the nausea. To help calm the nerves that are causing my hands to shake.

I head back to the dining room, all eyes on me as I settle into my seat. The box of alfajores sits in the middle of the table, but now I'm too uneasy to even eat one.

"Bueno." My mother sighs, defeated, as she stands up to start packing leftovers for everybody to take home.

Delfi and Agostina start to busy themselves, clearing the table. The men sit and chat with my grandfather, loudly, vivaciously. Not a care in the world. I stand to help, still uneasy, still confused.

We clean up the dining room and the kitchen, leaving everything as clean as we found it. This is part of dinner, too—always chipping in to help. My mother hands me a plastic grocery bag filled with containers of leftovers. I stuff an alfajor inside, and Cecilia throws in an extra one, giving me a wink.

"Chau," I say, giving her a kiss on the cheek. I make my rounds to say goodbye to everybody else. My brother and other cousins are starting to pack up as well. I make sure to grab my purse, leftovers, and the box, avoiding too much eye contact, desperately sidestepping the elephant in the room.

And when I walk out to my car, *I* feel strangely defeated. I think about the new weight that has settled onto my shoulders, the cross I'm bearing in these hand-me-down shoes, and I can't help but think that something heavy has just been added to my never-ending to-do list.

Chapter Three

Logan

THE AIRPORT IS SURPRISINGLY busy at this time of night as Tara and I walk down to baggage claim in silence. We're both tired from the weekend, and the long flight that included an even longer layover, even if we couldn't beat the price.

We spent the weekend in San Francisco at an intensive tango workshop teaching basics, fundamentals, advanced steps, and even hosting a milonga for the final night. It was a good time, as it always is, but my feet are tired and I'm sore.

"So, that was it," I say.

"That was it," Tara agrees.

Before we booked this weekend, we decided it would be our last workshop together. Silas, Tara's long-term boyfriend who's been crawling his way through medical school, is awaiting match results that will either keep him here or take them both to another state. Tara and I chose to keep teaching our local classes until that news came, but as for travel and competitions, we're done.

Our bags come down the conveyor and we grab them before walking outside to the curb.

"God, I was just getting used to that gorgeous San Francisco weather," she says. "This humidity sucks."

We're back home in Florida, greeted with humidity in late August.

"Didn't Silas sign up for Arizona?"

"It's dry!"

"I'll get a car," I say, laughing.

Her long sigh could be mistaken for exhaustion, compounded from a long travel day, but her shuffling feet as we stand on the curb are saying otherwise.

"You okay?" I ask.

"I'm tired."

I should probably go to bed, but all the travel has just left me wired and restless and hungry. I don't want to go home just yet. "Want to go to Waffle House?"

She gives me a small smile.

"Come on." I jerk my head in the direction of the car that's just pulled up. "Let me buy you some hash browns."

"I could go for a waffle," she reasons.

Our luggage gets thrown into the trunk and we hop in, setting our sights on those bright yellow lights.

***

My hash browns are piled onto my plate, a mess of smothered, covered, and chunked. Tara is picking at a waffle.

She clears her throat. "So."

"So. Something's up," I say playfully.

"Silas matched."

My eyes meet hers. Silas didn't know where he was going to match, and he was worried about uprooting his and Tara's life. But she's been the positive support in his corner, ready to jump into whatever adventure is next for the two of them. We knew there would be a change, but it's a much different animal when it's happening in real time. When I'm halfway through bitter coffee and a plate of greasy hash browns awaiting news.

"Where?" I almost don't want to ask.

"Arizona," she mutters.

"You did sound defensive," I joke. "That's great, Tara." I give a smile, but it might look forced. My hand shakes a little as I drink my coffee. Caffeine was a bad idea this late at night. "When?"

She takes a breath. "Twelve weeks."

"Shit."

"I know, I know." She winces. "I found out over the weekend, but I didn't want to tell you until we got back home."

I don't know what else to say. Why does this feel like a breakup? Not that Tara and I ever dated, but our partnership has spanned six years. We've always kept things professional between us, but she's also my closest friend.

"So, what happens now?" I ask.

She looks down at her cup. "Gonna finish up my master's."

"That's awesome." My smile isn't forced this time. I'm genuinely excited for this new chapter of her life.

She shrugs, taking another bite of waffle.

"Knock it off. This is great news."

"I know," she murmurs.

"Are you sad about leaving?"

"Of course, I am." She doesn't look at me when she says it.

"But?"

"But I think it's time."

I just nod and let out a deep, almost achy, breath. "I might be getting there," I tell her, putting words to a strange feeling I've been harboring.

"Don't say that," she argues, her eyes sad.

"Why not?"

"I don't know," she sighs. "I don't want you to abandon dancing."

"Like you're abandoning me?" I joke.

She pins me with a look and purses her lips to keep from laughing. I give her a smile in return. I'm mostly just fucking with her at this point. She knows that, but it doesn't change the fact that her news is almost setting me adrift into one big, unsure ocean.

"I feel like a giant asshole for doing this," she laments. "I know that it sucks on your end, but I want you to keep going."

"Don't feel like an asshole," I assure her. "We knew this move was happening."

She reaches over to grab a scoop of my hash browns instead of responding.

"Maybe it's time for me, too, Tara. Maybe this has just run its course. Look at what happened last year." Our last competition was a year ago, and it was a mess.

"Maybe this move will be good for both of us, then. Maybe what you're feeling isn't you, it's me." She looks down at her empty mug, twirling it back and forth. "I haven't been giving it my all lately."

"Neither have I."

Tara's got a plan; she's getting out of this now. She gets to start a new life, but in the process, she's leaving her old one behind.

"Maybe I need a new life, too," I argue.

"No, you don't." She shakes her head.

"I don't know," I shrug. "I'm just feeling disconnected with it, I guess."

We've fostered a wonderful, thriving community here. We've made friends, taught a large number of classes. But it just hasn't been as fulfilling lately. It stopped being fulfilling a couple of competitions ago. And it was clear after the last one that I was done.

Tara watches me as she chews, a concerned look in her eyes.

"I'm alright," I tell her. I just need a nap and a day to reset. I finish up my coffee. "Give me a couple of days. I'll get over my shit."

"I don't need you to get over your shit."

I look at the time, now well past two in the morning. "I think I need to sleep now."

"Same." She sits up straight and lifts her coffee cup. "Here's to the next twelve weeks."

I tap it with mine. "Let's go out with a bang."

What am I going to do? What is my plan? I never thought too much about it, but lately it's all I've been privy to. I've been doing this for twenty years. When I discovered professional dance, it saved me. But lately, so much of it has felt like drowning. Like taking step after step to nowhere. What else is there after this? And what happens when it doesn't give me the same feeling it did when I was a kid? Or when I was on top of the world? What happens if it doesn't fill my cup like it did? What then?

"Hey." She breaks me out of my thoughts. "You'll fig-ure it out. You always do."

But this time I'm wondering if I really will. I don't tell Tara any of this though. I just hug her goodbye and head home to my bed.

When I get home, my older brother Gavin is sprawled

on the couch, remote in hand, flipping through Netflix, watching absolutely nothing.

"What are you still doing up?" I ask.

There's a box of pizza on the coffee table, the pie mostly eaten. A bunch of empty Dr. Pepper cans are littered around it.

"And what the hell happened here while I was away?" I look around, inspecting the mess.

"Got laid off," he answers.

"What?" I must not have heard that correctly.

"I got laid off," he says a little louder, a bit firmer.

"Shit, for real?"

"Yep." More remote clicking.

"Why?"

"Company layoffs. Downsizing. Severance package. Blah blah, all that shit."

Gavin has been at this company doing client relations for years. He works nights and weekends, putting in eighty hours a week, traveling nonstop. He handles client functions, makes all kinds of money. He thrives in it, I think. At least, he did. He likes being important. He likes closing deals. He probably likes being away from home.

"How was your trip?" he asks.

"Alright," I answer.

"How's Tara?"

"Leaving," I tell him.

"No shit," he says with surprise in his tone.

"Yeah. Silas got residency in Arizona."

"Ah, damn. Sorry." He looks at me briefly, then turns back to the TV.

"It's alright." I sit down on the couch next to him. "She's ready to move on."

"Mm," he mumbles in agreement. "I get that."

"You okay?"

"Yeah," he sighs. "Yeah. I'm okay. I just need to sleep it off. Figure this shit out in the morning."

"Could you talk to somebody? You were a top earner for them. They can't just cut you like that."

"They can. And they did."

"Damn. Well, severance is good." But I know he's thinking about out of control rent prices, the bills. Our shitty landlord that never repairs anything. Things I never gave a shit about until we moved in together and he was breathing down my neck about savings accounts and finances. I always found a way to just make it work. Maybe that's the privilege talking. The fact that I always had my older brother fighting for me, watching out for me.

Maybe I need to do a better job of watching out for him, too.

"We can look for something new in the morning," I offer.

He just nods but doesn't look at me. "What time is it?"

"Um." I check my phone. "Almost three."

"Should probably head to bed."

"Yeah. Yeah, me too."

We throw the pizza box into the fridge and head to our rooms. I leave my luggage in the corner by the door.

We'll deal with it all in the morning.

Chapter Four

Julieta

We wore the same size: nine. That was always a running joke, because Agostina is a size ten and Delfi is an eight, and so I was the shoe twin.

These shoes are a perfect nine: stretched, worn in, loved. A simple heel— maybe three inches at most—a curved front with some very small embellishments. Sturdy leather soles for gliding along the floor.

They're beautiful. There's no denying it. Maybe part of that is the sentiment talking, but I can't stop looking at them.

I think about watching her dance now. How elegant and powerful she was. And I think about how she made all of those moves in these very shoes, the ones sitting on my lap at this moment.

I'm home, in my carefully curated downtown condo, the one only three miles from my office. Where I don't have mismatched picture frames covering every corner of wall space. Or a leaf in my kitchen table to extend it for company. It's not loud and booming, not filled with the sounds of conversation and music.

This home is quiet. It's simple. It's efficient. I liked that at first, how I could finally hear myself think after so many years growing up in a boisterous household, but right now it feels uncomfortably desolate. *Too* quiet, *too* simple. It might as well be a hotel room.

And these shoes deserve better.

Why the hell did I get her shoes?

I set the box down on the coffee table and bring my laptop over from my desk. I want to see her again, if only for a couple of minutes. If only through a screen. Nobody knows that I keep her old YouTube videos bookmarked for viewing whenever I get particularly sad. Or when I've had a long week. When I just need a little comfort in the form of her dancing. Nobody needs to know that I hold onto it like a child.

Delfi was the first to find these videos, one night when she took to looking up Argentinian travel guides and stumbled upon videos of Argentina's most famous female tango dancer in between. There were only a handful then, but every now and then a new one will pop up—an old competition, a compilation of certain moves, a study on pivots.

I pull up the videos now, cueing up the first one. There she is: as graceful as ever, like seeing an old friend. And there are the shoes. Steps back, steps to the side, steps forward. A glide, a turn. I know these moves by heart now.

I know the timing of them. At the one minute and fifteen second mark, there's a perfect turn. At the two minute and twelve second mark there's a dramatic pose.

I can feel my body slow down as it sinks into the couch. Like the equivalent of a warm cup of tea or the softest, plushiest blanket, I sink into this video, the dance, and the music.

The video ends, but a new one starts to play. One I haven't seen before that was recently uploaded.

A compilation of celebrated dancer Celestina Rossi at the San Diego Tango Festival in honor of the upcoming festival this winter.

Suddenly, I'm eight again. I'm bright-eyed and captivated and so deeply sad. I miss her so much, a deep grief that has burrowed its way into my heart and made an uncomfortable home there.

My grandmother started dancing when she was around twelve during what was considered the golden age of tango. As she got older, she would sneak away to clubs at night and dance with whoever was willing to dance with her. And during those nights was how she met my grandfather, who had found himself in these clubs because his father played in the bands. He always tells the story of how he felt an immediate connection when he saw her, and by the third time they had run into each other, he was in love. And he told her as much. My grandmother laughed in his face, but she kept dancing with him. And she kept meeting up with him. And then they got married and competed all over the world. For my grandmother, tango might have seemed like the love of her life, but she always said it gave her the love of her life. And that held its own value.

My eyes then turn to the shoes on the table next to the laptop. As I look at them in the box, I can't help but wonder what they would feel like on my feet.

"Well, they're mine now," I say to myself. "I guess I could just …"

I take them out of the box, hands shaking, delicately holding them. I'm almost waiting for them to turn to dust in my hands. A trick, an illusion. This whole thing has been a dream.

As I slide into the shoes, they feel perfect. Almost *too* perfect. Scarily perfect. The indents of her toes are embedded into the soles and mine fit into the space effortlessly. I stand and walk around, turning and twisting, striding from one end to the other. I could wear these shoes every moment of every day and feel entirely comfortable.

These shoes have seen the world. They've seen joy and wild abandon, power and grace. These shoes have had a *life* and now they have somehow managed to end up here, with me.

I put the lid back on and carry them with me to my bedroom. Once I set them down on the nightstand, I turn my lamp on. I can't bear to put them away in the closet. Not now, not yet. So, I sneak glances at them while I brush my teeth, the start of my nighttime checklist. I think about the feel of them while I wash my face, step two. But I don't grab my cases, and I don't look through any folders, and I don't think about work.

I think about the shoes. And I leave them there on the nightstand right next to me, the very last thing in my line of sight until I eventually fall asleep.

My alarm wakes me blaring at five am, and I stumble out of bed, still exhausted. I don't want to move my body. It takes effort to do anything. When I look over and see the box on my nightstand, everything comes flooding back, as if I assumed the night before was some highly realistic dream.

I shower, get dressed, check my emails—three from Barbara—and brew coffee into my mug. The drive to work is mindless. I might as well be sleepwalking. I sip on my coffee as I listen to some news podcast, zoning out in the process. I go over my mental to-do list again: the notes from Barbara, the clients I need to contact, the standing meeting with Yuli's Latina networking group tomorrow.

And once I get to the office, say my good mornings, and get another to-do item tacked on by Barbara, I fall into my chair and take one long deep breath in.

***

"Julie? Julie?"

I don't know how long I've been staring into space, but Larissa's concerned face that comes into view might be telling.

"You okay?" she asks.

"Yeah, sorry. I'm alright," I respond.

"How's the case coming along?"

"It's coming. Yeah, it's good. Working away at it." I might be nodding my head too vigorously, so I stop, which just makes every move I make that much more jarring.

"Alright." She sounds unconvinced. "Want to head to lunch in a bit?"

I check my watch, nodding again. "Sure. Give me ten minutes?"

She gives me a small smile, walking out of my office and next door to hers.

Ten minutes later, we're outside at the picnic tables. There's a welcome breeze today and dark clouds in the distance, signaling the incoming afternoon rain.

"So, he took me to a dance class! A ballroom dance class!" Larissa says as she unpacks her lunch.

"Oh?" I must sound more interested than I ever have in Larissa's dating life, so she keeps going.

"Yeah. Some ballroom down on Tenth Street. It was fun! Well, what am I telling you for? You know all about that." She waves it off.

Larissa was working here when my grandmother passed

away two years ago and I had surprisingly told Larissa the brief details of her life—celebrated tango dancer, beloved grandmother. Maybe I was just looking for somebody to share something with, somebody besides my own family who had their own stories, were dealing with their own grief. I had to be there for them, and my grief was lost in the shuffle, so I talked to Larissa about it instead. Quick, short tidbits so I wasn't taking up all the conversation, but enough to get it off my chest.

"I've never done ballroom classes," I reply.

"Well, that makes sense. You wouldn't need to!"

"I don't know about that," I add.

"I love those stories you told me about your grandmother," she practically swoons. "Well, this date was not that. You ever date somebody who takes you to a competitive activity, but he doesn't like to lose?"

I think about Jeremy—my last boyfriend who was certainly competitive, but hardly took me anywhere. I shake my head. "Can't say that I have."

"Not that a ballroom dance class is competitive, but he sure acted like it. Like he needed to be better than everybody there. He couldn't look like the new guy, or a novice, Heaven forbid." She rolls her eyes, dipping a carrot stick in ranch. "And when the instructor corrected him and complimented me, he almost lost his shit." She laughs. The aggressive crunch of the carrot breaks through her words. "I shouldn't be laughing at that, 'cause honestly, what a fucking tool."

Her dating stories are not unlike Agostina's dating stories. The plight of trying to meet somebody in your thirties: the societal expectations, the metaphorical clock. Hell, our family loves to desperately throw the word *husband* around. "You remind me of my cousin," I tell her.

"Is she also a hot mess? Is that what you're saying?" She laughs again.

I chuckle at that, quick and low. "No, no." She's a vibrant force to be reckoned with, I want to tell her. "She is bold and brave to continually put herself out there. That's what I mean. All these losers are missing out," I tell her instead.

Larissa giggles in response, but it's soft around the edges when she says, "Thanks, Julie. Same to you."

"I guess I'd have to go out and actually meet people for that, though." I give her a tight smile. An uncomfortable realization that perhaps good things come to those who actually go out and *do*. "So, what kind of dancing did you do?" I ask, bringing the conversation back.

"Oh! Well, there were all the classics ... the waltz and the foxtrot and the *tango*." She emphasizes the last word, and it hits something in me. It quickly reminds me of the shoes, the ones still on my nightstand, still in the box, still taunting me.

"Did you like it?" I find myself asking her.

"I did! I mean, the company sucked, but it was fun."

She shrugs.

"That's good," I nod, but I can't shake the feeling I'm getting now. I look at the time. Lunch break is over. "Well, time to head back."

"Yeah," she sighs. "I'm almost done with the documents for the Lorenzo case, so I'll bring them over to you by the end of the day."

We gather our leftover lunches and slowly walk back into the building side by side.

"Start on the notes for the Turner case when you can, please," I call out, heading right to my office. And when I enter it, I get back to my own pile, my own to-do list, my head down.

Except the shoes pull me from my work. The conversation at lunch is still wedged in the back of my mind. It's all a distraction I can't afford, but I think about the women in my life that got up and made shit happen without any fear. My grandmother, who decided to take up dancing as a young woman and continue on to compete. Who traveled all over the world and created a life she wanted to live. My mother, who packed up her family and built a life in a new country.

And I look at myself in the mirror and wonder where the ball got dropped. My life is one comprised of guilt and fear. I live in calculated decisions and apologies. I don't jet set around the world. I certainly didn't start a new life in a new country, relying on my own strengths and the kindness of strangers to get by.

All I've got is a list I've been checking off intently every day of my life to make my parents proud, a job I work way too fucking hard at, and now some shoes.

But what if.

I look around the office, find everybody deep in their own work, then pull up Google to search for tango classes near me. A small list comes up. The number one hit is that ballroom where Larissa went on the date, but another one in particular catches my eye. Something like what I'm looking for. Dance classes specific to tango, a couple of miles from here in a dance studio in downtown New River. A new twelve-week session starts this Thursday with—according to the website—renowned tango dancers Logan Beck and Tara O'Byrne.

That's too soon. I would have to coordinate with my clients, figure out my schedule and the timing of it.

Twelve weeks of the fundamentals of tango, it reads. *Each week will focus on a different technique. We will work together to give you confidence, make you a strong tango dancer, and most of all, have fun while doing it.*

That's a tall order.

But what if I put aside some of the logical thinking for a minute? Clearly nothing is logical if I'm even entertaining doing this. Maybe I like the idea of being a strong tango dancer or gaining confidence or, shockingly, having fun. I don't even know what that word means anymore.

I hover above the *Sign up now!* button, my heart racing as I consider doing it. What if my family found out? My fingers twitch just a little. Should I even be spending money on something so frivolous? My hand moves off the mouse. Maybe the shoes weren't meant to be worn, just admired from a distance.

"I can't do this right now," I whisper, just in case anybody else can see what I'm trying to do on my computer. In my own office. Behind a locked door. I'm getting paranoid.

A quick knock breaks me out of my stupor. I rapidly minimize the screen.

"Come in," I say, trying to sound as calm as I can.

Jim pokes his head in, paperwork in hand. "Hey Julie, could you stay late on Thursday?" he asks, not really waiting for an answer. "Barbara said you didn't have anything else going on and you'd say yes."

Of course, she did.

"I can't," I blurt out.

"Oh."

"Yeah, I forgot I have … something important that came up." I must look pale as a ghost.

"Oh." He's surprised. "Okay, not a problem. I'll get Larissa on it." He walks away, leaving the door ajar behind him.

I look back at my computer, pulling up the website I couldn't let myself exit out of.

Maybe the shoes *were* meant to be worn. What if they

are a sign to take command of my life? What if I want to do something for myself for once? Something I can love, something that can bring back some zest for life. Something that can help me reclaim my time. No emails, no messages, no phone calls from Barbara.

No assumptions that I have *nothing else going on.*

What if I took one step outside of my comfort zone? Just one step.

Would it change everything?

Fire at my fingertips, I click on the *Sign up now!* button and quickly fill out the form. Once I submit it, I step back and try not to think about the most impulsive thing I've done in about ten years. You'd think I just decided to rob a bank.

Maybe abuela wanted me to do this. Maybe she didn't. But maybe the more important part is that I want to. *I think.*

Maybe I want to try.

Larissa peeks her head in. "Hot date?" she says with a smirk.

I jump, startled from her accusation. "No, no. Just ... a family thing."

"Oh." Her face falls. "That's no fun."

I feel guilty for lying, giving her an answer that could easily dismiss her. But Larissa is kind and thoughtful, and she tries. And she indirectly put this idea in my head, so I can't help but change my answer and tell her instead, "I'm trying something new."

Her face lights up. "As you should," she responds supportively.

"I'll let you know how it goes." I aim for friendly.

"Can't wait!"

"Sorry Jim threw more work your way."

"It's fine." She shrugs. "Better to be productive here than to be out on another disappointing date."

"Yeah, I guess." Now I feel guilty about doing this, about having somebody else pick up my slack. "Well, let me finish up what I can to keep your work to a minimum."

"Thanks, Julie," she says, a grateful smile on her face as she leaves my office and heads back to her own.

And then I make it a point to work until I'm the last one in this building to make up for the time I'll be spending away from it.

CHAPTER FIVE
Julieta

I'M WEARING MY POWER pants to this first class. Well, my high waisted trousers that Agostina lovingly refers to as my power pants. The ones I didn't realize I always wore on court days. Maybe I picked them today for an extra boost of confidence.

I rushed out of work, almost embarrassed, as I left my surprised coworkers behind to make it on time for this six o'clock class. Larissa whispered, "Take me with you!" as I gathered my things and walked out the door.

I quickly park, and before I get out of the car, I shakily place the shoes on my feet, heart pounding as I do.

The website said you didn't need a partner for the classes, but I still see couples paired up and chatting when I walk in. I might be the youngest person here, except for the blonde woman greeting me who seems closer to my age.

"Hi! Are you here for the tango class?" she asks enthusiastically.

I nod, walking up to her slowly. "Hi. Yes."

"Wonderful. Welcome! What's your name?"

"Julie Martí."

She checks down a list on a clipboard. "Perfect. My name is Tara. We'll be starting shortly so you can get settled in studio B with the other students."

"Okay, great. Thank you."

This was a bad idea.

I feel very much like the odd one out. Everybody seems to know each other, chatting and laughing. Most are wearing tango shoes, some are even wearing dancing dresses. I'm out of my element.

This studio is like any other unassuming dance studio: wood floors, a wall of mirrors, bright lights, plenty of space. I linger in the back, unsure of how to proceed, holding on to my purse like a lifeline.

Tara seems nice enough. Maybe she won't notice if I quietly slip out now. She's speaking with an older woman in a form-fitting dress with roses all over it. I'll just pretend to search for the bathroom and calmly walk right out. I walk backwards, slowly making my way to the door, ready to run for the hills. And when I turn around to walk out, my face comes into harsh contact with ... a chin? A neck? What did I just run into?

"Woah, there." A deep male voice says while hands grab hold of my upper arms to keep me steady. "Is class over already?" he asks, and when I look up to meet his face, his smirk tells me he's joking.

"Oh. I just ... needed the bathroom."

"Ah. Right through there and to your right," he says, pointing toward the hallway just outside of the studio.

"Thank you," I manage to get out, face probably turning beet red.

I walk to the bathroom quickly, splashing water on my face to snap myself out of it. It's one class. For crying out loud, I can do one class. Maybe I can partner up with that guy I just ran into.

I make my way to the studio again and get situated in the back row and out of view.

"Good evening, everybody. Welcome to twelve weeks of the fundamentals of Tango," Tara states at the front of the class. "This is a recurring class that we offer here in the studio so I know some of you, but I do see new faces. My name is Tara and I co-teach this class with my partner, Logan."

Of course, it would be the guy I just face planted into. Of course.

Logan is up front next to Tara now, his messy dark hair like he just rolled out of bed, a fitted white t-shirt, and loose-fitting black pants. She's in a stretchy black dress that looks surprisingly comfortable.

The students say hello back, and judging by the enthusiastic reply, it seems Logan is quite popular in this crowd. Understandably so, I guess. He's attractive.

"For this class, we are going to focus on teaching basic steps and getting you comfortable with tango," Logan starts. "Dancing shoes are ideal, but if not, any comfortable footwear will do the trick. You need to feel confident in moving around so please wear loose or stretchy clothing to allow for movement. We start at six and it runs for an hour. We do ask that you silence your phones as well, if possible."

Tara smiles, and with a nod says, "Let's begin."

"With Tango, there is a leader and a follower," Logan tells the class. "People think it's always the men that lead and the women that follow, but tango has a long history of men dancing together to practice. And as time has gone on, it is not unusual to see two men or two women dance together, where one gravitates to leading, and one prefers to follow. Here, we welcome whatever you would like to do."

I don't know what I'm doing. I don't know that I want to be a leader, so I aim to follow instead.

"For the purposes of this class, Tara will teach the follower steps, and I will teach the leader steps."

"Tango is considered a walking dance," Tara says. "So, we're going to begin with the foundation of the dance, the basic step."

"The basic step is an eight-count step and it looks like this." Logan shows us the move as a leader, and Tara shows us how to do the step as a follower.

"Now, let's go slow. One." She takes a step. "Two." She takes another. "Three, four. Five, cross over. Six, step back.

Seven and eight."

We follow, all of us solo to start. I watch my feet, how they move in these shoes, and I'm struck by how good it feels.

It's almost unbelievable to be here, doing this. I never thought I would. I figured these dreams would have stayed with eight year old Julie, falling away with everything else I loved when I was young. But here, learning steps, wearing these remarkable shoes, it feels like I'm close to something I've been unknowingly chasing for a long time. It's almost too overwhelming, and I worry I might shut down.

Logan and Tara continue to speak, Logan mostly showcasing steps, slowly adding on to them, and letting us practice several times. He talks about the differences in Argentine tango versus ballroom tango. He speaks of the competitions he's done, the formalities of it. He even mentions how, "even though this isn't a history class, we can certainly take a minute to understand and appreciate the origins of tango. How it came to life in the impoverished neighborhoods of Buenos Aires, pulling inspiration from African and European dances."

The thing is, I don't know Logan, but I know he is a very talented dancer. That much is evident. And he could surely give the Wikipedia rundown of Argentine tango. But what else is evident to me now is how much I can sense the soul of it, the heart of it. And how a strange thing is happening to me in these shoes. It sounds ridiculous. Hell, it feels ridiculous. But I feel powerful. I feel graceful. I feel ... free.

"Now, we're going to do something called a practice hold or a practice embrace," Tara says to the class. "The practice embrace is not a proper tango hold. It's meant to give you more space to practice the steps, to work on them as a beginner with a partner. You're welcome to pair up with whoever you'd like for this exercise."

Some students pair up with their dates, others pair up with other students, and I'm left lingering in the back.

Well, this is awkward.

But then Logan walks over to me, stopping to get the attention of a male student that was next to me in the back row.

"Would you like to partner up with Ethan?" he asks me.

"Sure," I respond. It saves me the embarrassment of dancing by myself. Ethan comes over to me, and we position ourselves ready to dance.

"Hey, I'm Ethan."

"Julie," I say in greeting.

Logan nods and continues his walk around the room, helping other couples.

"Hold onto each other's upper arms like so." Logan demonstrates with Tara. "Try to keep your spine straight and your chest open. Keep your elbows up and give yourself space."

"As a follower, sometimes it's easy to want to cave in,

but don't be afraid to open up," Tara says, widening her arms and keeping her back straight. "Allow yourself to take up space here."

Is she still talking about tango or my life?

Ethan and I take our positions, and this feels much more intimate than I imagined it would. Not that I imagined much, but I'm almost too shy to be this close to a stranger, putting myself into awkward positions with him. I aim to focus on my steps, to keep my head down to look at my feet.

"So, is this your first time?" Ethan asks.

"Um. Yes," I manage, working on the basic eight count, stumbling a little as I go.

Our faces are close enough that even talking feels intimate. I pull my face back to answer but all it does is mess up my form.

"That's okay. It takes a while to figure it out. I wasn't very good at the beginning either, but I think I'm one of the best ones now," he says as I try to keep my head down. Whatever cologne he's wearing is harshly offensive to my nostrils, and his steps are hard to keep up with. He seems like the kind of guy Larissa ended up on that date with.

But the next voice I hear isn't his. It's Logan's, right at my side.

"You know, the thing about tango is that it should involve relinquishing your ego," Logan says out loud to the class. "In order to be a good partner, there should be a compromise. Teamwork is meeting where your partner is at. It's choosing to not humiliate or upstage the other." He turns to my partner. "Ethan, this is her first class, so you need to meet her where she's at."

Now this is really awkward.

"Julie, try to keep your spine straight," he says to me in a softer tone, placing his hand lightly on my back. It feels warm, like there's an underlying current of electricity coming from his palm. "Lift your elbows up and try to keep a box frame here to give yourself room." I nod in response, but then he turns to Ethan and says, "Watch the basic step as a leader again."

Logan takes my hand, stepping in to hold me in a practice embrace. "It should look like this." He then leads me with precision, one basic step together. It's only a couple of seconds, a brief eight count, but it pales in comparison to what I just danced.

Is *this* what dancing should feel like?

Well, no wonder he's the professional.

Logan releases my arms, and it leaves me feeling inexplicably dazed. Ethan and I come back together, working on our moves, maybe awkwardly laughing through it. I'm almost desperate to take the reins and lead him myself.

I listen intently, and I continue to practice the moves little by little. Tara and Logan walk around the studio looking at form, stepping in to help. She keeps a friendly, approachable smile; he's humming a song. Tara gives me a small smile of encouragement as she approaches. And when Logan comes over again, his brow furrows slightly, his mouth set in a firm line.

Am I doing something wrong? I stop for a moment.

"No, keep going," he says.

So I do, and he continues to look at me with that intensity. I will myself to not think about him, or Ethan's less than desirable leading, and focus on my feet instead. One foot in front of the other, cross over, feet together, and back. He wordlessly walks back to the front and calls out the end of class.

When Ethan and I finally part, he stumbles and steps right on my shoe.

"Ah, shit," I wince, leaning down to grab my foot.

"Oh no, I'm sorry. You're alright, though?" he asks, but doesn't wait for a response.

"Mmhmm," I mumble, nodding with a tight smile.

"So, for the end of class, we like to do a review," Logan says at the head of the class. "Tara and I will dance the moves you've learned today. We'll dance slowly so you can see them and then we can have everybody partner up again and try if you'd like."

Tara sets up the speakers to play a song in tempo. The music starts on cue, and I am not prepared for my reaction. There's an overwhelming sense of pride in the unmistakable sounds of piano and bass and violin. The rich, bold, incredibly romantic music loved so deeply, so fiercely by my grandmother is now here. The music I would hear in my dreams as a child is now in this small dance studio, the sound booming from the speakers. I *feel* it within me, setting me alight.

I catch my reflection in the mirror in the front of the room; I look terrified.

Logan and Tara stand facing each other then bring their hands together. Her arm wraps around him, and Logan's arm wraps around Tara, his hand set in the middle of her back. They do the basic step and cross, and I watch, soaking it all in.

I love to watch tango. It's wildly romantic, sensual, passionate—all the things that I'm not. It's a little like watching something you shouldn't: intimate moments between two lovers. And on top of that, Tara and Logan make a beautiful couple. Their moves are fluid and graceful. Her turns are elegant, his steps are in perfect rhythm. I could watch this all day, this mesmerizing dance I've somehow been tied to all my life.

Once they finish, we applaud them, and they break away to let us practice. Ethan comes back to me, and we move in our practice embrace, the same steps over and over again.

Soon enough, class is over. And I breathe a sigh of relief that I made it through my very first one.

"That's all for today," Logan calls out. "But we've got more weeks ahead of us, and it's going to be a great time.

See you all next week."

The students recite their goodbyes as they gather their belongings and head out the door. I practically lunge for my bag, reaching for my phone that I'm not used to being without for longer than mere minutes. And there I notice three missed calls from Barbara, six new messages from work, and two messages from Agostina and my mom. I quickly look at them, but none of them seem important. Nothing from work that couldn't have waited.

The wind has been taken out of my sails with a force. I couldn't even get an hour to myself. Not one hour to myself without the world needing me for something. Maybe I could just cut my losses now.

These classes are frivolous. More reason to admit it.

I glance up and find Logan and Tara looking at me, standing side by side, both of them smiling as they say, "See you next week."

"Oh. Yes. Next week." I nod, picking up my bag.

No, probably not.

Chapter Six

Logan

I'M STILL WATCHING THE door long after the class has filed out. Why does it feel so stuffy in here?

"Has she danced before?" Tara breaks my trance with the question.

"What?"

"Julie?"

"I don't know. I think so." I shrug.

"She did good," Tara says.

"She wasn't bad," I say dismissively.

I'd rather not think about it. She *was* good. She needs to polish up the basics, but that comes with practice. What she has is a fire within her. Something I saw in her eyes when she looked at herself in the mirror, when she focused on her feet, looked on with determination.

"Ethan could still use some work," I tell her.

I paired her up with another student, wanting to keep a distance and watch from afar. He needed a bit more help than she did, but when I stepped in to show technique and offer guidance, I wasn't expecting to feel ... *that*.

Tara huffs out a laugh. "He was fine."

"Anyway." I wave it away, packing up my belongings and getting ready to head out of the studio. "We need to let them know you're leaving."

"We will. Let's tell everybody next week."

"We should plan something. Maybe a goodbye milonga."

She lights up at that. "Oh, that would be fun."

"Your last one before you leave us to do way better things," I tease.

"You are dramatic as fuck, Logan," she laughs.

"But am I wrong?"

She just pins me with a look. One that says shut up. Or you're not wrong, but I'd rather not admit it. Or I'm going to miss this place, too.

"You alright?" she asks.

"Me? Yeah, why?"

She shrugs. "Just checking in."

"I'm good," I answer, but I know she knows I'm not being honest. She won't push either, which is a relief right now.

"Call me if you want to chat."

"I will." I nod, not making eye contact with her.

"See you tomorrow, then." She gives me a quick hug before heading out to her car.

***

GAVIN AND I MOVED in together five years ago. I don't know how much he likes it, but when he was traveling for work, he was away enough to probably not care.

Our two-bedroom suits us fine. I made the move out here first when I was twenty, finding a better tango community and better opportunities for dance. Gavin found a way to transfer within his company and followed. Soon enough, he was asking if we should just live together, since he was hardly home anyway so why was he bothering to pay so damn much in rent? Rent prices are ridiculous, I won't argue that. Our so-called luxury apartment is hardly luxurious for what we pay, but we've been here too long to want to move anywhere else. Besides, the location is great.

Our parents divorced when we were much younger and it was so messy, so rage-filled, that I think we both saw no choice but to get out.

I park my car and shuffle to the door, unlocking it and stepping in. Gavin's on the couch again, something I haven't quite gotten used to yet. There were so many times I would come home to an empty apartment, or to Gavin in his room working, or at the dining table on his laptop until late at night, not talking to anybody. Not giving me a second glance.

We're back to Netflix, apparently.

"What's up?" I ask as I step out of my shoes.

"Remember Woodstock 99? There's a wild documentary on it right now." There's some semblance of excitement in his voice, but it might sound forced.

"Oh. Cool." I don't know what else to say.

"Also, did you know that otters love to play in toilets? I watched that documentary earlier."

"Are you drunk?"

"Unfortunately, no." He keeps his eyes on the TV.

If I didn't know any better, I'd say he looks … sad. He looks lost.

"How was your day?" he asks.

I walk over to sit on the couch with him. "It was good. Started up a new session."

"And Tara's still leaving?"

"Yeah, she is." I nod.

"You okay?"

"I'm *fine*." Too many people are asking at this point. "Just going to figure out what I'm doing next."

"You're going to stop teaching?"

This question from him feels more accusatory than he probably means for it to, and I never quite know how to answer it.

"Yeah, I think so," I say, sighing. "I don't know, maybe not." My response is a jumble of words that make no sense to me, let alone him.

I don't know why I say it, or why I'm fighting any of it.

Maybe I am just having a minute like I told Tara that night at Waffle House. I need to get over my shit, get over this hump of whatever and keep moving forward.

The truth is the last competition we were in, we didn't even place. Tara and I had worked on that routine the bare minimum. She decided to head back to school for her master's and I had picked up another job as a choreographer for a local dance group production. We'd both struggled with finding the time and energy. And when we competed, it was clear that the want was not there like it once was. Some critics had things to say. They always do. Like how our routine had become derivative and stale, how the spark seemed to be dwindling.

"Where were the champion dancers tonight? This is not the Logan Beck and Tara O'Byrne we once knew. This is not good."

Those words still play on in my mind every so often, reminding me of the failure. Pushing on it like a fresh bruise, recklessly wanting to feel the pain. I was embarrassed by that result. Angry. I had let myself down, and I had let Tara down. I had, indirectly, let Gavin down, too. I told myself I was done with it, and I wasn't going back. I wasn't going to throw myself into that again, bruising my ego for whatever I was chasing. That was the last one.

"Want to watch this show with me?" he offers.

I can't remember the last time we just hung out. I can't remember the last time we've talked this much. "Yeah, sounds good. I'll grab some beers." I head to the fridge, pull out two bottles, and bring them back over to the couch.

Gavin and I sit on opposite ends, and he presses play.

Tara's leaving, so I don't have a partner. A new session just started, and Gavin is home, sitting on the couch with me, while we drink beers and watch some bullshit on TV.

Maybe it's time to really move along and find something new. I've been doing this since I was thirteen. I can't do it forever. But even as I think it, I feel a lump in my throat start to form. That's a long time to do something. To be attached to it. To have it define me.

After my part time stint last year, the local production said they would gladly offer me something full time. The same theater would eagerly take me as their production manager. The options are there. I just have to take them.

CHAPTER SEVEN
Julieta

EVERY SIX WEEKS, I show up at the salon for my regularly scheduled hair appointment. A trim, an upkeep. It's a comforting routine. One that I can always count on, one that is safe and predictable.

"Hi Jenny." I greet the girl at the front desk. "I have a ten o'clock with Cristina."

She checks me in, but Cristina walks by, waving.

"Hey Julie. Go ahead and take a seat. I'll be right there," she says.

But when I comfortably walk through the salon I've been to a million times and sit down in the same salon chair—the fourth one in, the mirror decorated with colors as vibrant as her hair—I start to feel antsy.

I start to feel ... *un*comfortable.

All around me stylists are chatting freely with their clients who know the routine. This is a classic Saturday morning. The salon smells faintly like hair products and lotions. The blow dryer is always on somewhere, white noise that lingers in the background. I look at Cristina's station, the combs she always uses, the hair dryer set in its holder. The stylist cart, the clips. I feel a crippling desire to take those sharp scissors, shiny and glinting with the reflection of the lights, and chop all this hair off in an instant. To get up and run out of here.

So maybe the classes were a bad idea. I knew it from the beginning anyway. My job can't handle my absence, and my family would ask too many questions about this and never let me live it down. I was worried and with good reason.

Doesn't matter that I felt an inkling of something finally. Or that I spent an hour not worried about anybody or anything but myself. None of it matters when I've got responsibilities to tend to, other priorities to address.

Maybe that was too much too soon. Too impulsive, too rash. Maybe I should aim to make a different kind of change.

"Hey girl. How are you?" Cristina says just then, coming up behind my chair, probably saving me from myself. She grabs the apron and ties it around my neck, securing the clips at the back.

"Good, good." I swallow.

She brushes my hair back; this routine is a familiar one with her, too. She knows what to do. She does the same damn thing every six weeks. But even then, every six weeks, she always checks.

"Just the trim, right?" She pumps the chair up with her

foot, looking at my reflection in the mirror.

Maybe this time, I need to break the routine.

"I'm not sure."

She pauses, hands on the back of the chair.

"I need a change, I think."

"A change? What kind of change?" Her eyes widen. She's excited now, chewing her gum with more vigor. She loves change in the form of a drastic haircut.

"I was thinking a cut." I answer slowly, unsurely. I actually don't know what I'm thinking cause I wasn't thinking anything until about two minutes ago.

"Okay!" She bobs her head up and down and runs her manicured nails through my long hair. It's down past my shoulder blades right now, a length that I usually tie back or up for work. Long hair that at times is more of an inconvenience than a pleasantry. "How short were you thinking then?"

Well. How short *was* I thinking? I look in the mirror, hair fanned around my shoulders hiding parts of my face. How long have I hidden myself? How long have I lived in the solace of a safe haircut? Of a safe life? Perhaps too long. So, I lift my hand up and point, channeling the strength I use in work. One clear cut decision, delivered with a confidence I certainly don't feel but am trying my best to convey.

"Like ... about here," I say. And when she sees my hand pointing to right above my shoulders, signaling for a fresh cut bob, her face breaks out into the most excited grin like a kid on Christmas.

I take a deep breath as she begins. It's just hair. This isn't me getting up and moving to Alaska or something. This is just a haircut. If it's terrible, it will just grow back. I could even have her put in extensions.

But no. I want this.

I want a change. I need a change.

I am so tired of this mundane, repetitive life. I am so tired of safe and simple and six-week maintenance appointments. I want the spontaneity that Agostina so proudly wears. I want the happy-go-lucky life that Delfina has created for herself. Even my younger brother who got the easygoing parents without any of the guilt trips to do well in school, go to college, make money. I want my own life to be one that I'm proud of, because I'm starting to realize how not proud of it I feel.

The snip of the scissors sounds harsh against my ears as the wet clumps of my hair slide down to the floor. Like something symbolic in the pieces that are falling around me.

This isn't about the hair. I just think it was the easiest target. Maybe the one closest to me at the moment. So, this could be a start. Tango might have been the first step, but perhaps that was the misstep. This could be the do-over.

The tango classes were a nice thought, though. I guess I didn't expect to feel so much. I didn't expect to leave so

... full of life.

In my thought spiral, I don't notice that she's done. She spins me around, my back to the mirror.

"Are you ready to see it?"

"Not really," I blurt out. This may have been a bad idea.

Cristina just laughs, taking it all in stride. "I would never steer you wrong, girl." She spins my chair around and when I look in the mirror, I know that she's right, and I can't help but smile, too.

A choppy bob cut right above my shoulders. My natural rich brown hair color accentuated with some beachy waves.

"Do you love it?" she asks in her ever-present excited tone.

That girl in the mirror, she looks like she's ready for something new.

"I love it."

Chapter Eight

Julieta

I'M STILL GETTING USED to my new hair. The ends that used to touch halfway down my back now tickle the sides of my neck, but I can't deny it's been a welcome addition to this end-of-summer heat.

I walk briskly down the sidewalk to the entrance of The Ivy, a trendy restaurant downtown in the financial district where Agostina works. I like to stop in every so often to say hi and chat, usually meeting Delfi here to spend some time together outside of family dinners. Once I step in, I wave to the hostess and signal that I'm headed to the bar.

Agostina has worked here for seven years now serving and occasionally bartending. She's hoping to make it to head bartender, but for now she just fills in when she's asked to. I'm nervous about what her reaction to my hair will be, my heart beating in my chest as I make my way to a barstool. She looks up then, just as I adjust in my seat.

"Oh shit!" She gasps in surprise, reaching out to touch my hair.

I roll my eyes, but secretly want the praise. The validation that I made the right decision. So much for wanting to live my own life.

"Midlife crisis looks good on you, Julie."

"Hi to you too, asshole."

She laughs at that, leaning over to give me a kiss on the cheek. She eyes my hair again, a smile still gracing her face. "It looks really good."

"Thanks." I blush. "How's work?"

"Not too bad. About to get busy. We've got some bigger parties coming in in about fifteen minutes."

The bar is a large rectangle, with the top made of polished dark wood and seating on either side. There are glass shelves of liquor suspended in the middle, twinkling lights wrapped around to add a cozy feel. The lights reflect off the bottles, making everything glow. I'm sure she's tired of looking at it, but for me, it's always been a little bit magical.

Bar patrons are scattered about, drinking and chatting, picking at food. Trevor, another bartender, is mixing drinks for guests. Everything is still relatively calm and quiet. My eyes scan the crowd, people watching, and along the other side of the bar they snag on a familiar face. Messy dark hair, lush lips. And when we make eye contact, the furrowed brows give him right away.

I notice a drink in Logan's hand as he's lifting it to his lips to take a sip, and that's possibly the reason for the smile he gives me now: a small one, tucked into a corner of his mouth, but showing a lot of restraint.

"Julie," he says with purpose.

The bar area between us is maybe a generous twelve feet, and I can hear him clearly. I'm almost taken aback by the fact that he remembers my name. It was only two days ago, I know, but still.

"You cut your hair," he adds.

My hands fly to my ends, and I'm suddenly self-conscious. This was too short. *Shit.*

"It looks nice," he tells me reassuringly, eyes sparkling.

Agostina is busy making drinks for a bar that is quickly filling up so she doesn't hear him say this, and I'd like to keep it that way. I'd like to keep this my secret for now.

"Thanks," I manage quietly, then as discreetly as I can shake my head to get the message across that we should act like strangers. But in that moment, his date, the beautiful Tara sits down next to him and smiles right at me.

"Julie!" she says by way of greeting, in a joyous voice like she's so happy to see me.

Agostina's ears perk up as she walks over to our side of the bar, dropping off my usual glass of wine, and I refrain from slamming my head onto it.

"Clients?" Agostina asks in casual conversation, uncorking a wine bottle in a swift move and pouring two glasses for a couple that just arrived.

I shake my head more vigorously now and they finally catch on.

"Oh, no, no. I was talking about somebody else, sorry!" Tara says, stuttering her way through, but I don't miss the smile that graces Logan's lips as he takes another sip. The one that wraps around the rim of the glass, curving so slightly, mouth opening to drink.

Honestly, I'm the worst. He's got a girlfriend, and she's sitting *right there*. I've got no business thinking about his smiling lips, for crying out loud.

"So, when's your flight, T?" I ask to change the subject, using her nickname.

When Agostina was in middle school, she went through a phase where she hated her name and wanted to be called Tina. Once she got to high school, everybody just started calling her T, and it stuck.

"Tomorrow afternoon."

She's taking a quick trip to visit a friend in Jersey.

"Come with me," she says casually.

"I can't. I have to work." It's always the same story. She pushes me to do things with her; I have to inform her that I have responsibilities.

"You know you get paid time off right? You are aware that you are allowed a vacation?"

Responsibilities have loopholes, too, she reminds me. I take a sip of my own drink ready to end this topic of conversation that I dragged us both into.

"She's got better sense than to go on vacation with you, that's the problem," I hear a voice from behind me say. It's

Manny, T's best friend and coworker.

"Hi, Manny." I give him a kiss on the cheek and a smile in greeting.

"Is Delfi coming tonight?" He asks as he grabs a tray of cocktails.

"She's running late, but she should be here soon."

"Don't you have tables to tend to?" T asks.

"Listen to her," he says to me. "Not even lead bartender yet and it's already going to her head. I'll be back in a bit!" He waves as he walks away.

"You don't have to come with me, but you still have to take me to the airport," Agostina adds in as a reminder.

"Yes, I know," I sigh.

Shortly after, Delfina walks in, stopping short when she sees my hair.

"No way!" she shrieks. "Your hair looks so good!"

The whole bar can hear this compliment. I sneak a glance at Logan and Tara who have looked up from their own conversation in curiosity. Logan gives me a small smile, and I whip back to Delfi, face flushed.

"Thanks," I mutter, running my hand through the strands again. She adds her hand, messing with the ends, running them through their fingers. She beams at me, as she always does. Delfi is one big ray of sunshine, always has been, even as kids. I smile back at her, like we have our own language between us.

"Hey bartender!" she calls out, adjusting on the

barstool.

"You're so cute," T says, deadpan. She leans against the bar and Delfi gives her a kiss on the cheek.

"I'll take a mojito, please," she calls out in a sing-song voice.

I sip my wine, chuckling as I do, taking this opportunity to calm my nerves.

"Want to get something to eat? I'm starving." Delfi grabs the menu and looks through it, her eyes perusing the items, lip tucked between her teeth as she does.

"Whatever you want is fine," I say agreeably.

"Hey T, can we get some calamari and the crostini, please?" she calls out. "You want anything else?" she asks me.

"Get the truffle fries. I want something snackier."

"You got it," T says, walking away to put the order in.

Agostina makes her rounds along the bar, checking on the patrons. A couple orders some appetizers, a lone bar guest asks for another bourbon. She brings Delfi her mojito, icy and refreshing in a tall glass, a bright green sprig of mint sticking out of the top. The parties have started to trickle in, making the space louder, laughter and chatter bouncing off the walls. But I'm acutely aware of Logan on the other side of the bar, his presence its own sort of pleasant heaviness.

"How are you doing over here?" Agostina asks Logan. He looks like he's debating whether to get another drink.

"We'll take another round," he decides. "Thank you."

"Oh, the cute ones are out tonight," Delfi mumbles under her breath beside me. It smells like mint and citrus.

"He's taken," I blurt, and sip my wine.

"He is? How do you know?"

Just then Tara sits back down from wherever she was, adjusting in the stool, smiling wide as T brings their drinks over.

"Oh. She's pretty," Delfi says with a sigh.

"Yep."

She turns on her stool then to face me, gripping my arm lightly. "So, tell me about the shoes! I've been freaking out since Monday, and you've barely answered my texts."

Right. The shoes. *The* shoes. "I've been busy," I reason. "Besides, nothing to tell."

"Are you kidding? Did you try them on? Tell me you tried them on."

I sigh. "They fit like a glove."

"Oh my God, I knew it! This is so amazing!"

"Anybody ever tell you that you speak in exclamation points?"

"All the time." She smiles wide, unfazed.

"What's all the screeching over here?" T chimes in, back in front of us to bring the truffle fries.

"The shoes!" Delfi says in response.

"Oh damn, that's right. How are they? They probably fit you like a glove, don't they?"

"Perhaps," I eye her, shoving fries into my mouth.

"What are you going to do with them?"

"I haven't thought about it yet," I lie.

"You have to dance with them!" Delfi says loudly beside me, resolute in her idea. I can only imagine the looks we're getting now from the professional dancers across the bar that I am actively trying to avoid.

"You should dance with them," T says in agreement, vigorously shaking a cocktail shaker above her shoulder.

"Isn't that kind of silly?" I hedge. My family, as loving as they've always been, have also been highly critical of anything I was interested in that didn't involve my studies. Is dancing kind of silly? Or is that the judgmental voice in my head that has grown louder than my own?

"No way. We would do the same damn thing," Delfi responds, then grabs my arm again with a gasp. "We could all sign up for dance classes."

"Oh, no. I don't know about that." I go pale as a sheet.

"I can't believe we've never even considered it."

T pours the cocktail, thinking it over. "I could look into something after my trip. Sounds fun," she shrugs.

"What sounds fun?" Manny chimes in behind us, back again and giving Delfi a kiss on the cheek.

"Tango classes!" Delfi screams to the whole bar again.

"I dated a dancer once. He was a hot mess," Manny says, arranging drinks on a tray. "Sign me up for tango." He nods, grabbing the tray and leaving just as quickly with it to his tables.

I chance a look over at Logan and Tara, still sitting side by side, but a man has walked over now and given Tara one very big kiss on the mouth.

I immediately sit up straight, suddenly confused. Suddenly inexplicably interested in whatever is happening.

Logan shakes his hand, and the man sits down with them. I lean against the bar, palm tucked under my chin. I pretend I'm snacking on the calamari but keep looking up in interest. Could they not be dating? Why the hell am I so invested in this right now?

Amid my very amateur sleuthing, my phone lights up on the bar with a message from my ex, Jeremy.

"This asshole again?" T asks, catching the notification on my phone before I can move it out of sight.

Jeremy dumped me eight months ago. Well, it was more mutual than anything, I guess. Both of us had demanding, full-time jobs. It was a struggle to balance both, and maybe we had an understanding that we were both just coexisting in the relationship. Ours was one where I wanted more than he was giving, settling for anything I got. It was, as I look back on it, mediocre at best. Doesn't mean the breakup didn't suck, though. Losing a piece of somebody's affection. And it doesn't mean that he doesn't still text me every so often, asking what I'm doing, or if I want to meet up for a drink. The no-strings sex was fine, but even that had become a little boring, a little predictable. A little ... unsatisfactory on my end. Maybe he wasn't wrong when he had said to me months ago, "There isn't any passion here, Julie."

But there is a familiar warm body and a familiar, comfortable bed. There's somebody on the other end saying okay. Just going with it, like I do everything else. Just looking for the affection again, the part I don't want to admit out loud.

"You're still stuck on him?" Delfi asks.

"You should be one to talk, Delfina," T says, with a knowing smirk, probably a jab at the crushes Delfi tends to hold on to.

"It's fine," I tell them.

"Yeah, that's the problem, Julie. It's fine. You don't need *fine*. You don't need basic ass Justin."

"Jeremy."

"Whatever."

She walks away to refill more drinks when Delfi chimes in. "He wasn't a bad guy, but yeah, he kind of sucks. And while I think you should definitely have your fun, this guy isn't it."

"I'm not looking for fun," I lie again. It sounds even more pathetic than I thought it would.

"Why not? Why don't you give yourself some joy?"

I look at her—sweet sunshine Delfina—and I wonder how it's so easy for her. How it's so easy for all of them. For T and Delfi and my brother and my mother and even

Leo, who got out, who got his own happy relationship, his own successful life.

Have I become too numb to everything that I just take whatever comes floating my way? That I just keep saying okay because it's easy? That is certainly easy, isn't it? I can't continue to be on this end saying yes.

What do *I* want right now? To be a different me. To be passionate and fun and to do the things I want to do. For me.

I catch Logan's eyes across the bar again, the drinks warming up his smile, and I make a decision then: Maybe what I don't need is easy. What I need is difficult and challenging and hard for me. Like a last-minute decision to get a haircut. Like a zero-hour decision to sign up to dance. Like keeping it going. I'm going to keep the classes going. I will at least see them through to the end of the session.

I give him a smile in return.

And then, another hard thing: for the first time, I leave Jeremy's text unanswered.

Chapter Nine

Logan

I LEAVE TARA AND Silas at the bar and make my way to the bathroom. It's been a long night; a long week really. And that's evident on my face when I catch my reflection in the mirror. Tired eyes, shoulders slumped. I feel like a wreck.

As I step out of the bathroom, I run into Julie making her way down the long narrow hallway leading to the restrooms.

"Oh. Hi." She stops walking when she sees me.

She's backlit by the dim lights lining the hallway, the outline of her almost elegant as she stands before me. It was a surprise seeing her tonight, but not an unwelcome one. She looked like she had a nice time, for whatever that's worth.

"Julie," I say again. Like I don't tire from saying it.

We stare at each other for a brief moment, unsure of how to continue this exchange. When she asks, "How are you?" it comes out in the most awkward tone, like she's trying to be professional and friendly all at once. I can't help but laugh.

"I'm alright. This is a nice place. Looks like you had a nice night."

"I did. Did you?"

"I did," I nod.

"Sorry about your date."

"My date?" I ask in confusion.

"She was kissing another guy?" She points behind her to the bar where Tara and Silas are still sitting, probably all over each other, feeding each other martini olives.

I can't help but laugh at this again, too. Tara as my date. Though I guess to any other eye it would look like that. That's the power of good partners, I guess.

"Oh, God no. Tara's my dance partner and we're friends. Nothing more."

She rears back slightly in surprise. "Oh."

"I don't date partners." I don't know why I say it. It's not *not* true, but what does it matter if she knows? And I can't deny that I've slept with enough dancers anyway.

"Oh, right." She clears her throat and frowns. "Makes sense."

"So, will I see you next week?"

"Yes, you will," she says with conviction, standing up even straighter.

"Good." I tuck my hands into my pockets, now fidgety under her stare.

"Good," she nods.

"Do you need a ride home?" I peer at her while she

stands still in front of me. I don't know how many drinks she's had, but I'd like to make sure she makes a safe choice.

"I don't get into cars with strangers," she answers succinctly.

"A good rule," I smile.

"Anyway, I'm fine," she replies, but then adds in, "Thanks, though."

"Sure. Well, have a nice night, Julie," I say, making my way out of the hallway so I, too, can head home.

"Goodnight, Logan," she says behind me, in a voice that sounds both sweet and strangely seductive. The words float between us, making a space right between my shoulder blades, and then crawl up to ring in my ears the whole way home.

***

WHEN THURSDAY NIGHT COMES around again, I see the same crowd trickle in. The couples, the familiar faces. Some new students have hopped in on this session, and they look eager to start, excited for something novel. I've seen that look before, too. Women dragging dates, girlfriends aiming for a fun night out, engaged couples looking for a reception dance. And before I realize what I'm waiting for, I see her walk in. A flowery blouse and pants again. Same shoes I happened to notice last week. That bouncy haircut that frames her face.

"Hi, Julie!" Tara calls out to her.

Julie's smile is apprehensive. Still tight-lipped, but a little brighter this time around. Her limbs are a little looser, her back a little straighter. She sets down her belongings and finds a space in the back again. Ethan slides next to her, saying hello. She offers a hello back, but then immediately looks forward to the mirror, waiting for instruction.

This time we talk about the ocho, the step that involves pivots and a figure eight motion.

We refresh our steps for the eight step and the cross. We continue to work on the basics, Tara and I leading, teaching form. Again, I catch Julie and the concentration on her face, the focus on doing it right. There's something so passionate about it. It's making me feel a little bit off balance.

After Tara and I dance the steps, everybody pairs up and I find myself going back to Julie. But this time I want to get in right before Ethan can extend his hand out.

"May I?" I offer my hand.

"You want to be my partner?" she asks, surprised.

"Well, it does take two to tango."

"Clever," she smirks.

She gives Ethan a small shrug in apology and takes my hand.

We come together slowly, still in a practice embrace, her hands gripping my upper shoulders. And then we begin to move even slower while I let her adjust to the moves, to our bodies moving in rhythm. It doesn't take very long, our adjusting, because the weird feeling that's reemerging is now a little more recognizable: this feels familiar.

This feels like we've done this dance before, like our feet have met in rhythm before. Like my body settles into a place it has known for a long time. She welcomes what we're doing. She trusts it, I quickly notice, and that's a very big thing.

"You're doing great," I say.

"Oh. Thank you."

"What's your dance history?" I ask.

"My what?" She's trying to keep her focus on the steps, but that question might have taken her out of it.

"What else have you danced?"

"Oh. Well, I did ballet when I was nine. And then jazz when I was eleven. And then I quit and never looked back."

"Really? That's all?"

"Yes?" She makes a figure eight as I lead and watch her body pivot from side to side.

"Keep your chest forward toward me," I remind her. "You know tango." It's not a question, but an observation.

"I was exposed to it at a young age," she says between steps.

Her legs move along in a mesmerizing pattern. Her chest stays forward, her hips face the side and pivot. She might be counting the steps in her head, but like clock-work she's hitting every single one. I step side to side, shifting weight as I need to, allowing her space and time to hit every move. My hands twitch as I grip her upper arms in a practice hold, unknowingly squeezing to bring her closer.

"But you never danced it?"

"Kind of complicated." She keeps moving in rhythm as we're talking comfortably. This close I can't help but smell hints of perfume on her skin. "What about you?" she asks.

"I got into ballroom dancing in my teens."

"That's interesting."

I shrug. "I needed the structure of it. I liked that I could channel my focus into it."

"I can relate," she says softly.

"I have a feeling you can," I tell her.

She stills briefly, and I know she wants to look at me, but she keeps her head down, her feet in tempo. "No offense, but I kind of expected somebody older to teach this class."

Maybe she expected somebody older, or somebody different. This community is full of wonderful dancers from so many parts of the world. Dancers and mentors that I am lucky to call friends—Argentinians, Chileans, Romanians, even Americans like me taking to dance and competition.

I huff out a laugh. "I get that sometimes. I'm thirty-three, but some days I feel ancient."

Argentine tango was always my favorite, so I decided to focus on it the most when I started really dancing. The love for it fueled me through my teen years when I needed the focus, to later in life where it continued to be a lifeline. Right now, it's teetering on the edge of exhaustion. I've been giving my all for so many years, some days all I feel is my body breaking down. My alarm clock reminding me to get out of bed, but my body fighting it every step of the way. My heart saying, *you loved this, remember?* and my brain saying, *what does it matter anymore?*

"I'm a year older than you so if you're ancient, what does that make me?"

"Prehistoric, probably," I joke.

She lets out a surprised gasp, something close to a snort, and her smile starts to unfurl. My eyes track the movement, my own smile mirroring hers, my heart speeding up as I watch.

The song ends, and we part. I give her a bow in thank you, wondering why, right now, my body is saying, *bring her back, do it again.*

I head back up to the front of the class where Tara and I discuss next week's steps and agenda.

"Once the twelve-week course is up, we host a fun milonga night with students and other regulars in the tango community. Tara and I have been doing this for several years now, and it's always a great time. A night of social dancing, drinks, usually some locally made empanadas. A great time all around."

The class breaks out in scattered applause and cheers.

"That being said, we've got some news to share," I start.

"As some of you may know, my boyfriend, Silas, is in medical school," Tara cuts in. "He just got matched for residency and ..." she pauses to take a breath. "We'll be moving to Arizona in ten weeks."

This news is met with gasps and congratulations, surprised *ohs* and sad *aws*. I even see Tara wipe her eye as she thanks them, taking one more breath. I happen to notice Julie, eyes wide like in shock, clapping along with everybody else.

"I will be here till the end of the session. And not to get too ahead of myself, but I do want to thank you all for being such a wonderful community."

"This milonga will be a goodbye party, too. Let's make this a big send off for Tara," I add in. "Thank you for a great class. See you next week."

The crowd disperses, most of them coming up to Tara to give hugs and chat. Shortly after, they grab their belongings and walk out the door. Julie grabs her bag and checks her phone, frowning once more, then says goodbye as she follows the other students out.

"You okay?" Tara asks behind me as I'm looking at the door.

"Yeah. Good." My response is almost robotic.

"Uh-huh," she says like she doesn't quite believe me. "What?"

"Maybe your future is in Pro-Am," she laughs.

"Oh yeah? You pawning me off on amateur dancers now?"

"Just one," she says pointedly, laughing again.

"Oh, shut up." I move and start gathering my own belongings. We fall into silence as we both pack up together. There's been something else on my mind, and I don't know how to bring it up, but with that ProAm comment now may be a good a time as any. "I've been looking for some jobs."

Her eyebrows lift. "Really?"

"Just looking."

"For what?" She stops packing up to face me.

"I don't know," I sigh, frustrated. "Something normal? Something that doesn't involve so much travel."

She eyes me thoughtfully for a beat. "You're really having a hard time, huh?" Her voice is tender, but we both know that question is rhetorical. And after the last competition, maybe I just need to let myself know when it's time to quit, too. "You've got to take care of you, Logan. I get it."

"I don't know what I'm doing yet, anyway. Like I said, just looking." My statement sounds non-committal, because it *is*. Frustratingly so. When I take one step forward, steadfast on making a change, something brings me back.

Something else makes me waver.

"How's Gavin doing, by the way?"

She knows about his layoff. Maybe she notices the similarities in the two of us now looking for new jobs. Or maybe she just wants to let me off the hook for now.

"I ... don't know," I say. "The other night, I came home and we sat down and watched TV together."

"Huh," she mumbles curiously.

"I know." I nod in agreement. "And it was nice."

"Is he job searching, too?"

"Not sure." He might not be, but I'm not going to pressure him into any of it. If it's evident that I'm having a hard time, it's sure as hell evident that he is, too. "Are *you* okay?"

Tara sighs loudly. "I know it's the right thing, but it still sucks," she says.

"I know. They all love you. They're going to miss you."

"I'm going to miss it here, too," she says quietly.

We've been partners for six years, but we've known each other close to ten. Tara and I met at a tango festival, and then kept running into each other after that. It's a small community that way, always running in the same circles. I always trusted her; we always had fun. When her longtime partner decided to retire from competing, we decided to partner up. And there was no stopping us from there.

But everything comes to an end, especially in this business. We've seen many retire or move away. We've wit-

nessed divorces and petty arguments break up partner-
ships. We've been privy to too many messes, so we always opted to stay truthful, to keep it professional, to
stay friends. And to go out there and kick ass. We spent
years competing, teaching, traveling to festivals, hosting
our own weekend workshops. Now here we are.

I always thought this would be part of my life forever,
but that's not the reality.

"We've had a good run," I say, lightly teasing.

"You're not getting rid of me that easy, asshole."

"Unfortunately."

"You'll find my replacement soon enough anyway."

I laugh. "I'm not looking for a replacement. I'm looking for another job, remember?"

"Whatever you say," she shrugs, as we both walk out of
the studio and head home.

Chapter Ten
Julieta

"You're in my way."

"Oh! I'm sorry." I'm looking at the spices in the grocery aisle when a woman pushes her cart up to me. I take a step back and allow her to pass directly in front of me, sighing deeply as she does.

I head down the ready-made foods aisle, grabbing packaged salads and quick meals for the week and whatever snacks I can find on sale. My hectic schedule doesn't allow for a lot of cooking time, so dinners usually involve premade foods or something in the slow cooker that Delfi got me for Christmas one year.

I grab bags of chips and pretzel sticks, plus Delfi's favorite hummus. I stock up on the cheese T really likes, beers and LaCroix for my brother, always keeping things available for whenever they show up unannounced.

As I turn the corner, I bump into another cart headfirst, an embarrassing yelp coming from my mouth.

"We've got to stop meeting like this, Julie." Logan. Bedhead hair, mischievous grin, warm eyes, tall and lean and ... hell, I'm checking this man out in a grocery store.

It's a Saturday morning, and suddenly I feel under dressed in my bike shorts and faded t-shirt that I threw on before leaving the house.

"What are you doing here?" I stupidly ask.

"Probably the same thing you're doing." He points to my cart.

"Right." I sneak a peek at his. Pop-tarts. Cinnamon Toast Crunch. Uncrustables. A teenager's dream.

His eyes narrow. "I can feel you silently judging my cart right now."

"Oh no, I—"

"Which, by the way, is full of very delicious foods that truly should not have an age limit no matter what society says. But that's probably a conversation for another day."

"Probably." I find that I'm smiling, so I give a little more in return. "I wasn't silently judging your cart. I've always been ... fascinated with other people's grocery carts. Since I was a kid. Probably because what we had in my house was so different."

While my friends ate meatloaf dinners at the reasonable time of six o'clock, my dinners consisted of my mom's guiso or a crispy milanesa at the very reasonable Argentinian time of nine o'clock.

"You mean, your household didn't contain the gourmet delicacy of an Uncrustable?"

"I've never even had a peanut butter and jelly sandwich."

He gapes at me. "You're kidding."

"No," I shake my head, smiling.

"What sad, sad world are you from?"

"Argentina, actually."

His smile drops, then turns into a look of pleasant surprise. "Shit, seriously?"

"Yeah," I nod.

"Vos sos Argentina?"

This makes me smile bigger. He's spoken some words in Spanish during class, and it took me a little by surprise when I first heard them.

"Y no me dijiste nada?" he teases.

He speaks it well, and funny enough, with a clear Argentinian accent. "Your Spanish is impressive."

"Gracias," he says, mirroring my smile. "I don't know. Part of me felt like a hypocrite immersing myself into the dance and culture and not knowing the language. So, I learned it." He shrugs like it's not a big deal, but it really is.

"Why do you say it like that? That's amazing."

"You're the real deal, though. Why didn't you mention you were from Argentina?"

I shrug. This topic always pushes me into uncomfortable territory.

"That's really cool," he says, almost admirably. "It's a beautiful country."

"That it is."

"Ah, and you were probably looking for an Argentin-ian instructor, weren't you?"

"Instructor? Oh, no. No. I don't really know what I was looking for. I kind of signed up on a whim."

"You don't dance like you signed up on a whim."

"I think that's a compliment?"

He chuckles. "You're good. Are you coming to the milonga?"

"Me?" I ask reluctantly.

"Yeah, you."

"Oh, I don't know."

"Why not?" he asks casually.

"Just wasn't planning on going that far with it, I guess."

"Well, what *were* you planning on doing with those vintage shoes you wore to a tango class you signed up for on a whim?" His voice is light, teasing, suggestively deeper.

I have no response to this. All I can do is look at him while he stares back, waiting for a response, knowing he's caught me, smirk right on his lips. It's probably that smirk that will do me in. It's surely that smirk that has me enter-taining anything he's saying.

"I'll think about it," I tell him, which is true. I will think about it. For all of two seconds and then toss it right out of my mind. Dance classes are one thing—an hour a week that acts as a distraction from my hectic life, a reprieve from the busy and the nonstop. A time where I can give in to what I want. I've allowed myself this.

But a milonga? An immersion into the community? A deep fall into it? That's too far. That was not part of the plan.

Certainly not in those shoes.

And if my family found out, who the hell knows what they would say. What my mother would have to say about her daughter following in her own mother's footsteps. And I know that is the ridiculous part, that I have my family's voices in a constant loop in my head. That those voices stop me from doing so much in my life.

I'm thirty-four years old and the voices in my head tell me no.

"Those shoes are from the nineties, by the way," I say, maybe a bit defensively.

"As much as it pains me to say, the nineties are considered vintage now."

"Wow, I feel old." And then surprisingly lean into the playfulness as I add, "Prehistoric, even."

He lets out a loud laugh, eyes crinkling at the corners, and I almost feel victorious in having made him laugh. Our bodies are closer now, leaning into each other. I could tell myself it's to make room for other shoppers in the aisle, but there's no denying how my body curves toward him like he's got his own gravitational pull.

"Anyway, think about it," he replies, a shrug like something could be so simple. So easy. He and Agostina would get along great. "I'll see you next Thursday."

"You will."

"Maybe get yourself a peanut butter and jelly before then. I don't want to have to dance with somebody with such an unrefined palate."

I can't help but beam at this again, more grinning than I've probably done in the past two weeks. That's a rather depressing thought.

What isn't a depressing thought is how he said he wants to dance with me again. And how he said I'm good. How he thinks I should join the milonga. How he noticed my damn shoes.

I like dancing with him, too, and the shoes give me enough confidence to do it.

I see him look in his cart and tilt his head like he's thinking about something. "Better yet ..." he says, then grabs a box of the Uncrustables, breaking the package open to get one out.

"What are you doing?" I look around the store wide-eyed, prepared to find an employee lurking in a corner ready to pounce.

"Consider it an emergency situation. Like one of those moms that has to crack open a box of crackers for her hangry toddler."

"And I'm the hangry toddler?"

"Yep." He puts his hand out, the Uncrustable sitting

right in the middle of his palm.

"It's still frozen."

"They're actually better that way. Insider secret."

I take the package from his palm slowly and unwrap it gently, almost like wanting to prolong this bizarrely touching moment we're having inside of the grocery store.

"I opened a bag of chips halfway through shopping once," I tell him.

"I knew you had a wild streak in you."

I chuckle at that, taking a bite of this peanut butter and jelly concoction in my hands. I chew thoughtfully, the salty bite from the peanut butter playing against the sweet jelly wrapped in a doughy, still slightly frozen, piece of bread. He stares at me, anticipating, waiting for what will surely be a mind-blowing experience.

"It's not bad."

"Not bad?" He sounds appalled. "This is the greatest culinary invention in history, probably only second to twice baked potatoes."

I snort. It's not bad. But what's even better is the thought of it. The sincere way he offered me one, the experience he's pushed me to have, gently, carefully. Sweetly.

"Thanks, Logan." My face hurts from how much it's been smiling, stretched into a joyful grin.

"Anytime, Julie," he says tenderly, as his face mimics mine. I'm starting to really like the sound of my name on his tongue.

I hold the remaining sandwich in my hand, not clamoring to eat more, but not wanting to throw it away either.

"Want to split the rest?" I offer.

"I'll never say no to an Uncrustable." We laugh as I tear it in half and pass a piece over to him. He finishes the rest in a handful of bites, smiling while he chews. His eyes light up when he smiles like that. Small crinkles at the corners, and his face softens even more. He is handsome. And fun-loving, and good-spirited. All the things that are evident in his face now, though not necessarily always. Out-of-studio Logan is much looser around the edges than in-studio Logan. Though I can't say I hate either one.

"So. Tara's leaving. That must be hard," I say.

"It's alright. It's life." His voice sounds tight.

"I guess so. Will you find a new partner? How does that work?"

He hesitates before answering, and I worry I've overstepped. "Um. Not sure. Sometimes it takes a while to find somebody you can vibe with. It's not so easy." He shrugs.

"Oh. That makes sense." Except I don't know how much sense it makes. My grandmother danced with my grandfather the majority of her career. But maybe he's right. There's certainly a connection that needs to be had.

"Alright, well I'll see you Thursday, then," he says.

"See you Thursday," I nod and wave my goodbye, walking toward the bread aisle and feeling his eyes on me the whole way there.

Chapter Eleven

Julieta

"The limes go on the other side. No, not there. Other side." T's voice sounds clipped, all business, as I walk up to the bar. "Hey Trevor, can you show Gavin where the boxes go in the back?"

As I sit down on the barstool, I notice the new face behind the bar. Tall, lean and polished. They walk to the back, chatting quietly, and I notice T prepping glasses and garnishes for the night with her stoic, resting bitch face.

"What's going on?" I hedge.

Delfi slides up next to me then.

"Fucking Steve, that's what," she retorts. "Brings in his buddy as a new hire, and has me train him for a position that *I* want."

My eyebrows lift in hearing this.

"What a fucking surprise. Steve and his bullshit strike again." She huffs out an angry breath, moving bar glasses around with force. "Why the *fuck* am I still here?"

Trevor and the new hire walk back over, just as a couple settles in at the bar. T moves to making our usual drinks and greeting the couple. As she comes over with our orders, the new hire slowly moves in.

"Hi, I'm Gavin," he says, stretching his hand out for a handshake. All those sharp edges: a sharp jaw, taut cheekbones are juxtaposed with warm eyes and a soft demeanor as he introduces himself. There's something strangely familiar about it.

"Julie," I respond, taking his hand.

"Delfina," she says with an overly friendly smile.

"My cousins," T adds in firmly.

"Nice to meet you," Gavin nods, then turns to T and lifts up extra bottles. "Where do these go?"

"In the storage closet," she responds curtly, and he walks away, leaving the three of us in a strange silence.

"Hm." Delfi breaks it.

"Don't," T says quickly.

"He is ... *good-looking*."

"Christ. Pretty sure Samantha already dropped her panties somewhere, and Manny has a sudden desire to upsell drinks to all his tables."

Delfi snorts a laugh while I hide a smile behind my own drink.

"He's also trying to steal my job," she hisses under her breath.

"Okay, I need some snacks for this show. Let's get the calamari," Delfi says. She holds up the menu, looking through it as if we're not here all the time. "Want to try the burrata? Or maybe a flatbread?"

"That sounds good," I say.

T takes our order and continues with her night, chatting with her regulars, making drinks for the tables as she goes. Trevor works alongside her, and Gavin watches everything, getting acclimated to T and her own brand of chaos.

I turn to Delfi. "How was your week?"

"Oh, it was fine." She waves it away. "How are you? How have things been?"

While I've been feeling so mentally drained and unhappy at my job, it's only been accentuated by the fact that I now have something fun in my life. Something that allows me to feel excitement instead of indifference, or stagnation, or irritability.

"Oh, you know. Same shit." I shrug. Doesn't mean I'm comfortable telling them about it, though.

"How's Babs?" T asks me, using the nickname she's given Barbara.

"One of these days I'm going to slip and call her Babs and she's going to key my car and fire me."

"I don't think she has it in her to key your car."

"I've seen her do worse for less. Just last week she screamed at Jim in front of the whole office and told him he would be uninvited from the holiday party."

"She's so miserable." T scowls.

"I had a boss like that. It's never good to be in that

environment," Gavin chimes in. I didn't realize he was listening, but now I feel concerned that he might have heard something he shouldn't have.

Agostina just gives him a very hard look, one that screams, *nobody fucking asked you.*

But Gavin just shrugs, unbothered. "I'm just giving my two cents."

"You can keep them," she retorts.

Trevor laughs in the background. "He's not afraid of you, T."

"I know," she mumbles under her breath, giving him a look from the corner of her eye. "It's bad for business."

The bar is starting to really fill up now. Stragglers from a large party in the party room, couples and friends ordering drinks and bar bites. T moves effortlessly through the bar as she always has, efficient and quick and damn good at her job. Trevor and Gavin move quietly in the background with her. Gavin is focused, learning, the perfect complement to her organized chaos.

Manny comes by checking on his drinks, saying hi to us in passing. "Dale, rubia. I need my drinks for table 32."

T just ignores his comments, setting down the two drinks in question.

The night continues in a blur until everything starts winding down. The din of the restaurant falls into a more agreeable sound. Low murmurs, a slower rhythm. I should get back to my cases. I should work on some tonight. But for once I think, *maybe tomorrow. Maybe this weekend.* Tonight, let me enjoy this. Delfi and I are just relaxing, and I'm not in a hurry to go anywhere, to just sit in the pleasure of it. I've got a near-empty glass, and our snacks are mostly gone. T is quietly wiping down the bar, showing Gavin how to start closing everything.

"We're headed next door after this," T says to the guys working around her.

"Count me in," Delfi says.

The restaurant closes at ten o'clock, so they will usually clean up and head over to the bar down the street. It's tucked away off the main road and conveniently stays open until two in the morning. I always opt to go home, but tonight I'm feeling energized. A little more alive. A bit more enthusiastic than I have been in quite some time.

"Can I join?" I blurt out.

Delfi and T's eyes widen, and I almost shrink down in my stool for asking.

"Fuck yes," T responds enthusiastically, and my answering smile is quietly filled with relief.

"You look good, Julie. Something going on?" Delfina asks.

"Not sure how offended I should be by that question."

"She's just living life with her snazzy new haircut." T winks at me. Maybe that's it. Maybe I'm just playing the role of new me. Maybe once my hair grows back this roller-coaster might end, but for now I might as well hold on tight because even I don't know what's getting into me.

***

DELFINA AND I FIND ourselves at the bar next door close to eleven, T trailing behind with Manny and some of the kitchen crew. They all wave to the bartender once they walk in, some lining up at the bar, some sitting on stools, others taking their drinks and snacks to the outside patio area. This bar—not fancy in the slightest, with a gaudy nautical theme and names carved into the wood tables—is a neighborhood and staff favorite.

"Hey Derek, let me get two glasses of the IPA on tap," T calls out to the bartender, ordering drinks for her and Manny. She turns back to Delfi and me and asks, "What do you want?"

"Get us the same thing," I answer.

Meanwhile, Trevor calls out, "Hey T, grab me a vodka Sprite," before walking to the back patio with Manny and Delfi tagging along.

T's eyes turn sharp at something over my shoulder, but she quickly swivels back to Derek at the bar, adding on to her tab.

"Hey everybody. I invited my brother, too, if that's okay," a voice behind me says. "This is Logan."

Logan?

We all turn to find Gavin standing with his brother, who happens to be none other than *Logan*, and when he spots me, his smile slowly grows wider. The crowd mumbles scattered "heys" while Gavin comes closer. And before this can escalate to allow something else to slip, I stick my hand right out and say, "I'm Julie."

"Hi Julie." He smiles, shaking my hand briefly, eyes lingering.

How the hell do I end up seeing this guy everywhere?

"We've got a table out back," T says to them, balancing beers and mixed drinks expertly in her hands, then turning to walk away.

"I'll grab the rest," I call out as I set my elbows on the sticky bar littered with paper coasters. There's a jukebox in the corner, a fancy one that you have to download an app for, playing an eclectic mix of loud music.

"What do you want?" Gavin asks Logan.

"Whatever you get is fine," he responds as Derek sets the remaining drinks down in front of me. I can see their similarities standing this close—their tall and lean figures, their sharp jaws and broad shoulders. Gavin is still in his bartending uniform consisting of his white button up shirt and black slacks. He's lost the tie, though. Logan is in a basic shirt and shorts, something simple, but he wears it so well. He's effortlessly cool, so comfortable in his body. Maybe that's the dancer in him, I don't know.

I grab the drinks and hear Logan's voice beside me.

"Need help?"

"I've got it, thanks." I lift one in brief cheers, then turn and walk to the patio.

The outdoor patio sits under an awning with several high tops and low tables around the perimeter and three pool tables off to the side. It's surrounded by bushes and greenery, and twinkling lights hang from the awning. Manny found their usual high top near the pool tables and snagged one for playing. T is getting her cue set up while Manny racks the balls. I walk over to join Delfina, passing her a beer.

"Damn. Good genetics," she says, eyeing Logan and Gavin stepping outside with draft beers in their hands.

"I know."

"Wait. Isn't that the guy we saw last time?"

"Is it?" I feign interest and take a sip of my drink. "How do you even remember that?"

"Can't forget a face like that."

Another pool table has emptied out, so when the brothers walk up to our table, Gavin asks, "Anybody want to play?"

"Sure!" Delfina answers. Logan takes her seat, leaving the two of us at the table.

I take one long swig of my drink then set it down gently, the condensation already growing on my glass on this humid night. The rotating fan in the corner above our table is occasionally throwing a welcome breeze my way, my hair swaying with it.

"Should I be concerned with how often I've been running into you?" I ask Logan while looking over at Manny gloating over his good shot.

"Should I?"

I crack a smile. "So, your brother is the new bartender."

"Guess so. He got laid off from his other job, so I mentioned the restaurant last time Tara and I were there."

I watch Gavin miss a shot. "That sucks about getting laid off." I think about what I would do if I got laid off. Probably cheer. Probably decide to reinvent my life. Or, realistically, probably just daydream about it and go get another office job.

"And what do you do? Considering how often I've run into you I don't really know much about you."

I turn to face him then. "I'm a lawyer."

His eyebrows shoot up briefly. "That's fancy."

"Is it?" I guess it is on paper, but most days it feels less than fancy when I'm elbow deep in paperwork, up late at night sacrificing sleep and social time for it.

"I can see it." He nods, taking a sip of his own beer.

"See what?"

"Your personality matches," he chuckles.

"That's depressing." I scowl.

"Oh, not in a bad way. Just ..."

An upbeat song starts to play on the speakers, something from that jukebox. T and Manny start to dance, and

I can't help but smile.

"And those are your friends?"

"Cousins. Well, Agostina is. She's the blonde. Everybody just calls her T. And Delfi is the brunette." I point to Delfina playing pool with Gavin.

"Ah, got it."

"Manny is a friend," I explain. "And your brother's coworker," I add.

"Yeah, guess so," he chuckles. "That's nice." He smiles softly.

The moment we had in the grocery store feels like ages ago. I almost wonder if I imagined it. The bubble we were in then seems to have burst now, out in the open, with so many other faces around.

We look at each other, and I wish I knew what he was thinking.

"Tell the truth, now. How many boxes of Uncrustables did you buy after that first bite?" he asks, smirking.

I slowly smile at the question, the topic that makes me think maybe he's been thinking about me, too. "I bought them out," I say, grinning as I sip my drink.

"The only appropriate answer."

The grocery store might have been one time, but the dance classes have been consistent. And with all these faces around, I can't help but feel a little uneasy.

"Don't tell them about it," I say then.

He meets my eyes in question.

"The dance classes," I clarify. "I'm sorry I've been acting like I don't know you."

"I'd tell you I'm not offended, but I *am* confused." He gives a quiet laugh.

"It's ... complicated."

He eyes me curiously. "Family usually is."

I sigh loudly. "Complicated like you're so sure they love you unconditionally, but sometimes things sure do feel conditional."

The look on his face mirroring mine looks like he might have his own experiences, own grievances with it. The complications of family. The hard parts of it. The good parts, too.

"I love my family," I start. "So much. But they're also a lot. I like to think my cousins would support me no matter what, but who knows what would happen if the news inevitably traveled up the chain." I take another sip, looking over at Delfina aiming for a corner shot. "Like I said, this whole thing is complicated."

"Have you thought anymore about the milonga?"

Of course, I have. And of course, the answer is still no. "Yeah."

"But you're not going to do it."

"What does it matter to you? You get commission on how many people show up?"

"Yeah. I've got bills to pay."

"Seriously?"

"No," he laughs. "I just think it would be good for you."

"And what do you know about what would be good for me?" I snap back.

His smile drops abruptly. "Not a thing."

"That was so shitty, I'm sorry." Where did that even come from? "I appreciate your enthusiasm for this, I do. And I don't expect you to understand my resistance to it, but I just don't know how ready I am for something like that."

"I'm sure you're very busy," he says in understanding. "I see you check your phone all the time. You frown at that thing more than any disappointed parent would."

I sigh in exasperation. God, what must I look like to the outside world? An overworked, boring business professional whose profession matches her boring ass personality? This is starting to get really pathetic.

I want to keep this conversation going, but Gavin and Delfi come over now, commiserating on a good game.

"Wanna play, asshat?" Gavin asks.

Logan laughs, "Nah, I'm good. See if she wants to," he says pointing to another coworker Samantha.

Gavin smirks and heads over to her, walking past T whose mouth turns to a scowl almost immediately. I bite back a laugh.

"I'm going to grab another round. Do you want one?" Logan asks.

"No, thank you. I'm probably going to head home after this."

Once Logan heads inside, I watch Gavin start a game with Samantha, while T and Delfi come back to the table.

"Making friends?" T asks upon sitting down, with a smirk.

"Being friendly," I tell her pointedly.

"He looks like he's being friendly, too." She lifts an eyebrow.

"He's thirty-three."

"And?" She asks like she fails to see any problem.

"He's younger than me."

"Seriously?" Delfi says almost in disbelief, or maybe it's renewed interest.

"Oh, shut the fuck up, Julie," T cackles. "Jesus Christ, stop making excuses. You need somebody to have fun with."

"I know how to have fun by myself."

"Oh, do you? When was the last time you had any fun? Before tonight."

I keep my mouth closed. I meant it when I said this whole thing is complicated, for so many reasons. I'm not interested in giving my secrets away right now. I don't want to talk about it, about all the fun I've been having at this tango class. About the fun I've surprisingly found outside of it, with a certain someone that is walking back over to the table with a drink in hand.

"It's time for me to head out anyway," I say, wrapping up this conversation.

"Me too, I think," Delfina agrees.

"Fine. Manny and I will keep this party going in your honor." T says.

"Be safe," I tell her, giving her a kiss goodbye on the cheek. "Text me when you get home."

"I will," she sighs. Years ago, I would have driven myself crazy trying to control what any of my other cousins, or siblings, did. I would have tried to control the drinks, the partying, the late nights. I would have tried to reason with them, get them to come home, too. I realize now I can't control them, I never could. And besides what did it get me? Sitting on the sidelines of someone else's fun. Trying to attach rules, trying to keep everything comfortable for me.

I'm older now, but I still want a text when they get home.

"Nice meeting you guys." Delfina waves to Gavin and Logan, now quietly chatting in a corner. I wave, too, leaving words between Logan and me unsaid. Leaving them lingering in the currents between us: his eyes that hold the smallest twinkle, the smirk that is showing restraint from becoming a full smile, the hand that is waving back that once held me close as we danced. This is a strange secret to keep, I know, but as conflicting as the whole experience has been, it has been no less fun.

So, for now, I'll keep thinking about the dance.

Or maybe, I'll just keep thinking about him.

I don't really know why.

***

I CUDDLE UP ON the couch with my laptop and a glass of water, googling Logan Beck like I probably should have done some weeks ago. The search results are not surprising: accolades that feature both him and Tara, his own website, the dance studio's website. Seems like he's taught at different ones throughout the city. Dance shows and events. Features in international championships. And then videos.

I cue one up and press play, a local competition from about two years ago, him and Tara taking the stage. I look on, mesmerized, this feeling not an unfamiliar one, and *yet.*

I haven't felt this in so long, the feeling of my heart being pulled from my body. The silence in the room, the desire, the burning. The way my legs are twitching. I haven't felt this since ... well, since I was eight.

It's incredible to watch, really—watching somebody do something they love and watching them do it so well. He's dancing with Tara, strong and powerful Tara, who holds the power in this dance. Perhaps that's been part of the appeal for me: how a woman's body can move so sensually, say so much. How much power it can carry throughout a song.

I notice then that this festival is one my grandmother attended several times throughout the years. As a dancer in the beginning, and then later as a guest judge. She invited me once when she had traveled to the States for it. I was in the thick of studying for exams, elbow deep in the stress of law school. By that point I was in my twenties, but I took one night and went, pushing aside my responsibilities for just a moment. And I adored it, watching these couples dance, in gorgeous glittering dresses and three-piece suits.

Of course, once my mother found out I'd skipped out on a morning class because I had been out too late the night before, I never heard the end of it. I was destroying my life, she'd said. I was throwing away my chances at a good career. I was being careless with my time.

"Pero Maria, por favor," my grandmother had chided. "Déjala." Let her be. She's young.

But after that, I couldn't let myself get off track. If only because I didn't want to hear the shit anymore. If only because I kept being reminded how much my family had already sacrificed for me to have this opportunity. And how dare I not be grateful?

Sometimes it felt like the guilt trip wasn't worth the fun I was having otherwise.

Would the guilt trip be worth the fun now?

Either way, I'm opting not to tell her. I'm choosing to keep this for myself. And even though my grandmother isn't here to see this, she left me these priceless shoes. She'd probably want me to do this.

At least that's what I'm going to tell myself.

"They are fantastic," I hear somebody in the video whisper.

She's right. And there's a frightening feeling building within me that makes me think how much I'd like to be up there, too.

My phone buzzes with an incoming email, an inconvenient reminder from Barbara that there is too much to do, too much going on and leaving the office early is 'not indicative of those who want to be here.'

Logan telling me about Gavin's layoff was an unrealistic daydream. This email from Barbara is a harsh reality. What would happen if I got fired? What would it look like if I had to sit my family down and tell them that I was let go from my job? The intrusive thought is a jolt of fear to my heart.

When I graduated college and law school, my brother joked how I was the golden child that could do no wrong. He was so proud of me, he'd said. He always looked up to me. My parents were equally impressed, so proud, so honored. My mother consistently reminded me how smart I was, how she always knew I would do great things.

But what they didn't know, what they couldn't know,

is just how stifling it is. How difficult it has rendered my life. And how I haven't noticed the extent of it until recently.

Julie with the new haircut wants to create a life she's proud of, just as she has silently wanted to do her whole life.

I *want* to do great things.

Suddenly, I feel a rush within me, almost like the swelling of a wave, the rising of a tide. I'm going to do it. I'm going to chase this one thing that is making me feel like something more. That is finally making me *feel*.

Months ago, I would have folded at the sight of this email, but right now, I'm going to figure something else out. I'm going to fight back.

Chapter Twelve

Logan

Before our parents' divorce, there was a lot of fighting. Loud accusations, angry screams, flying objects. Afterwards, things weren't much more peaceful. The thing nobody talks about with divorces is how the children become the pawns in it. Or maybe they do, but I was too young to realize that's what would happen. Gavin got stuck taking care of me in the aftermath, but I wanted out of the house as often as I could manage. Our neighbor Alison's house was always a bit of a refuge for me. She had a British father who would make us large plates of fries doused in malt vinegar for a snack. She had Nintendo and cable, and we spent a lot of time riding bikes outside. It was there that I also learned she took ballroom dance classes at the city rec center. And one day, not wanting to go back home, I opted to tag along with her instead.

It was a whole new world. Deborah, the instructor, probably taking some sort of pity on me, let me sit in, and it changed my life.

Because I was young enough, there was some sort of

discount when signing up. I pooled most of my allowance with some extra money Gavin gave me to pay for that first session, and I never missed a day. Not one day. I would hitch rides with Alison, and I would listen to Deborah and focus and learn every step. God, I loved it. I looked forward to that day of the week more than anything else. Maybe I loved it so much because of what it meant to me—a place of solace in between a shitty home life—more than what it actually was.

Except I kept going and going. I went on to compete, even with Alison as my partner sometimes. I kept climbing and climbing, holding on to the love I had for this dance with white knuckles. The thing is, once you do something long enough, even if you once loved it so much, it can wear on you. It gets tiring; It becomes a burden. Soon enough it's an ugly shadow casting everything in shade. The past couple of years have moved at a slow pace. Going through the motions: workshops and travel, festivals and shows. Like crossing off a to-do list out of habit.

And now here I am, suddenly looking forward to these sessions again. I could reason that it's like the equivalent of putting in your two weeks, knowing you'll be out soon enough. Except I haven't been job searching. Not really, anyway. Haven't had the time. No, this is something else.

And she just walked through the door.

Today Tara and I are teaching giros, turns in tango. Julie has moved up a row in the class, still focused on her feet in the mirror. Still determined to get the steps right.

"Logan and I are going to show you a proper tango hold today. You can practice this with a partner and get acclimated to it."

Tara steps next to me, and I put my arms out like in an embrace. "For the leaders, your left hand will reach up just above your shoulder. You don't want to go too high, it should be a comfortable height for you and your partner. And your right hand will come around and settle on the middle of your partner's back."

I continue. "For the followers, your right hand will meet your partner's left hand in a hold, again just slightly above the shoulder, and your left hand will come around to settle onto your partner's upper arm, similar to the practice embrace."

Tara and I show the hold in action. "This is an open embrace, which is where we will begin." Tara and I step closer, temple to temple, chest to chest. "This is a close embrace. We'll work our way up to this one." I smile.

And after Tara and I demo the steps, I see Ethan jump right in to ask Julie to dance. Maybe I just envision the quick look she gives me, but she moves closer to him, and they begin.

One of our regular students, Leonora, walks up to me confidently, asking to be my partner.

"In a minute," I tell her. "I'm going to walk around and check on everyone."

She pouts, and I pair her up with Carla to practice the steps while I keep my eyes on Julie and Ethan as much as I can.

His hands are all wrong, wrapped around her like that. His body is too close to hers. I walk over and adjust it.

"You don't want to be so close. This is an open embrace, Ethan," I tell him, my voice inexplicably clipped. "Spine straight. Don't act like a magnet to her." Which is nothing if not hypocritical because lately all I've felt like is a magnet pulled to her presence.

"Keep your hand here." I position her arm, reveling in the softness of her skin I get to touch again.

"Okay." She nods, doing as I say.

They continue to dance, both looking straight ahead, practicing the moves over and over.

Once the song is over and Tara and I have said our goodbyes for the week, Julie comes up to me.

"Can I talk to you for a moment?"

I'm surprised, maybe a little concerned. "Sure. What's up?"

"So. I've decided to attend the milonga at the end of the session," she starts. "But—"

"You can be my date." I hear Ethan's voice out of nowhere, a playful tone like he might be kidding, but I'm not quite sure.

"Oh." Julie says. And that's all she says for a moment.

"Usually, you *ask* somebody to be your date, not just

state it, Ethan." I try to keep my voice equally light and teasing, but I'm annoyed. It's basic fucking etiquette, really.

"Want to be mine?" He tries again, smirking.

I think a vein just popped in my forehead.

"Um. Okay," Julie answers apprehensively, then turns to me. "But, I was going to say, I'm having a hard time with the scheduling of this class. It's interfering with my work, unfortunately, so," she clears her throat, "would you happen to offer private classes?"

"Hey, that sounds good," Ethan chimes in, inviting himself.

The words are on the tip of my tongue—*No, I don't do private lessons*—which is the truth. I haven't done them in years, and I have no intention of starting anytime soon. But all I feel right now, besides the absolute dissolving of any fucking logic or reason, is my body and mind screaming, *don't take her from us.*

And maybe it's how she's uneasy, already anticipating a no. Maybe it's how I can recognize the look on her face as something I once felt. Or the look on Ethan's face that is saying something else altogether. I want to wipe that one off his face.

Maybe it's how I can feel my entire body zing with an awareness. *We want her back*, it's saying. *We want her near.*

And so, I tell her yes. She's stepping out of her own

comfort zone, I can tell. She's giving up a little bit of control. I can guide her through this.

"I can give you private lessons," I respond, and I'm sure that somewhere Tara has probably fainted.

"Really?" She smiles like I've given her the best gift.

"That's great," Ethan says.

"Great," I manage to say.

"Great!" Tara adds, a little too loudly.

"What would work with your schedule then?"

"I usually have to stay late in the office, so would there be an option to maybe push the time back later?" she asks hesitantly.

"We could stick to Thursdays after group class. So around seven thirty? Would that work for you?"

"I could do that," Julie agrees.

"Sounds good to me," Ethan adds in. I almost forgot he was here, wanting in on this. He turns to Julie and says, "Let's exchange numbers, and we'll go from there."

"Oh. Alright," she seemingly agrees.

"I've already got your contact information in the sign-up forms," I throw in smugly.

What the fuck was that? What the hell is happening to me right now?

Tara is probably asking herself the same question.

And sure enough, once they leave, I get it. "What was that?" she says, mouth agape.

"I don't know. I couldn't *not* do it," I tell her. "I could use the extra money, anyway." And that's true. But something else is a driving force. An ugly sense of jealousy, like my body and my brain are both ganging up on me, making me say stupid shit that I'm going to end up regretting later.

"You think maybe you're offering help that your ass can't cash?"

"What does that mean?"

She doesn't answer, instead just studies me for a moment then says, in a tone that suggests she's not thrilled about this, "Go easy on Ethan."

***

WE'VE BEEN WAITING FOR twenty minutes and there's still been no sign of him. I should have started fifteen minutes ago, but Julie wanted to wait. To give him the benefit of the doubt. Like he even deserved any of the benefit.

But about eighteen minutes in, I think she realized what was happening—phone in hand, texts unanswered—which left her looking defeated and left me feeling seven kinds of angry.

"I'm so sorry about wasting your time like this," she says apologetically. "This is ridiculous."

"It's alright." I keep my voice light, but I'm biting my tongue. "He wasn't a good partner for you anyway."

"Why not? He seemed like a nice guy. He knew the

steps; he followed them fine."

Because I didn't like how he looked dancing with you. All wrong.

"And then he ghosted you."

"Maybe he didn't like dancing with me," she shrugs.

"Then he's definitely not a good partner for you."

She sighs. I can tell she's upset, and what's worse is she feels guilty. "Maybe I didn't know the steps well enough."

"None of this is your fault, Julie."

"I'm just trying to do something for myself here. Is this a sign from the universe that I'm asking for more than I deserve? Am I being knocked down a peg? Should I stay in my lane?" Her laughter is tense, her mouth is clenched.

"Sounds like this has been difficult," I start, trying to decipher what she's said. "Would you like to keep the private classes going then?"

"Why bother?" She asks bitterly, and it's a feeling that I know all too well.

"Because you deserve the joy of dancing."

She stills. "What?"

"I felt that way once, too," I tell her. "This career can have a lot of ups and downs. You know what my old mentor told me once? *'You deserve the joy of dancing.'.* She was right. She was always right. And now I'm letting you know."

Her eyes soften at that, they way mine probably did when she told me those powerful words.

"He wasn't a good partner for you. You lost him, but you've still got me." I swallow.

"You," she repeats flatly.

"Are you gonna look me in the eyes and tell me we're not good together?"

She opens her mouth to speak, but she shuts it just as quickly, looking stunned. What even possessed me to say that? My mouth has zero filters around her.

"Logan," she begins, and the reaction to her saying my name is another sharp zing. "When I signed up for these lessons, I had another idea in mind. I didn't mention it at first, but..." she trails off, looking like she's unsure of what to say next. She steps side to side, restless and fidgety, and it's got me curious.

"But?"

"There's a competition. One for the San Diego Tango Festival. Have you heard of it?"

Have I heard of it? Uh, yeah. I nod in response.

"Right. Of course you would have," she mumbles. "Well, I want to do it."

Shit. I did not expect it to go this way. My raised eyebrows might be showing that.

"I need a partner, and ..." she shuts her eyes, like it must pain her to be asking for help like this. "Well, I was going to ask Ethan, but as you can see ..." she waves her hand around the empty studio.

I can sense what's coming, the impending question

that I hope I'm reading wrong, but probably not.

"If you think we're as good of partners as you say, would you be interested in doing this with me?" I might hear a tremor in her voice.

How did we get here?

"I ..." I told myself I'd never go back to San Diego. I told myself I was done with it. "Why do you want to do that one specifically, if I may ask?"

"Personal reasons."

That's all I'm getting? I'm quiet for a moment as I try to figure out where to even take this conversation.

"Like I said, I was going to ask Ethan about this, but clearly that didn't work out. If you don't want—"

"I'll do it," I blurt. *Fuck.*

I almost instantly regret it. But then I look at her and I decide to stop fighting with myself. I decide, impulsively, to join in. She wants to do this, and, for reasons I'm trying to untangle myself, I can't say no. So, something short of rash and ridiculous and probably fucking stupid, I'm going to do it with her.

"I'll be your partner and we'll compete together." Fucking hell, if Tara could hear this now.

"Really?" she asks quietly, hopefully, then looks down at her shoes.

"This is important to you, and I want you to experience it, so why not?" That sounds reasonable.

"And we'll keep doing the private classes?"

"Yeah. You and me. Fuck Ethan." This gets a chuckle out of her. I'd join her if my chest didn't feel so tight. "We'll work on a routine and get you ready for San Diego."

She takes a deep breath before she answers with a smile. "Alright."

But that alright sets me on edge. That alright makes me feel more alive than I have in the past year. That alright sets my whole entire heart in motion, like it's waking up from one very deep slumber.

"Alright, Julie."

And right when I think it's the end of it, she keeps going.

"Teach me," she says, firmly this time. Like she knows just what she wants. "Teach me how to be a good tango dancer. Teach me how to do it right. I want to know everything." She's voracious in how she tells me this, like she's starving for all this knowledge.

I haven't seen such energy about dance since I started dancing myself. There's something about the way she's approaching this experience that is refreshing. It's genuine and vulnerable and exciting. Fiery and passionate. And it might be making me love this dance again.

"This class was on the house. Let's start fresh next one."

I can't deny that I'm excited, that I'm ready to dive in. But there's an underlying current of nerves, something that's got me feeling jittery and reckless.

It's always been about the craft, and suddenly, it feels

like it's not.

Chapter Thirteen

Julieta

"I Googled you the other day," I tell him, standing in the middle of this dance studio facing the mirror. This place seems much bigger with fewer people in it. The mirror feels much more intimidating when it's just me staring at it, waiting for direction.

I still can't believe I'm doing this. I still can't believe I asked. I figured I could run it by Ethan during the private class if it went well, but it clearly didn't. In the middle of that mess, I realized maybe it could be Logan instead. I was prepared for a no; there was no way he would agree to it. Except that he did, and now we're here.

It seems like one impulsive decision has led to a plethora of them. One after the other, like this is who I've been all along. The rush of signing up for lessons in the first place was the beginning of a whole mountain of them: classes and a haircut and a plan to go to San Diego. Who am I right now? I'm still not sure how I'm going to get that news past everyone, but maybe that's a problem for Future Julie.

"Oh yeah? Find anything fun?" he asks.

"Some videos."

"Do tell." He narrows his eyes.

"You were incredible." I sigh.

"Just lots of practice," he says casually, unbothered.

"Don't be so humble," I call out. "You're a wonderful dancer. You're good with your feet." I point to his. "There was one video where you did a giro and ocho. I loved how you did it, how your feet stepped in line. Tara is fantastic, too. She's so beautiful, so graceful. What a great partnership you two have. Or, had." I wince.

He doesn't say anything in response, just smiles as he listens to me ramble on. And at this point, I am absolutely rambling.

"You've traveled all over the world, it seems like. You've won championships."

"Tell me more about your research," he grins.

I have the decency to blush at least. "It's very admirable, your success."

"Mm. Success is relative." He comes to stand next to me, looking at me in the mirror as he speaks. "You're very successful, too."

My parents think so, I want to tell him.

"We'll start with a warmup and then some basic moves," he says, redirecting the conversation to why we're here.

We go through the moves slowly, Logan detailing every step and proper form. We're starting from the beginning again, but I don't mind. I like this thorough exploration of the dance. I like it with him.

"Let's do a proper tango hold," he suggests.

His arm comes around behind my back, and mine finds a home along his upper arm. He's attentive as he touches my spine gently to adjust my posture, and the heat radiates throughout my body. I look up to meet his eyes, silently asking for validation that I'm doing this right. He looks at me, and quickly nods, like almost encouraging me to keep going. I step closer, leaning into his space, and I find that I really like it here. *This* feels intimate. This feels ... special.

I'm looking over his shoulder, our faces almost cheek to cheek, when he gives the next direction.

"Basic step," he says.

We move together on the basic eight count as he leads. Such a different experience from what I've danced so far. Maybe he was right to have me forget about Ethan.

"Remember, slow and quick," he adds, leaning into my ear. "Every slow is two beats, every quick is one. Think of that as you walk."

We refresh the steps for the basic cross, the ocho, and the giros briefly. I revel in this dance with a proper tango instructor, one who leads like he means it. One who meets me where I'm at.

Towards the end of our time, he grabs his laptop and sits down on the floor, pulling something up. I sit with him, drinking some water, and catch myself staring at his long limbs, his loosely defined muscles, his body moving fluidly.

"Does anybody else in your family dance?" I ask.

"Nah, not really. Gavin can do some basic steps, but he's not big on ballroom. More of a silent supporter." He chuckles. "What about you?"

The question inexplicably catches me off guard, and I almost choke on my sip of water. "Oh, um. My grandmother."

"That's nice. Yeah, it was very popular with that generation. Is she an avid dancer?"

I smile now—a small one, close-lipped—and nod. "She was."

"Oh, I'm sorry."

"No, don't be," I wave off. I don't usually talk about her, but in this scenario, it almost feels sacrilegious not to.

"When did you move here?" he asks, and I'm grateful for the subject change.

"I was five."

"Wow, you were practically raised here."

I can only nod in agreement, this statement so common, then drink some more water as he continues doing whatever else on his laptop.

"Truthfully, I haven't done private classes in a very long time," he says.

This surprises me. "Why did you agree to do these then? You didn't have to."

"I wanted to." He looks at me for a moment before turning back to his computer screen. "So. Homework."

"Homework?" I ask, surprised and maybe slightly appalled.

"Work on the steps we learned today at home. Practice, practice, practice," he recites. "And, if you feel so inclined, Google some more videos," he smirks. "Maybe look at some other dancers. I could give you a list of some favorites?"

"No, no," I smile. "Thank you, but I've got it."

"Great." He gives me a grin in return. "We're going to work on the basics, get them very polished, and then little by little work on improvisation, and then eventually, a routine."

"Wow," I say, almost tentatively. Maybe I'm in over my head.

"You can do it. One step at a time. That might be a tango pun."

I laugh. "This was good. Thank you."

"It's only gonna get better." It sounds like a promise, and I shouldn't love how good it sounds. There's a sudden swoop low in my belly like I'm sitting at the very top of the rollercoaster, ready to fall.

"Right. See you next week, then?" I grab my bag.

"Wouldn't miss it."

Chapter Fourteen

Julieta

"You're too ... stiff."

I scowl. *Well, then.*

"Why are you so stiff?" he asks, perplexed.

"I'm not trying to be stiff," I answer, defensively.

"Move your limbs."

"I *am* moving my limbs."

"Just ... okay, let's try this." He demonstrates a couple of exercises and warmups to get my arms and legs moving more freely.

I might be too nervous, doing these dances with him now privately. Sometimes I look at him dancing—the flawless delivery, the fluidity—and wonder how I could even match up.

"Bet you're wishing you didn't offer to do this," I mumble.

"Not even a little bit," he says firmly.

I start to backtrack, but he keeps going.

"We aren't joining the tango Olympics here. It's a fun competition. For amateurs."

"Right," I answer almost embarrassingly.

"And I agreed to be your partner because I wanted to. I don't do things I don't want to do. Remember that."

It's surprising to hear it. What a wonderful feeling that must be. *I don't do things I don't want to do.*

Logan sighs loudly, then takes a minute to, I assume, think.

"Okay, we're going to try something else." I see him walk over and grab what looks like an extra t-shirt from his bag. "Can I put this over your eyes?"

"You're going to blindfold me?" I ask, skeptically, as I look at the shirt in his hands.

"Can I?"

"Well, you're the professional, I guess."

But he doesn't rush to do it, instead just eyes me for a beat. I shouldn't do things I don't want to do, either, but in this instance, with him next to me holding this piece of fabric almost as a sort of peace offering, I find that I want it.

I swallow, then tell him, "Go ahead."

As he gently slips the fabric over my eyes, his fingertips brush against my hair, and my scalp erupts in goosebumps. He ties a knot in the back tight enough to be secure.

"I don't want you to look down at your shoes, or at me, or the mirror. I want you to feel the music. Trust your feet, and trust your body. I'm going to wrap my arm around you now, and I'll help you do the same." He takes my arms and positions them properly, his skin something warm that I get to explore through feel, and then we begin.

I start rough: stepping on his foot, tripping over nothing, missing a step.

"Dammit. Sorry," I say.

"Take your time. I'm right here."

But as it goes on, I start to find my confidence. I start to figure it out.

Maybe it's the not looking, the feeling, the trusting. The rhythm I have to follow with my own body and then his. I walk, I turn, I sidestep and move backwards in an ocho. He leads me as he always has: gently, slowly, confidently. And as we're temple to temple, intimate in our embrace, his deep voice is a reassuring sound in my ear.

"Very good."

"Perfect."

"Just like that."

With my eyes blindfolded, and his breath on the shell of my ear, these words can almost take on a whole new meaning.

This is just a dance. He's a professional. But it doesn't stop my body from responding the way it does—a shiver and a trail of goosebumps on my arm. A racing heartbeat, and a secret wish. Thank God I'm blindfolded so I can be saved the embarrassment of him noticing and looking at me. Once the dance comes to an end, I pull back but keep the blindfold on as I wait for more instruction.

"That was great. Let's do it again," he says eagerly.

And so, we do. I wrap my arms around him, and his find a comfortable home around me.

A walk, a sidestep, an ocho, a medio giro. Again, and again. The feeling is now fiery, deep in my chest and finding a way through my veins.

His tone is low in my ear as he takes the blindfold off. "That was even better." Our eyes meet, and his are a shade darker than I remember, burning into mine. "One more time without it. With music."

I can do nothing but oblige.

The song starts, playing loudly through the speakers. This song is all longing and seduction, a slow rhythm meant to make for a deliciously slow dance. I walk to him slowly and we come together in an embrace. His fingers lightly brush against my ribs, moving to my back.

This is a surreal moment, grasping the elusive feeling I've been chasing since I started. The harmony in how we are dancing, the anticipation of each move, the follow-through. I'm letting the music move me. I'm letting it dictate as I follow.

I envision every step, I sweat with every turn. I stay focused but loose, allowing myself a moment out of the rigidity. I dream of his every step and fall in line accordingly. He leads like he was born to do it.

This time as we dance, I play the part. I let myself believe it: that I'm his, that he's desperate for me. That I will most certainly fall to pieces if he leaves me. That I do nothing but dream of his hands and his eyes and his lips. But I'm finding that with him it's not too hard to pretend.

He is temple to temple with me, eyes closed like he's savoring all of this, too. We sway and sway, and glide along this floor like we own it. He's not offering any words of encouragement or otherwise, there's just the music and our silence. All we want to say is being said through this dance. All I want to convey is being freed through these moves.

And when we stop, the music comes to an abrupt finish that should end with a pose, but we don't break away. We stay, mere inches apart, out of breath, staring. I feel elation. This overwhelming, expanding feeling in my chest that is desperately looking for an outlet.

Logan's smile unfurls slowly as mine follows, and his eyes fall to my mouth. The feeling, slippery and explosive in equal measure, finds an outlet in the form of a hug. One big, warm hug where my arms wrap around behind his neck, and my body takes space right next against his. A surprised grunt slips out of his mouth as I practically jump him, but his responsive arms reach around to hold me, squeeze me, and just like this I can feel how fast his heart is beating. How it sounds as fast as mine. How the dance really took it out of us.

"Thank you for today," I tell him against his shoulder, my voice muffled.

"Thank *you*," he says quietly.

"Are hugs okay? Does this break some sort of professional code?"

He chuckles quietly, rubbing my back gently. "Hugs are great."

I peel away from him as I reluctantly say goodbye. I wish I could stay here forever. But I take my belongings, and my smile, big and bright, and I float home.

So much for not feeling anything. Right now, I feel *everything*.

Chapter Fifteen

Logan

It's past eleven in the morning when Gavin stumbles out of his bedroom, yawning.

"Late night?" I ask from the couch, huddled over my laptop working on a class syllabus.

"Mm," he mumbles in response.

He's been coming home late most nights, a different schedule than what we've both been used to.

"How's work going?" I ask.

"Good, actually." He makes himself a big bowl of Cinnamon Toast Crunch, our favorite with stockpiled boxes in the cabinet. "Really good."

"Yeah?"

"Yeah." He nods. "Well, Steve's a fucking mess, but it's ... different. I'm still getting to talk to people, meet people, but it's a little chaotic and fun and just something new." There's a light back in his eyes, something I didn't fully realize was missing until just now. "My body's sore as shit and I get home really late smelling like a fryer, but I'm having a great time." He smiles around a mouthful of cereal. "How about you?"

"Same," I laugh.

"Oh yeah? How are the lessons with Julie?"

"They're going really well." I choose my words wisely.

But there's no denying that they *are* going well. The last class took a turn into unpredictable territory. I don't know what I was thinking blindfolding her, but it helped. It fucking did something, that's for sure.

And that hug? She *hugged* me.

It's been one thing dancing with her, holding her close in a proper tango hold, but that was a kind of intimacy that left my body craving more. I'm not *not* a hugger, but the feel of her chest pressed up against mine, and her arms holding me tight like she couldn't bear to let go, broke something open in me. I didn't want it to end.

With each class I see her let loose a little bit more, and it's only fueling this fire. She's got power, more than she notices. She's got an energy. It's like she's been pressed into a box for so long, I wonder what would happen if somebody let her out.

"Is she better than Tara?"

"She's different." Not that I would compare the two, anyway. There is no comparing them. Tara has had decades of experience, and at the end of the day, Julie is still an amateur. "She's a different dancer than Tara, but—I can't believe I'm saying this—I might feel a stronger connection with her. There's a chemistry I feel like I've been missing."

"Chemistry is good."

I scratch the back of my neck. Chemistry is not what I was expecting. "Tara and I were great partners, but we're tired. She's acknowledging it; she's taking a step back. I don't blame her."

"But Julie?" he asks with a smirk.

But Julie. Fuck, Julie is giving everything, and I can't stop now. Not yet.

"I thought I was done with it, too," I say. I know it's not really a direct response to what he's asking. But what I mean is that maybe these classes with Julie are somehow throwing me back in.

"Life surprises you sometimes." He smiles around a mouthful of cereal like he knows what I mean.

"How's it going working with her cousin?"

He pins me with a stare. "Don't ask."

"That bad?"

"Nah," he says, smiling to himself. "Not that bad."

He yawns again, pouring more cereal into the bowl.

"Hey," he says. "I like this. You being home more. Me being home more."

These moments between us aren't new, but it's been so long I kind of forgot how comforting they could be.

"Me, too," I say.

But with that, I have to get up and get ready to go.

***

"How are the private classes going?" Tara asks once group class is done. The students have filed out, leaving us alone and the studio empty.

"They're good. Good." I nod in response. That's believable enough, right? That shouldn't result in any extra questioning. I've kept her up to date with the basics: Ethan bailed; Julie wanted to keep going, but things have gotten admittedly a bit more complex.

"Good," she repeats skeptically. "Uh-huh."

"We've got the third one tonight."

"So, she was just looking for classes that worked with her schedule?" she asks, digging for more information.

"Yeah." My voice cracks. I rub the back of my neck, clearing my throat. "Actually, she asked me to compete with her in San Diego."

She meets me with stunned silence.

"I don't know," I groan. "I don't *know*. This is so different from everything I've been feeling." I run my hands through my dark hair, pulling at the ends in frustration, making it even messier. "This seemed important to her. I can help her."

"You can," she says then, her voice firm, her eyes soft. Before I can say anything else, she adds in, "I've got to get going. Meeting Silas. But keep me posted on this. Please."

She gives me a hug goodbye and slips out quickly.

I have always liked the stability and precision of this dance. During separate houses and holidays, alternating weekends, and parents bad-mouthing one another, this dance kept me grounded and centered. But Julie's making me feel off balance now. She's starting to chip away at this numbness. Making me a little more reckless.

"Alright, what are we doing today?" Julie throws her bag down as she walks in, a night and day difference from when she first walked into this studio, looking for a way out.

She slips out of her blazer and there's something about the act, the jacket sliding off her shoulders in slow motion and exposing her soft arms, and me watching, that is making me feel ... *starved*. Desperately hungry as my eyes study every curve of her. I turn to look away, busying myself with the music selection.

I clear my throat. "We're going to work on boleos, ganchos, and enganches today."

"Sounds like a lot," she says.

"You can do it." I stand to walk over to her and can't help but smile. "So, I'm going to lead with an ocho, and then quickly whip you around. You'll twist your body, kicking your leg up."

I show her the steps in the mirror, first solo, and then in position, leading her and guiding her through them.

"The gancho is a hook, so your leg is meant to hook

around mine," I state. "I'll lead you in an ocho, but on one step you'll swivel a bit farther, and my leg will step into place behind you, and it will allow for you to kick up between my legs."

Again, I walk her through the steps slowly, repeating them over and over.

"Make sense?"

The first time we try together, she kicks me right in the calf.

"Oh shit, sorry!" she says.

"I'm alright," I wince. "Let's try again."

And so we do. Again and again. She's agitated, and she seems off.

"Dammit," she hisses, looking at her feet in the mirror.

"Just take your time," I remind her calmly.

But her steps are stilted, just a beat off. She's trying to rush through it like she's trying to get this lesson over with. None of the confidence she walked in with is showing now. It seems like this sudden addition of new steps has thrown a wrench in it.

"Hey, let's take a water break," I offer.

"No, I'm fine." Her voice is clipped.

"Julie, come on," I push.

"No. I have to get this right."

"You don't have to do anything right now," I say softly, a contrast to her firm tone.

"Yes, I do." She's adamant. "This competition is in

eight weeks. I don't even know what the hell I'm doing."

She stares at her feet in the mirror, working on the moves over and over. Her body seems tired, lacking energy. There's something in her face: maybe anger, but deep down, disappointment.

"Who are you trying to please?"

"What?"

"Who is it that you are trying to please in taking these classes? Your family? Or you?"

She doesn't answer, instead just pins me with a look then turns away.

"The correct answer is yourself."

Frustrated, and tired, she gives in, sitting down and taking sips of water.

"I'm sorry." She sighs. "I'm having a hard day."

I sit down across from her, keeping a small distance. "Work, or ...?"

"Work. Life. I don't know." She frowns, defeated. "I don't like making mistakes."

"Nobody does, Julie."

But she shakes her head like that was a stupid response. "I feel like I *can't* make mistakes."

That I understand, too.

"I can't make mistakes, and I can't do anything wrong because if I do then it's clear that I shouldn't have been doing this in the first place. And if I can't figure it out, then maybe I'm wasting my time. And maybe I'm not even worthy of the time spent on this hobby."

"Fuck."

"Sorry, I shouldn't be saying this."

"No, tell me more," I say. "Get it out."

She gives me a small smile. "I don't like being vulnerable either."

"We don't have to talk about that, then. Let's talk about something else."

But she just shakes her head instead, with knit brows. She remains quiet for some minutes, sipping water, looking down at her shoes.

"I don't think I've ever prioritized my own happiness." The way she says this sounds like she just made a revelation, something from deep within that hurts to dig up. I didn't expect it, and it hurts to hear her say it. "Some days it feels like I have to ask permission for joy."

"Is this joyful?" I want her to say yes. I want to know that what we've been doing has been bringing her well-deserved happiness.

Her answering smile is small, and it doesn't quite reach her eyes.

"You've got permission to be here all you want, as much as you want."

"I know this is a lot of me rambling, and maybe none of this even makes sense to you." She waves her hand. "I just don't want to let her down."

"Who?"

She looks at me like she misspoke, and she shakes her head. "My family."

"I get that."

"I don't want to let you down," she says softly, vulnerably, and it burrows into my heart.

"You could never let me down Julie." Heavy words for what seem like a heavy conversation.

"You say that now." She smirks.

"You could make a million mistakes," I tell her. "There's no letting me down." That might have been too much, but there it is again. Reckless. No filter. She makes me feel excited. A kind of desperate that I like. A lot.

"I don't want to waste your time," she quietly admits. It sounds stressful, this pressure that she's been carrying and living under for so long.

"Julie, there is no time wasted when you're here. You're learning something with every class. You're dancing. You're trying something new. That's all this is about. Everything else is icing on the cake."

"These shoes were gifted to me. So, I'm trying to honor that. I'm trying to make my family proud. I want to make sure I don't take them for granted."

"They were a gift, not an assignment."

She sighs like I don't understand. "I don't want to waste it."

The thing is, I do understand. Maybe only a little, but I do. The crushing pressure, the high stakes, the expectation to always do well, to make sure you're making people proud. I'm just seeing in her what I've felt in myself—the exhaustion, the complicated emotions, the yearning for something more. "We all have our reasons," I tell her quietly.

"What's yours?"

My phone lights up just then, a message from Gavin: GOING OUT TONIGHT. COME WITH.

He's listed a place down the street from the studio, a local bar with live music on certain nights. Maybe we could both use the break, I reason.

"Let's do something else," I say suddenly. She looks to me again, waiting for me to continue. "Class time is almost up anyway. What if we call it a night and take this on the road?"

She blinks. "What? Where?"

"Just down the road to the Alley Cat. Ever been?"

"A couple of times," she says, confused.

"My brother is out tonight. It just gave me an idea to go and unwind a bit?" I pose it like a question, unsure if this is even smart.

Her brow furrows. "I don't know."

"Just figured you could use a break. And my brother is cool. He doesn't meddle, or anything. Keeps quiet." I know she doesn't want her family to know about the tango classes, so I'm trying to acknowledge it and cover my bases as I can.

The look on her face is one of gratitude, maybe a little sheepish. "Is … that alright? I'm not looking to take up your time."

"You're impossible." I laugh. "We were just talking about this." My laughter subsides as I study her face, my eyes clocking every inch. There's that feeling again—that hunger, that want. The lines are getting blurred and right now I feel like the catalyst, muddling all of it as I go. "I like you taking up my time," I say softly.

Her mouth unravels into a smile, a blush creeping up her cheeks as her eyes meet mine. I see her debate it as she looks to the door then back to me. She checks her watch, biting her bottom lip, deep in thought. I'm suddenly aware of how my body is leaning toward her in anticipation, desperately wanting her to say yes.

Soon enough, she agrees. "Yeah, alright."

I jump up and start to gather my things, perhaps a bit too eagerly. "Grab your bag and follow me." I walk with her out of the building and into the night.

Chapter Sixteen

Logan

"Would you like to drive separately?" I offer.

She thinks this over before answering, almost definitively, "You can drive, I don't mind," and I feel like I've won a bit more trust.

"Let me clean this up," I mumble, moving the passenger seat mess to the back and wiping the front seat so it's good for her to sit.

She gives me a close-lipped smile bordering on a smirk as she gets in.

The drive is quick. Once I park, I look out toward the place and notice it already overflowing with crowds on the wrap-around outdoor patio that contains bar stools and high tables. The large window against the wall is open to the bar inside, and the bright neon lights cut through the otherwise dark night. I'm trying to gauge Julie's reaction, but now that we're here *I'm* second guessing if this was a good idea. Brave face forward, we step out of the car and walk inside.

The Alley Cat is tucked away a couple of miles from

the studio, down a quieter street that caters more to the locals. There's a DJ on tonight and loud crowds gathering around the bar, the tables, even the small makeshift dance floor.

"Oh," she says. but it doesn't sound like disappointment. The inflection in it, it sounds excited.

We grab a table in a corner, a little quieter and away from so much action. I notice Gavin quickly, and I walk over to say hey, letting him know I'll be at another table. He waves to Julie and then turns to continue conversation with one of his new coworkers from the restaurant.

"What would you like?" I ask her.

"I guess I'll just take a beer for now. Thanks."

A server brings our drink orders, and we sit in slightly awkward silence.

"What are you thinking?" I want to know.

"I'm thinking the me from a month ago would be wondering if this was a good use of her time. I should be home working on cases."

"But the Julie right now?"

"She's ... cautiously optimistic." She laughs.

"And she laughs!"

"Sometimes." She gives me a smile.

"This place is loosening you up already and it's only been ten minutes." I grin.

She sips her drink, smiling as she does. And then she scans the room, her eyes snagging on something and growing wide.

"Ah, shit. Gavin's here with a bunch of coworkers, huh?" she nervously asks.

I look over my shoulder to see what she sees and find her cousin laughing with others, and Gavin not too far away.

"Fuck, sorry, I figured this would be a safe place to hang out," I say, apologetically.

"God, it's fine," she huffs. "I'm being so ridiculous, I know." She sets her head down on her hands, moving side to side in frustration.

"Julieta! What the fuck!" A loud voice cuts into our conversation.

I do a double take and find her cousin at the table gawking at us, holding a bottle of beer.

Julie lifts her head, smiling in a tired, exasperated sort of way. "Hey, T."

"I see how it is," she says, but she doesn't sound upset. There's a slight smirk as she looks between us again.

"It was a last-minute plan," Julie says.

"A last-minute plan?" Her jaw falls open. "You don't do last-minute plans."

"I might have suggested the last-minute plan," I add in, lifting my hand to intercept. Her eyebrows lift at this.

"Well, that just means I'm going to be texting you every night to come out with me, then," T smiles. "Looks like you're busy making friends now, though."

She walks away, leaving a strained silence between us

that I worry is about to feel suffocating except Julie just sighs and laughs. I smile at the sound of it, at the thought of her breathing a little easier.

"Give me a minute and we'll join them," she says. "I don't want to keep you from hanging out with your brother."

"Oh, don't worry about that. He's enjoying the company of everybody else just fine."

She laughs quietly at that.

"So, tell me about your family then, *Julieta*." If I found myself saying Julie too much, I can't imagine how annoying I'm about to get knowing her full name.

She grins as she sips her drink. I might even see a blush bloom on her cheeks.

"That's a beautiful name. Why call yourself Julie?"

"Easier," she shrugs. "People take it for what it is. They don't comment or inquire."

"What was it like, moving here?" I ask, quickly adding, "If you don't mind me asking."

She sighs. "Hard."

It's all she says, and I take that as a cue to move on. But then, to my surprise, she takes a breath and keeps going. Elbows rest on the table, her hand loosely cups the glass as she twirls it back and forth slowly.

"Maybe not hard at the beginning. I didn't really get it at the beginning. But soon enough I was asking to go home. I was wondering how long we were going to stay here. Except this was home now. It felt like I had been suddenly plucked out of my comfort zone and dropped into a new place, one where I didn't know anyone or anything, and I didn't speak the language. None of us got it at first, but we adapted as we went on. My cousins and I are all close in age, so we stuck together. I kind of fell into that role of caring for them. I was handed a lot of responsibility, and I was expected to follow it. We figured things out together. Watched a lot of MTV and American TV shows at friends' houses."

"And you never had a peanut butter and jelly sandwich."

She laughs at that again, a sound I never thought I could care about so much. She's letting her hair down a little bit, and I feel like I'm getting caught in the web of it.

"You know how they say it takes a village to raise a child? It really does. I remember my parents working so hard all the time. They would rely on neighbors to babysit, or friends they made at church to take care of us in a pinch. I mean, it was the *vintage* nineties so a different time, but they really did lean on that village, so to speak.

"But it was difficult. Everybody assumes you can just move to this country and get all the benefits and steal jobs and whatever else everybody wants to yell about, but there's a lot of legal drama involved. There's a lot of uncertainty, there's a lot of paperwork. And money. So much money. There are so many hoops to jump through. It is a *fight.*"

Maybe it's the change of scenery that has her opening up and sharing all of these stories, but I can't help but listen closely as she draws me in.

"And I would be remiss to not mention all the other cases that weren't like mine. That were harder because they were detained and waiting, hoping for an answer. For something. We had such a hard time, and yet we were some of the lucky ones." She takes a sip then gets quiet, letting the conversation fall into silence.

"Sorry. This feels strange to be telling somebody about," she says, sitting up straight, like she was in a trance before, and she's snapped out of it. "But I guess it's been so many years at this point, maybe I'm just removed from it enough."

"Thank you for sharing it."

"There's a very tangible self-preservation that I think remains in me." She furrows her brows. "My whole life was hesitation. My whole childhood was balancing what I could and could not do, unlike my friends who were free to do whatever they wanted. So, it's easy for everybody to say, 'Just go for it! Just do it!' but the trauma doesn't forget that for many years you couldn't. You just couldn't do any of it. The trauma doesn't forget that."

"What made you want to do this?"

"I don't know. I think I wanted to channel some of the bravery from my family? Or create a life I can be proud of?

Or try to find something to bring me joy? Take your pick."

"All of the above," I murmur. I feel like I could be the one saying those things.

She lets out a big breath, a forceful whoosh. "I need a shot."

My eyebrows lift. "Well, okay then."

T comes over then, balancing several shots in her hands. "Ask and you shall receive."

"Seriously? Are you lurking in the shadows?" Julie asks incredulously.

"Of course, I am. I hear the word *shot* and it's my cue to appear."

Julie takes the glass warily, lifting it to her nose and sniffing it. "What the hell is this?"

"Chuck Norris. Cheers losers!"

I grab the glass and shoot it back in one quick gulp, the liquor burning all the way down. My eyes water slightly. I see Julie do the same, watching her throat as she swallows, glassy eyes mirroring mine. I try to savor the mess of flavors only to detect something which I think is ...

"Jesus, is that hot sauce?" She slams the glass down on the table, making a grimace.

"Ugh, that was awful." T winces, too. "So. Gavin's brother. We meet again."

"Agostina," Julie says in exasperation.

"What? I'm being friendly," she tells Julie defensively, then turns to me again. "Manny heard Gavin say you're a dance instructor."

"Yeah. I teach tango."

Her jaw drops. She looks over to Julie, and I realize then I've probably put my foot right in my mouth.

"You're a tango instructor? Oh shit!" T says. "Julie!" She's talking loudly now, however many drinks and shots in at this point. "Julie loves tango."

Julie's eyes widen, a silent plea that I can imagine means, *Please, don't say anything else.*

The DJ plays a new song, something loud and poppy, and T excuses herself to go find Manny and dance.

"See you on the dance floor!" she calls out, and I just laugh politely in response. When I turn to Julie, I expect to her to laugh with me, or to catch her rolling her eyes once more, or perhaps even expelling one deep breath that we got over that hump.

But instead, I see that determination in her eyes again as she tells me, "I love this song." And then she gets up and walks right onto that dance floor.

CHAPTER SEVENTEEN
Julieta

I'VE ALWAYS LOVED TO dance, but never did it enough. Well, until recently I didn't do it enough. Didn't go out enough. Didn't do *anything* enough. The constant theme.

Logan is watching me now. I catch his eyes, and it's certainly enough to warm me right the hell up. I might be reading into this too much, but when is the last time somebody looked at me that way? When's the last time I spent time out with these people I love, dancing the night away?

So, I let myself be a little free again. I let myself grip onto the wild abandon I do nothing but chase. And I let everything get just a little bit looser.

"Yes, bitch. Dance with me!" T yells over the music and I lean into it a little bit more, move and sway.

"Are you okay? Sorry, I saw your arms flailing around and thought you were calling out for help," Gavin says to T as he hops over to us on the dance floor.

"Get fucked, Gavin!" She smiles, as she shimmies away,

dancing to the beat of whatever drum.

I just shrug, continuing to dance to the song as I follow her.

"Making friends?" I ask.

"I could ask you the same thing," she counters.

"It's nothing," I'm quick to say, but I catch Logan's eyes once more as I spin and land on them, and it feels like hitting a brick wall. Sudden and jolting. Shaking me up, bringing me to my senses. What am I seeing in them? What destruction am I barreling into?

I might be too many drinks in.

But the drinks keep coming, showing up in my hands, and I sip out of habit. Sip to quell the guilt and anxiety of being out. Sip for the fun of it.

The music gets louder, the beat thumping throughout this space. The lights are just dim enough that it makes everybody look mysterious and enticing. But the only one I'm drawn to here is keeping his eyes on me as I move.

Once I'm drenched in sweat, I head back to the table for a break, greedily taking the cup of ice water Logan offers me.

"Having fun out there?" He smirks, leaning closer to me.

I give a shy laugh in response. "This was a good idea."

"I'm glad you're enjoying it."

"Are you too refined to dance to pop hits in an alley bar on a weeknight?"

He laughs out loud. "No. It's just been fun watching you."

I'm definitely too many drinks in for these comments.

We fall into a safe silence, people watching. The DJ plays a slower-paced song, something popular, something ... rather sexual. It's late, and it's loud, and there's a whole lot of grinding happening on the dance floor. I find myself lost in the rhythm of it, swaying along with the crowd.

"You know what I love about tango?" I start. "The passion, the sensuality. How the woman holds so much power." I take a breath. "I long for that kind of power."

He doesn't hide his surprise in hearing what I just said. I don't know why I said it. I'm running my mouth.

"You're a lawyer, Julie. You're powerful," he says, like it should be so obvious.

"I'm not powerful. I'm just doing my job."

"You're passionate."

"That's laughable. My ex told me when he broke up with me that I had no passion, that there was no passion here." Now I'm really running my mouth.

His mouth might be a snarl. "That's fucking awful."

"He's a prick!" T screams, seemingly out of nowhere.

"Sounds like it."

I shrug. "I mean, I don't think he was wrong."

"Julie," he chides. "Jesus Christ."

"I don't know. There was certainly much left to be desired," I say, considering. "Maybe I haven't had good enough sex to indulge in passionate tango. Maybe that's my problem."

Logan almost chokes on a sip, coughing as he does.

I just look at him, wondering how the hell I allow all this shit to slip from my mouth whenever he's around. All of this has been looking for a way out for so long, dancing on the tip of my tongue. The alcohol has let everything fall out. Or the sincerity of him, whichever. Which is probably why the next thing I blurt out is the most truthful one by far.

"I hate my job!" I tell him, words probably slurred. "I mean, I love that I can help people. I love that I have the ability to do that. But the rest of it? I hate all the paperwork, the politics. I hate my boss." I'm just going for it now. "I hate that I want everything to be done right so I sacrifice my time every single day for it. That I'm the one making sure everything is okay. I'm pulling the weight. Nobody is asking me to. At this point, they all just expect it. Like T doesn't expect me to show up for stuff, or Delfi always expects me to have some miserable story about my job. It's all expected—for me to stay late and work on cases."

My phone chimes with a new message from Barbara, as if I summoned her. Maybe she's in a corner watching me.

"And to respond to messages at 10 pm." I hold my phone up.

"Shit."

"Yeah." I take the last gulp of my drink, setting the glass down a little too hard, rattling the already shaky table.

"I'm organized. And efficient. And I can handle everybody else's things, while never allowing the space for myself. I'm the perfect employee."

Logan just looks at me, his mouth a firm line. His eyes are sad, and it's breaking my heart to see it. I want to fix that, too, but instead I just stare back, lost in them.

"I spent so much of my life being told to not waste time on frivolous things," I say.

"And dancing is frivolous?" he asks.

"Dancing is very frivolous."

"Do you believe that?"

I shake my head and give him another truthful answer. "I don't know what I believe anymore."

"You deserve so much more than you've allowed yourself."

I just nod. Sure, I might think I deserve things, but then I also think I'm asking for too much in simply asking for *anything*. Like when I told him I hadn't prioritized my happiness. The realization of that statement is an overwhelming weight to carry, leaving me wanting to crumble underneath it.

He swallows before saying quietly, "You deserve to prioritize your happiness and your joy. And if nothing else, you deserve somebody that's going to prioritize *you*, Julie. That wouldn't leave anything to be desired." The words almost get lost under the loud music.

Maybe he's had too much to drink, too, though all I've seen him with is water. But still, I certainly have, and that's what I blame it on when the vision of Logan on his knees, at my feet, suddenly appears. And how the craving for it quickly grows into an almost desperate longing.

"You shouldn't have to ask for permission for any of that," he tells me adamantly.

Suddenly, the boisterous bar around us is quiet, and everything is frozen, and all I see is him looking back at me.

He also wasn't part of the plan.

When did these feelings emerge? When did this change?

I can't deny something has always been there, simmering just below the surface. It feels like tonight is breaking me free, and who knows what else will come of it then.

"Panty Dropper!"

"What?" I'm harshly pulled out of the spell, looking in the direction of where that voice came from.

A tray of more shots is ceremoniously placed on the table by T.

"Seriously? How is your liver okay?"

She shrugs. "Better not to ask. Besides we're celebrating."

Gavin and Manny appear at the table now, too, grabbing shots from the tray.

"Celebrating what?"

"You leaving your house for once." She reaches for a shot.

"You're fucking hilarious."

"I know," she winks. "To being hilarious." She raises the glass up.

"And panty droppers," Manny adds, not referring to the drink.

"And panty droppers!" T repeats.

As I lift my own glass, I watch her eyes briefly meet mine, smiling. And then my eyes meet Logan's, who must have been watching me the whole time. I tap my glass with his, all the others following in a cheer.

"To joy," I mouth to him, and catch his answering smile, brighter than the neon lights in this place, and then we both down our shots.

"Okay, this one was better," I tell T.

"Much. Now, back to dancing."

"No. I need to go home," I say, but who knows what came out.

"Aw, really? But I was having so much fun with you."

"You were? Imagine that."

"Logan, could you take her home?" T asks.

"I'm fine," I tell him, dragging out the word *fine*. "Don't worry about it. Stay and enjoy the night with your brother. I'll get a car."

She laughs like I just said something hilarious.

"I've got her." He nods to T. He says his goodbye to

Gavin who wants to stay a little bit longer. He says his goodbyes to Manny and T, too, and then places his hand on my back guiding me as we walk out.

"You don't have to do this," I tell him, standing in the middle of the parking lot.

"I know I don't. I want to, remember?"

"Fine," I huff, defeated.

He chuckles. "Just get in. Tell me your address. You do know your address right now, right?"

"Funny," I say, squinting to look at the street signs. But they're all moving. And the trees are moving. And the buildings are moving. And suddenly, the cold gravelly asphalt is on my back and the sky, inky blank, is above me.

I hear a scuffle of shoes and feel an arm come around me. "Shit, you okay?"

"Mmm. This is nice." Logan's arm is tucked underneath me, and it's soft and strong. It feels supportive. I could just lay here for a while. I could take a nice nap here, under this arm.

I think I hear T then, her laugh and her straightforward communication. A couple of words like *fifth street* and *stop sign* and *seventh floor*.

"I'm going to pick you up now, okay?" Logan says. He hooks his other arm underneath my legs, moving me to the car.

"I can walk." I try to fight off, swatting at hands.

"Don't think you can, party animal." His voice is deep,

but playful.

"This is ridiculous. How did I even get here?" I groan.

"Might have been the Panty Dropper."

A laugh bubbles out of me as I cover my face with my hand. Logan gently sets me down in the car seat, an impressive show of his strength, and checks to make sure I'm alright.

"Good?" he asks softly, close to me, eyes studying my face. I nod as he reaches over to buckle my seatbelt, hands quickly moving over my lap when I'd really rather they linger. Has car safety ever been this hot?

I need to go to bed.

***

"Seventh floor?" he asks, heading to the elevators.

We walk slowly, side by side. My steps are crooked and he's hovering in case I take a nosedive on to the tile.

"I feel pretty stupid right now, by the way," I say sloppily. Not sure if he understood me, though.

"I'm having fun." He laughs, and it sounds so sweet.

I always ride this elevator alone. It's funny to think about now. I leave early in the mornings; I get home late. I very rarely find myself talking to people in this building, let alone any stuck in elevators. But here I am riding this elevator with somebody for once, and I'm barely holding it together with my stomach full of booze and my head swimming.

The ride up is painfully slow, and we stand across from each other watching the numbers go up. He's got his hands tucked into his pockets, effortlessly cool Logan, breathing evenly. A steady rise and fall of his chest, that same chest I met on the very first day of tango class. My eyes move downward to his feet, crossed at the ankles, and then up to his face, that smile tucked into the corner of his mouth like he's got a secret. Like he's caught me. One that might be screaming, *see anything you like?*

The elevator comes to an abrupt stop, a rude interruption, and the doors open to my floor.

"Apartment 712."

He walks me to my door, and I turn to lean against the wall. Suddenly all my senses are awake. I see how he keeps his body close to mine for safety, I feel how his hand lightly touches my arm for stability. I notice how he checks in to make sure I'm alright.

Except maybe I'm not fully awake, because I don't catch how I'm leaning into him, moth to his flame, until I realize he's still and I have to pull back, embarrassed.

"My keys are in my bag," I mumble, looking through my overstuffed purse for them. Now I've become antsy, ready to get in the house and die of embarrassment, and when I can't find my damn keys, I flip the purse upside down, dropping all its contents onto the hallway floor.

"Hang on, Julie," he says gently, leaning down to grab the keys that he's spotted in the pile. He calmly puts everything back into the bag and hands it over to me. Why do I feel like crying right now?

I really need to get into my house and get the fuck into bed.

"Which key?" he asks, holding them in his palm.

"I've got it."

"Let me," he says softly, with such kindness, that I can't do anything else but just let him.

"That one." I point to the silver key on the ring.

Once he opens the door, we walk in, and I find I can breathe a little easier.

"Thanks for bringing me home, Logan. Good night." I say it in a hurry, a mess of words, hoping to get him out of here quickly. I don't know what's going on tonight, but this can't be a thing.

"Hold on," he laughs quietly. "Let me just make sure you find your way to bed and don't end up face down on the floor somewhere."

I turn around to argue and quickly lose my balance, everything spinning.

"Whoa." He reaches out to grab my upper arms.

I can't help but laugh, catching his eyes which are also full of humor. Full of something else I can't quite place. "This is how we met," I say.

He smiles back, his hands squeezing my arms just

slightly. But the smile falters as he swallows and simply agrees, "Yeah." An acknowledgement, an understanding. That's all any of this is.

"The uptight, boring lawyer whose personality match-es her job and the fun-loving dance instructor," I keep going, laughing to make a joke out of it, but all I probably did was reveal how I've kept our conversations in my head.

He furrows his brow in response. "You downed a shot called the Panty Dropper while dancing all night in a crowd of sweaty people. I'd hardly call you uptight or bor-ing."

I chuckle, opening my mouth to tell him I was just kidding, but he keeps going.

"So, you've got some hang ups with your job, but I remember that conversation, too. And I saw you take my words the wrong way. It makes sense that you're a lawyer not because you're *uptight* or *boring*. It's because you com-mand attention. You don't even see it. You walk into a room with your head held high and your shoulders back." He pauses to look at me. "You command my attention."

I stare into his eyes, lost in this wonder of a person, and see the fire in them. God, what would it be like to have all his attention? What must that feel like? I want to know. I really want to know.

"Thought you didn't date partners," I blurt out and he goes still. I shut my eyes, wincing at the nonsense I'm spewing. "Shit. Sorry. I thought I was doing myself a favor by finally going out and enjoying myself, but right now, I'm really regretting drinking so much."

His body loosens up as he chuckles, soft around the edges, wholesome. Something I wish I could feel against my skin. His lips are parted slightly, and I feel possessed in how I'm staring at them, willing them to come closer. I watch his tongue dart out and lick his bottom lip. I could melt right here. This man is clearly so damn passionate and professional and warm and welcoming, it's doing nothing to quell my rapidly growing emotions.

His hands quickly squeeze my upper arms again, like he's talking to me in this way, too. But I don't know what any of it means. All I did was show my hand and right now my head is swimming with too much alcohol to even make sense of it.

"I don't know what the rules are anymore, Julie."

Am I drunk or does that sound like some sort of confession?

"I don't know, either," is the only response I can manage, and I say it out loud.

He lets go of my arms and drops his hands to his sides. Am I drunk or does he seem defeated?

"I should go to bed," I whisper.

"I should go, too," he whispers back.

"Thanks Logan." Everything is catching up to me. I'm exhausted; I'm a mess.

"Always," he responds, that small grin tucked into the

corner of his mouth. I want to press it with my thumb.

"Okay, goodnight." I shuffle my way to my bedroom, and once I spot my bed, I feel my body sag with relief. I kick my shoes off into a corner, throw my blazer onto my upholstered bench. I pull my clothes off and throw them across the room in record time as I fall face first into bed. Finally.

***

THE ALARM BLARING IN my ear right now is frankly offensive.

When I move to turn it off, everything else moves too. My head is pounding, a constant dull ache that feels like somebody is squeezing it like a stress ball. My limbs are Jello.

I am hungover as hell.

God, what other nonsense did I do last night?

I text Agostina: DID I DO ANYTHING STUPID LAST NIGHT?

She might not even be awake yet.

MORNING, SUNSHINE! OH, YOU HAD A GREAT TIME.

I groan as I read her text. I can't be doing these things, I'm not fucking twenty-two. I need to be more responsible. I need to use my time wisely, as I hear my parents' voices in my head.

Last night was ... well, it was fun. And different. A reminder of what I've always wanted to be: the carefree one that doesn't have to carry the weight of everything.

I grumble, rolling over to get out of bed, figuring out how the hell I'm going to make it through the workday, when I remember I left my car at the bar. "*Shiiit.*"

Right on cue, my phone lights up again with a message from T: Manny and I got your car this morning.

Me: You did? How?

T: We did it before yoga.

Me: You were downing shots called the Panty Dropper last night but this morning you were awake for yoga?

T: I contain multitudes.

Me: Thanks.

T: It wasn't a big deal. Logan told Gavin to tell us and we just made a plan, whatever. Gotta go cat cow.

I almost want to fight that nobody needed to get my car, that I could have figured it out on my own, but they did and now I don't have to. Now I have one less thing to worry about.

In bed, with my Jello limbs and my dull aches and my churning stomach, I think about how I have so much paid time off. Would the world really end if I just took it for once?

Before I can think too much about it and lose my nerve,

I call Barbara. I take a deep breath, this act making me even more nauseous.

"Barbara Prescott."

"Hey Barbara," I clear my throat. "Good morning. I'm so sorry to have to do this, but I am not feeling well. I can't make it in today."

"Oh?"

"Yeah," I push forward. "Must have been something I ate. Not sure."

"Fine. Can you work on your cases at home then?"

Can I? Probably. But do I want to? I feel my stomach churn some more as we have this conversation. "I'm actually going to take the day."

Her huff on the other line is loud. "Fine. See you next week." She hangs up, and the phone call is done. I feel the lingering guilt for a minute, but then it slowly starts to evaporate. Lifting and lifting until I feel free of it. Well, I feel like shit—my own fault—but I have banked sick leave and I'm going to take it. I'm finally going to take it.

As I crawl back into bed, the night comes back in pieces. Little ones, like dancing and loud music, laughing with Logan. Then bigger ones, like the elevator ride up, my purse spilling onto the floor, the feel of Logan's grip on my arm. How it all still feels so potent.

I pull up my messages and type out another one.

Chapter Eighteen

Logan

Julie: Thank you for having T get my car.

I read the text, and I can't help but smile. I know it's early. I know I'm about to push my luck, but I take the risk and call her.

"This is a bold move," she teases when she answers, her voice rough with sleep and—I can only imagine—one really bad hangover.

"I thought so, too." I laugh.

How much of last night does she remember? How much does she want to remember anyway? I might have said too much, lost in whatever moment we were having, but her drunken confessions threw me for a loop, too.

"So." I clear my throat. "About last night."

"God, how much of a mess was I?" she groans.

"You were a delight." I smile.

She snorts. "I'll take that as a five out of ten."

"The more important question is how are you feeling?"

"How do you think I'm feeling? Like shit." She laughs. "And can I tell you … I called out of work."

"Wow." I'm impressed.

"I *know*. Used a sick day and everything."

"Wild streak," I tease.

"You're a bad influence," she says. But with the raspy sound of her voice and the quiet cadence, it doesn't feel much like an accusation as it does an invitation to play along.

"I think you like it," I tell her.

And in that same quietly seductive voice she says, "I think I do, too."

I wish I could see her right now. I wish I could go back to last night and watch her again, her body moving on the dance floor, sweaty and messy and not caring about a thing.

"You know, it's okay to be a little reckless, but maybe pace yourself. Hangovers are not the same in your thirties."

Her answering laugh is loud, but I imagine there's a blush attached to it. One that follows her neck down, one I'd love to follow, too.

"Hey Julie," I start.

"Yeah?"

"I'm sorry I just left you hanging like that."

"You didn't leave anything hanging."

"I did," I insist.

"You were trying to get away from the drunk girl that was blabbing away. Nobody would blame you." She huffs out a laugh. "I crossed a line, and I made you uncomfortable."

"You didn't make me uncomfortable," I tell her.

"You sure looked it."

"You were drunk," I admit. I didn't know how to handle everything she was saying to me when she was drunk enough that there was a chance she wouldn't remember. "I don't know what you remember about last night …"

"I remember all of it, believe it or not."

Everything gets quieter; everything becomes amplified. The sound of her breath on the other line, the rustle of bedsheets where I assume she's sprawled out, the clearing of her throat. So that answers that.

"I meant everything I said," I whisper.

"I meant it, too," she reveals, and my eyes close at the sound of it. "So, what are the rules now?"

My mind is trying to catch up with my heart, that's the issue. This is foreign territory. This is … I don't know what the hell this is.

"There's a milonga tomorrow night," I say instead. "Come with me."

"Uh. Not sure if I'm there yet."

"You are. There's a practice session an hour before, and then the milonga runs all night. But you could stay as long as you wanted. It could help you get a feel for different styles, help you get comfortable. Really get your feet wet. What do you think?"

"I think this feels like a low blow asking me when I'm hungover."

I let out a small laugh. I haven't been to one in a while. I've felt oddly removed from it, and the thought of going with Julie ... well, it would be good for her. Maybe good for both of us. "People are non-judgmental. It's just meant to be a good time. Drink some wine—"

"Don't talk to me about alcohol right now," she groans.

"Eat some snacks."

"Also, no."

"There's a tango DJ. Does that sound enticing?"

"You're funny," She chuckles, but the following silence makes me wonder if she's thinking about it. "And I can practice before hand? With you?"

"Yeah, we can meet an hour before."

"Okay," she concedes. "What time?"

"Let's meet at six. The milonga starts at seven. Ideally you want to dress up for this but try to be comfortable. Oh, and it's at the Midnight Ballroom. Down on Tenth street?"

"Yeah, okay. I can do that."

I've got her, and now I need to keep going. "Want me to pick you up?" I offer.

"Seems to be the theme," she quips. "Sure, I would love that."

"Great. I can't wait." I bounce on the balls of my feet, the anticipation building.

"Hey Logan? Thanks for last night."

"For what?"

"You know what. You carried me into a car for crying out loud." She huffs out a laugh.

"Always. You know that."

Her answering sigh is loud over the phone as she says, "Yeah. I guess I do."

***

"Hey, do you think mom and dad gave you too much responsibility?"

"Uh ..." Gavin is on the couch, remote in hand, searching for whatever new Netflix documentary he's going to binge.

"Like, did they make you take care of me because you were the oldest?"

"They didn't make me." He shakes his head. "I wanted to. I had to. You know how things were after the divorce."

"Yeah." I nod.

"Why? What's this about?"

"Just a question. Did you ever feel like you couldn't prioritize your own things?"

"Are you okay?" he asks, mildly concerned.

"Yeah, I'm fine. I know you did a lot for me back then." He got a full-time job at eighteen, balancing school and work, offering to help me pay for the ballroom classes when the tuition increased. He wanted me to keep going—fully supportive, fully proud of me. "Did I take anything away from you?"

"I didn't *have* to do anything, Logan," he tells me, brows scrunched together. "I already said that. I wanted to do it for you. What's this about?"

"Maybe you felt resentful towards me, I don't know."

"Nah." He's quiet for a while, looking at me, his mind probably racing. "I did what I did for you because I wanted to. And I hope you know that. I got to live my life, too. I did plenty of things for myself. You didn't stop me. Mom and dad didn't stop me."

"Okay," I say, trying to ease out of the topic of conversation. "Well, I've got a full day of classes and then I'm headed to the milonga tomorrow night."

"Is this about San Diego?"

I almost flinch at those words but manage to shake my head. He's talking about last year. The competition that Tara and I made a mess of. But now with the promise to Julie, the weight of San Diego is that much more prevalent.

"I've been proud of you from the very beginning, Logan," he says clearly. "That shit isn't changing. Ever. We all have bad days. You're still alright in my book."

I scratch the back of my neck, probably a nervous habit at this point. He's said these things to me before. He said them then, a year ago, but with the both of us working on new trajectories of our lives, it seems oddly more genuine. "Thanks."

"Are you still searching for jobs?"

"I'm not going to work with Steve if that's what you're asking."

"Fair enough," he laughs.

"I don't know what I'm doing yet." Truthfully, I don't.

"Also, fair," he says. "Have fun at the milonga then. It'll probably be a late night for me, and a busy weekend, so see you when I see you." He lifts his hand in a wave, remote still in the other as he presses play on a documentary about koala rescue habitats.

"See you later."

Suddenly, everything seems so different.

Suddenly, everything feels like it's starting new.

Chapter Nineteen
Julieta

TIA CECILIA USED TO frequent milongas when I was younger, going out and staying until late. She would stumble back home laughing and humming to herself, her dress stretched out around her body like she'd been dancing all night. She always made it a point to wear something flowy or stretchy, something with give to allow for movement. I remember that now as I'm desperately searching my closet for something, anything decent, to wear. I find a simple black dress with thin straps, falling just past my knee, a slit up the side. A dress I bought on a whim for a date with Jeremy. I didn't end up wearing it, breaking up shortly after instead. That was probably for the best anyway, but this dress will do.

My grandmother's signature look was always a bright red lip. Didn't matter how the years crept up on her, she kept that signature. And I always thought it was the most sophisticated look.

I feel a little more than silly as I try to recreate it now. Deep, lush, ruby red painted on in strokes. Any other dancer could fashion a glamourous updo with their long flowing hair. My short bob gets pinned back with small pins, brushed away from my face. I step into the shoes, buckling them with the same nerves I felt the first time. I've been wearing them for weeks now, but this somehow feels more official. Headed to a milonga in these shoes feels like I'm really doing the thing.

When I look at myself in the mirror, the surprise is jolting. There's a steady acknowledgement that I look damn good in this dress. And Jeremy didn't deserve to see me in it anyway.

But Logan...

Well, maybe he'll like it. Not that I'm dressing up for him. But maybe he'll appreciate that I look presentable, that I'm properly dressed for the part.

Though after Thursday night, I don't know where anything stands.

One more look, one more turn in the mirror. Maybe I'm lying to myself. I should at least aim to be honest. There's no point in going down this rabbit hole searching for the authenticity in my life if I'm not going to be honest with myself.

The knock on the door breaks me from it and I race to answer, smile on my face. When I step out to greet him, his jaw turns slack, slowly perusing my body in this dress. I feel practically naked.

"Wow." There's a devilish smile in place now. "You look

great."

"Oh. Thank you," I reply, but the compliment makes me stand up straighter. It makes me feel like I'm getting it right. And this dress, I can admit, is for him.

He leans in to kiss me on the cheek in greeting and the move, familiar in every other aspect of my life, surprises me.

"You look great, too," I add in. And he does. With loose pants again, and a button-down shirt. It looks casual, yet somehow professional. Like he knows what he's doing just fine. He smells faintly like cologne, something generic enough that I've probably smelled many times over in the courthouse, but on his skin it smells bright and novel and deliciously sexy.

"Let's go dance." He smiles as he offers me his hand, and we walk to the elevators and out to his parked car.

"Okay, here's a quick rundown of a milonga," he begins as we drive down Seventh Street.

"I know what a milonga is."

"Do you know the etiquette?"

I eye him. "Give me a refresher."

"So, it's a social night for the tango community. That's it, first and foremost. Nobody is judging you, there isn't a prize to be won. This is just a good time. The fun thing about milongas is the casual aspect of it. You can people watch; you can drink your wine in the back of the room if you want. That being said, I'd like you to dance with different partners tonight, if that's alright. Get a feel for different styles."

He keeps his eyes on the road as he talks, but I can't help but look over at him: his hand loose over the steering wheel, his hair that same mess as always. He takes up space—in this car, in the studio. Wonderfully. And he does so without a second thought.

"The practica will help get you acclimated to the milonga style. There's a closer embrace and the steps are quicker and shorter. It's meant to be improvisational, fun."

"Fun," I repeat, with a tight smile, but the nerves are starting to emerge.

"The cabeceo," he keeps going. "If a man is making eye contact and you'd like to dance with him, you need to hold eye contact and give a nod. If you're not interested, you look away."

I just stare.

"You should wait until he approaches you, and then he'll lead you to the dance floor."

I can't help but snort in laughter. "Oh God."

"He can also verbally ask you, but it's not as common. But even in those situations, do not be afraid to say no. A no is very respected in a milonga, at least it should be. Also, no talking during the tanda."

The tanda I know. It's two to three songs in the same tempo that are played for dancing.

"One tanda is customary, and it's enough," he continues. "You say thank you once the tanda is done, and that is a means to an end. Two tandas ... well, that means he's probably interested in more than just a dance." He winks, mouth curved into a smirk.

"What year is it again?"

"Don't walk through the dance floor when getting on or off, try to walk around. And just have fun with it." He turns into the parking space effortlessly.

"Just have fun with it after you listed forty-seven rules for me to follow?"

He puts the car in park, then turns to look at me. "This should be a good time, something enjoyable, so let yourself have it."

We open our doors, stumbling out into the warm night, and I can't help but laugh in response again.

"What?"

"I don't know how I ended up in this predicament with you mansplaining a milonga to me, but here we are."

"Unless you're in the tango community, it's not the most common knowledge. Even to Argentinians."

"I guess so," I say. But maybe I would have hoped to know. I should have known all of this.

"You alright?"

"Just nervous, I guess." Just dragging up memories. Just remembering why I'm here.

"Hey." He stops walking. "You know you can say no to

me, right?"

"What?"

"You can say no."

"I know that," I respond, but the answer falls flat. Do I know that? Of course, I do, why is he saying this?

"I just want to make sure you know. Fun, remember? If it starts to feel like a chore, or like pressure, then you can step away. I won't be upset about it."

But what happens when I can't let myself step away? I think. "Okay," I nod.

"Okay," he replies with a deep breath, and he opens the door to the ballroom. Logan takes my hand, my very own lifeline, and we walk in. "Vamos a bailar."

Chapter Twenty

Julieta

"I found us a table over here if that works?" He points to a small round one. It's close enough to the dance floor to watch other couples dance, but not so close that we're in it.

We spent the hour before doing the practica, standard practice where I worked on getting used to a quicker, more improvisational technique.

"This is great, thanks."

"Would you like some wine?" he asks. "Or are you trying to take it easy, party animal?"

This makes me chuckle, something looser, as I answer, "I'll just take a cup of water."

"You got it. I'll be right back," he smiles.

He walks through the crowd easily, like he's familiar with all of this. People call his name, and he stops to give each person a greeting: a kiss on the cheek, a handshake, a hug. They look so happy to see him. He gets caught up in animated conversation, and there's something so comforting about it. About how embedded he is in it, how he knows the language and the customs, how they've welcomed him, too.

Older couples are standing around the dance floor, and the tango DJ is setting things up. The house lights are dim, and spotlights in muted red light up the space, making for something more intimate. Long tablecloths cover tables around the dance floor, streamers of fabric are loosely draped and hanging from the ceiling.

The music begins and the dance floor immediately fills like a flood. I've got a close seat, and the view is nostalgic. It's incredible, wondrous that I get to be here, too. My eyes don't leave the floor, or the dancers' feet. Everybody has their own style, I notice. Everybody has their own version of magic.

This feels like home. A home I didn't know I'd ever feel again.

Logan returns with a glass of wine and a cup of water, setting them on the table gently.

"Sorry it took me a bit. I got sidetracked by some regulars."

"That's okay. They looked happy to see you."

"It's been a while," he admits, then takes a sip of his wine. "Let me know when you want to go out on the floor."

"Soon. Let me get my bearings first."

An older man walks past our table, doing a double take, and I recognize him immediately as Javier, an old family friend.

"Julieta! Que haces acá?" he asks in a playful tone. It must come as a shock to see me here.

I can only laugh in response, as he leans down to give me kisses on my cheeks in greeting. "Vine a bailar," I tell him casually. *Of course*, I'm here to dance tango at the milonga on a Saturday night.

"Que bueno!" He turns to look at who he must assume is my date and stills.

"Logan? Cómo estás?" He shakes his hand, a genuine smile on his face.

"Re bien, Javier." Logan answers. "Cómo te va?" Yeah, that Spanish is still hot.

Javier looks between us, thinking who knows what, then turns to me. "Y tus viejos cómo están?" Javier asks me, inquiring about my parents.

"Bien, bien. Todos bien." I feel like a bobblehead with how much I'm nodding and smiling in this conversation.

He looks at Logan again, and I almost feel the words build up, the way I'm going to talk my way out of this. Defend it, deny it, whichever. But Logan just smiles at him, talking briefly about classes and tango and people I don't know. A whole community of people that I know nothing of. It should be awkward, like I'd rather sink in my seat, except that there is a literal seat at the table for me here. I get to be here as much as everyone else, and it's something I never quite realized I was missing. Soon enough, the conversation wraps up, and Javier says his goodbyes.

"Chau, Logan. Nos vemos. Chau, linda." He leans down to give me a kiss on the cheek, then walks over to a woman and offers his hand to dance.

"You know Javier?" I ask.

He nods. "He's big in the tango community."

"Ah, that makes sense," I say. "He's an old family friend. My parents met him at night school when they were learning English."

"I love that," he says warmly. "How about we dance now?"

"I would love to," I answer. "Oh wait, you're supposed to make eye contact, and I have to hold it and nod."

He laughs as he gets up from his seat, holding his hand out for me to take. I take it immediately.

The floor is crowded, but couples are keeping everything moving, and keeping their moves contained. Suddenly, thrown into the middle of it, my nerves decide to make a new appearance.

"I don't know if I can do this."

"It's just you and me, Julie. Just you and me here. Nobody else matters."

But I notice Javier on the outskirts. Friends about his age chatting, friends that maybe knew my grandmother and in turn may know me, and I just feel silly. Like I'm a poor excuse for a replacement, like I didn't deserve to get these shoes let alone dance with them.

So, while I would love to think that nobody else matters, right now, in my mind, in my line of sight, everybody does.

"Stay with me, Julie," he says right in my ear. "Take one deep breath." My body complies, almost frustratingly quickly. "Good, now take another one."

This one I pull from deep down within me, hoping to summon some of my grandmother's bravery, hoping to find some of my own.

"You," he whispers almost definitively, squeezing my hand, inching me closer to him. "And me."

And maybe it's the breathing, or the calm way he speaks to me. The way my body just molds to his in comfort and familiarity, this dancing position like muscle memory. Or maybe, I think, this is all I need right now.

You and me.

And the tanda begins.

CHAPTER TWENTY-ONE

Logan

THE MILONGA STYLE CAN take a minute to pick up, but I have no doubt that she can do it. The improvisation will do her good, the social dancing could be what she needs.

She's dancing with Roberto right now, an older gentleman who is gentle and accommodating. The look on her face could be one of concern, but her moves are fluid, her feet are in rhythm. *He's no Ethan*, I think to myself.

I try to keep her in my sights as much as I can, watching from afar, but somebody else pulls me into conversation. It's been a while since I've been to a milonga, and I've missed it more than I realized. This place has always felt like home.

"We've *missed* you," Susana says with feeling.

"I know. It's been a while."

"Heard about Tara," Victor adds.

"Yeah," I respond, but the commentary is getting old. Even Tara would think so.

"Is that the replacement?" Martina lifts their chin in the direction of Julie. "You work fast, Logan," she says, as they all laugh.

"Oh, not quite," I chuckle nervously, but I'm itching to end this conversation and find my way back to her. I don't like that they're calling her a replacement, likening her to something disposable. It feels disrespectful. It makes me surprisingly upset. And, even then, I don't want to get into the tricky chats about what's happening next, where I'll be, what I'm going to do.

"We're going to dance. Nice seeing you, Logan." Susana squeezes my hand and walks away.

I stay put, leaning against the makeshift bar with a cup of water in hand. I spot Julie dancing with somebody new, somebody younger. I don't recognize him, but I haven't been here in a while, and he may well be a regular in this crowd. His hand is flush against her back, and I watch it slowly inch its way downward. My chest suddenly goes tight as my hand grips the cup of water, my eyes burning a hole into his hand.

Julie looks happy as she dances, her gorgeous red lips stretched into a grin, her body pivoting side to side. I knew she would dance with different partners tonight. I *knew*. But right now, face to face with it, my stomach is in fucking knots.

His feet move in rhythm, matching hers, and for the first time in a long time, I feel a strong desire to take this back. To hold my ground instead of calling it quits. To keep this dance as mine.

Just as the tanda ends, Julie thanks him, but he doesn't budge. Yet, she looks around and when she sees me, staring right back at her, she holds eye contact. When I told her about the etiquette, I just wanted to prepare her for it, but I didn't expect to have such fun playing along. Like right now, where I can't do anything but hold her gaze. And when she gives me a nod and a smile, I know I'm done for.

"I think I'm having a hard time keeping up." She winces as I walk over to her. "Nobody wants to dance with me."

"That's not true." I offer her my hand. "Roberto seemed to have a great time dancing with you. And who-ever that guy was." I jerk my head in the direction of the person that was previously dancing with her, now on the outskirts looking annoyed.

"He was nice," she says. "Roberto was, too."

"Truth is, you will run into some who prefer more experienced dancers, who can't leave their ego at the door, but those aren't the ones you want. At the end of the day, tango should always be about surrendering to the music, and the joy of having a beautiful woman in your arms." With that, I wrap my arm around her, getting into position to dance.

"That's it, huh?"

"That's it. So, if it wasn't clear," I say in her ear, "I want to dance with you."

She smiles as her arm finds space around my shoulders.

"Much better," I say, when we're in position.

"Did you miss me?" she jokes.

"I did," I reply. But how do I tell her that watching her dance with a new partner was like a kick in the ribs. How do I explain it when I don't understand it myself? Luckily I don't have to as the tanda begins.

We're in a close embrace, arms wrapped around. I made do with quick improvisation, and she follows along, humming as she does. We're temple to temple, so if I wanted to lean over and tell her all my secrets I could. I could turn and whisper them right in her ear as we dance.

"Lean into me," I say softly.

"You're breaking one of the forty-seven commandments," she whispers back.

Dancing hasn't felt this personal in a long time. Everything feels that much better: the softness of her skin, the glide of her feet. The joy I feel again.

"You want to know why I invited you here?" I ask, in her ear.

"You told me it was to get comfortable."

"Well, yeah, that."

"And?"

"And I didn't want to wait until Thursday to see you," I admit.

She pulls back a little to look at me. "Bold move," she grins.

"You command my attention," I tell her again.

"Do I?"

I sigh, a breath pulled from deep within. "I can't help it. I want to give you all my attention." *I want to give you everything.*

When the tanda ends, I don't part. She doesn't move either. Instead, we smile during the transition period between the music, and when another tanda starts, I bring her in to dance again.

Breaking yet another rule.

***

JULIE AND I HEAD back to our table, sitting quietly watching other couples dance. I happen to catch the time—almost midnight—and watch her stifle a yawn.

"Late night for you?" I tease.

"This is way past my bedtime."

"Wild streak." I waggle my eyebrows while she gives a quiet laugh.

"Yeah, something like that." She takes a small sip of water, then quietly says, "I wasn't allowed to quit dance."

We're sitting side by side at this round table, legs hidden underneath the tablecloth, watching the dancers in front of us. Couples get on, some come off to take a break. She continues to talk, both of us looking ahead.

"All the recitals and strict teachers and kids my age who rolled their eyes at my improper form, who were practically offended at how unserious I was about ballet at nine years old ... after the pressure of it got to be too much, I told my mom I wanted to quit. I didn't like it; it wasn't for me.

"But classes cost money and time, and there were still paid sessions left. And so, I had to keep going because the classes weren't free, and there were kids who would have loved to be in my shoes, so maybe I should try being grateful for it. I was very ungrateful for even thinking about it. That sounds silly. It was ballet, not torture."

"But did it feel like torture?"

She lets out a soft chuckle, almost like a realization. "It did."

"Yeah," I say with a small smile.

"Maybe they did me a favor, teaching me not to quit everything. I don't know." She shrugs.

"Or maybe they didn't listen to your wants and needs."

"I was nine. I didn't know what I wanted."

I still don't know what I want most days, I want to tell her. "You were old enough to know you didn't want to do ballet."

"Maybe." She shrugs again. "You didn't have that issue," she jokes.

"No, my parents didn't care enough about me or my activities. They were too busy hating each other after the divorce."

"That must have been so hard."

"It wasn't fun, but dancing sort of became a lifeline for

me then. I looked forward to it, I loved being there. It made me feel welcome."

"I'm glad you had that. And you had Gavin. That must have been comforting, too. Big brother and all that."

"I want to quit dancing, too," I blurt out, almost out of nowhere. She looks over at me, probably taken aback by what I said. "*Wanted* to quit. I'm not sure where I stand right now."

Her surprised stare becomes soft, watching me, listening. She's been vulnerable with me, the least I can do is open up, too. "When Tara told me she was leaving, I wanted to jump ship, too. She's moving on to more exciting things, but when I leave this, what do I have left?"

"Oh, Logan," she says quietly.

There's my name again around that voice. There's that hunger. Like I want to hear her say it again as I kiss her and swallow it up, feel the taste of it in my mouth, too. I grip my cup of water again, like it's my own anchor, keeping me steady.

"What's changing your mind?" she asks softly.

"I think you might be," I confess.

She sits up straighter. "How so?"

"I'm having fun dancing with you, Julie."

"I'm having fun, too."

"I haven't had fun like this in a while. Tango hasn't been this fulfilling for me in a long time." It's the truth, unfiltered. She doesn't flinch; she just keeps listening, so

I'm inclined to keep talking. "You and me. This feels like a good thing."

But with the way she's looking at me, this feels a bit like throwing myself into the fire.

"Yeah," she breathes out. "It does."

Chapter Twenty-Two
Julieta

This, right here, feels like the best thing.

His eyes meet mine with a focused look, one I can't turn away from. His stare envelopes me in a rich warmth, like a big comfortable blanket, and I want to wrap myself around him. Feel his warmth all over.

"One more tanda. What do you say?" he asks then, voice low.

There is no answer but yes. Not now, and probably surprisingly, not ever. "I'd love to."

He takes my hand and leads me out to the dance floor. I follow every step, every turn. We move together in quick unison, and this feels better than it has ever felt. It's freer than it has ever been. I lean into him, suddenly unashamed of it, and he mimics it. Soon we find ourselves closer, much closer, temple to temple, my eyes closed. Our moves begin to slow, not quite following the beat of the song, and this feels like we've created our own bubble, our own little world in the corner of the dance floor.

The two of us move in tandem, slowly, deliciously, my

body fighting every bit of restraint to just press against his. He inches even closer to me, his hand pressing on my back to secure me to him, and I don't fight it. Our hips meet, our hands are pressed together. I breathe slowly and feel his own breath right on my neck, almost making me lose any willpower I am exerting right here. We are way too close for proper tango dancing. This is about to be dirty dancing at the milonga if we don't knock it off.

And yet, his hand on my back is still solid, and his heartbeat that I now feel through his shirt is racing. He must feel mine, too, furiously beating with excitement and nerves and a rush of electricity. Something has changed here, and I'm drowning in it. The rigidity, the lists, the constant careful planning I've lived within my whole life has started to break, and I want out of it. I want ... *him*.

"What are you thinking about?" I whisper into his ear, suddenly desperate to know, shamelessly breaking a milonga rule.

He breathes in deep, and a pained sigh falls from his mouth. He looks like he's about to respond, but the song ends, and it takes a second to break away. Once we do, the spell is broken. The trance we were in quickly falls to shards. I inhale through my nose, watching Logan watch me. If he was as affected as I was, he doesn't show it now.

He applauds the DJ, then smiles at me. "Your first milonga and you shut it down."

I can't help but smile back, one big grin overtaking my

face with happiness. "This was so much fun," I tell him genuinely.

"The best milonga I've been to," he admits.

The time is now one in the morning and everybody is gathering their belongings, hugging and kissing goodbye, making their way to the exit. We follow the crowds spilling out onto the sidewalk. Logan's hand sits on my lower back and, while he's done this before, I am now even more acutely aware of his gentle fingers, his palm almost flush against it. He moves his hand once we're outside of the building and I push the disappointment down.

In the end, this was a wonderful experience. This was a wonderful night. *This* she would have approved of.

At some point, the night turned rainy, a steady rainfall that is not letting up as crowds gather under the awning. Others are running through the parked cars, huddled under jackets, some under plastic bags, some with the foresight to carry an umbrella.

When did we all become so afraid of the rain?

When did I become so afraid of everything?

So, I look back at Logan, who's watching the sky, and I shrug, running right out into the rainy night. In a matter of seconds, Logan is by my side, laughing with me, following my slow jog.

"God, I love the rain," I tell him, my dress starting to stick into my skin. Rivets run down my arms and face, tracing the lines of my smile. It's coming from deep within, directed right at him.

His smile back is almost devious, perusing my soaked skin and my drenched hair. The wet ends are dripping down my back. Everything should feel uncomfortable, like I want to wipe my face and hair and arms, but all it feels is freeing. As freeing as this whole entire night has been.

My mother always used to say the rain was a blessing from the skies. Like when it rained the day of my LSATs, when it stormed the night before my first job interview out of college. The rain always did feel like a blessing in some ways, but right now, under this sky, after this night, it truly feels like the best blessing. Washing me clean, giving me new life.

As I continue to walk, I slip under the wet pavement and Logan immediately reaches his arm out to grab me, pulling me in right to him.

I gasp at the action. *"Oh."*

His other hand, now like the best habit, finds its way around my waist. My body reacts as it has all night: with fervor and fever and want. He dances a couple of steps with me, and I'm almost in awe of how my body falls into line with his. How familiar it has become, how much like home it feels. My answering laugh is light and bubbly and loud. Who knew I could even laugh like this?

"You," he says simply, dancing with me in messy rhythm.

"Me?" Our foreheads meet as we sway along the deserted sidewalk, the rain starting to let up.

"That's what I was thinking about. That's what I'm always thinking about." He studies my face, and our swaying slows significantly. "You. Always you. And this dance and this night and this goddamn spectacular dress."

Oh.

"You make me want to break all the rules, Julie," he whispers.

"We know how I feel about that." I swallow thickly.

He laughs softly against my mouth.

"So, I'll find a new partner," I rush out. A rash suggestion when the last thing I want to do is get farther away from him.

He shakes his head. "Can't let you do that now."

"No?" I should be embarrassed by how breathy and desperate I sound.

"Don't want you dancing with anybody else."

"I don't want to dance with anybody else." I shake my head.

His smile turns sexy, something devilish that I can just make out in the dim of the streetlights. "I didn't kiss you goodnight yet."

So direct, so clear. So damn *hot.*

"You didn't." Is my voice *breathier?* At this point it sounds like equal parts hopeful and horny.

My body, alight with absolute want, is burning. And then he adds to the flames and kisses me.

He starts slow—languid and delicate as his lips meet mine. Little soft kisses like he's getting acquainted, but as he presses closer, it becomes aching and demanding. Our mouths move in better rhythm than our feet. Logan kisses like he dances, gentle yet leading, firm and *passionate*. And like everything else between us, it feels dangerously addictive.

His hand, still firm at the small of my back, presses me closer, and I can't help but grab his dress shirt and pull him to me. His lips part, allowing for his tongue to meet with mine, brave and forward and possessive. I can taste the rain on his lips, and somehow, I want more. It isn't slow anymore. Now it's bordering on feral. A soft groan leaves his lips, and the sound causes a swoop low in my belly. My heart races. It feels like I've been struck by lightning. My fist is still gripping his shirt, his palm is still against my back. If I could get any closer I would, but our bodies are flush, leaving no space between us. This feels entirely surreal; this feels like the *best* thing.

Weeks ago, I was in bed by nine o'clock surrounded by cases. Now, I don't even recognize myself making out on a downtown sidewalk. My back meets the building, the bricks scratching my skin, adding to the sensation.

His hands travel down, settling right on my ass in this tight dress that is probably not leaving much to the imagination. I want his hands all over me in this dress. My sighs are probably telling on me plenty.

"I love that," he chuckles softly, pressing a kiss to my jaw.

"Love what?" I pant, now gripping his messy hair in my own sort of victory.

His teeth graze the skin below my ear, and I sigh again.

"That," he clarifies. "How happy you sound."

I don't know what to say, so I kiss him instead. He's not wrong, though. I can't remember the last time I was this happy.

"Tell me there's something here, Julie," he whispers, a sort of plea between us. It's almost begging, and it makes me want to grip his shirt tighter, pull him in closer. He leans over me slightly. My heart ramps up, beating loud enough to feel it in my throat.

"There's something here, Logan." My desperation has probably reached a limit, but I don't even care.

And his hard kiss against my mouth is all the response I need.

Chapter Twenty-Three

Julieta

When we walk into the elevator, we're met with a frustrating turn of events. A loud group celebrating Bailey's Birthday Bash—according to the glittery pink sash worn by the birthday girl—crash into the elevator, separating Logan and me. We stand on opposite ends, watching each other over the rambunctious group. His smirk remains on me and the heat between us must be off the charts by now.

Once the doors open, we stumble out, walking briskly to my apartment door, unclear where this is even going. At least for me. His hand reaches for mine, and it feels completely natural. We reach my door at record speed, but he just presses me against it, stopping me in my tracks, stopping me from reaching for my keys.

His mouth hovers above mine and I want to just melt into it, this feeling something lush like velvet.

"Want to come in?" I ask, against his lips. "You should, um … dry your clothes."

His answering laugh might be a little pained. It must be close to two o'clock at this point, way past my bedtime, but

I am absolutely wired. In response, he presses his mouth to mine, soft and sweet. But it quickly takes a turn into something deep and dirty, quiet groans, and his tongue meeting mine like he's ravenous. I know the feeling.

"I just want to take my time with you, Julie," he grits out between kisses, almost frustrated by his own logic.

"That's good. That's okay," I pant out. "Time is good." Maybe if I repeat it enough, I'll believe it myself. Even though all I want right now is to drag this man through my door and rip his shirt off.

"Nothing left to be desired," he mumbles against my neck he's sprinkling with kisses. "You deserve all my time."

Oh God, my drunken words have come back to haunt me.

"Shhh," I mumble, shaking my head.

He kisses me once more, sighing deeply. "Let me see you this weekend." His hips meet flush with mine, and I can't help but push back, feeling just how much he wants me right now.

I'm not rushing to leave his arms, not clamoring to let go of the death grip on his dress shirt. "Okay," I agree.

But neither of us stop. If anything, the kissing just intensifies, like everything is coming out. Like weeks of private tango classes have been the most intense foreplay.

He nips at my lip, then he moves down along my jaw, my neck, sprinkling me with the most perfect kisses. There's a rumble in his throat as I bring him back to my mouth, kissing him again.

But maybe he's right, keeping him here so late at night, so I pull away and grab my keys to unlock the door. His hands find my waist, continuing to kiss along my neck.

"I can't wait to come back," he mumbles against my ear. "Tell me I can come back."

I open the door and turn to face him. He grips the doorframe like he might rip it off the hinges any minute.

"You can come back whenever you want," I tell him, laying everything out on the table for the first time in a very long time. I will allow myself this perfect moment of joy.

But he just stares at me, holding eye contact, his eyes burning. I can feel the heat from here. I can feel the sizzle and spark that's molding between us. Maybe he feels it, too, because suddenly he blurts out, "Fuck it. Just a little bit longer."

I should be embarrassed by how I practically lunge at him, but he just catches me, mouth immediately meeting mine. This time I do drag him into my apartment, not parting for one second as he kicks the door closed behind him,

"Is this a good idea?" I ask, ever careful. Somehow the guilt is never too far away.

"This is a *great* idea," he replies. The way he says the words, with such sureness and clarity, strikes something within me, and I can't help but agree. This feels too good, too delicious, too much like *everything* to be wrong.

"God, this is a great idea," I repeat. I can't stop running my hands along his body, can't stop kissing him.

His hands are everywhere, too—on me in places they haven't touched yet. The boundaries placed by proper dancing and professionalism are being thrown out the window. It feels strikingly brand new, deliriously perfect.

"Tell me," he pants out. "Tell me what you want."

The answer comes out of me in a rush, no thought just feeling, "I want to be selfish."

I don't even know what I mean by it, almost ready to apologize for it, but he just kisses me harder and cradles my face as he says, "Be selfish. Be so selfish."

He bends down slightly, wrapping his arms around my waist, and quickly lifts me up. I yelp in surprise, but then fall into it because I can't get enough of him right now. Can't get enough of his warm skin and his soft lips and his body, so strong and sure, against mine. He starts walking eagerly, kissing wherever he can: my mouth, my neck, my chin. Messy and sloppy and exactly what I want. *This* is what I want—to feel so desired that nothing else matters.

"Hope I'm going the right way," he mumbles against my shoulder, and I let out a laugh. He steps into the guest room, the one everybody occasionally likes to crash in, and lays me down on the bed.

This room is mostly bare except for a bed with generic bedsheets and a closet full of storage bins that may topple over when opened. Generic artwork on the wall, a small window overlooking downtown, blinds shut.

"Guest room," I explain, reaching to get him close again.

"Oh. Do we need to move?"

"No no no, come here."

"Okay good, I don't want to move," he rushes out, and I giggle again. Light and effervescent and *happy*.

His hands are firm against my hips, pinning me onto the bed, and it makes me love this that much more. Like there isn't a question or a doubt. His thumbs graze hip bones, my body rolls to meet his.

"Are you tired? I know it's late," he asks, checking in.

More laughter, more joy. "I have never been less tired in my life."

"Tell me what you like."

The shame of my early adolescence comes back to haunt me with that phrase. What do I like? I don't know. I don't think I've ever been allowed to know. I learned to never ask for what I wanted, even though I wanted so many things.

But Logan here with me is so much more than what I would have hoped for otherwise. From the start he has been nothing but tender and gentle. It's not a surprise it would translate to here.

"I think ... maybe I'm still learning what I like, or don't like."

"Okay," he says, but it's not placating. It's him listening

and absorbing the information.

"I like ... I *need* ... foreplay."

"Jesus Christ, your ex sounds like a clueless, selfish ass."

"No, no." I put my hand over his mouth. "I don't want to talk about him ever again."

"Good." He kisses me roughly and something about it makes me feel so alive.

"Kissing is the best foreplay."

He smiles, nipping at my bottom lip. "It is, isn't it?" and he leans in to kiss me again, but this time slowly. He's not in a rush to do anything. The languid movements of it, the exploration of tongues and mouths. A delicate, sensual rhythm is starting to build and I'm feeling a whole lot of need climbing to the top.

"Tango is the best foreplay," I spill out, and he just laughs softly as he peppers me with more kisses.

"What else do you like?"

But with his mouth on me and his body next to mine, I want everything. I want too much.

"Just touch me." I sound impatient, but it's nothing but need.

"Where?"

"Everywhere."

And so, his hands make their way all over my body. They go up and down my arms, down my back, grabbing my ass. They continue up my thigh, bunching up my dress. The anticipation is delicious, his hands are addicting.

"Can I?" He motions to my dress.

"Yes." I respond quickly, but he slowly, slowly pulls my dress up. Every new inch he exposes, he kisses lightly. My knee, my lower thigh, my upper thigh. Higher and higher, making everything build, making me crazy for it. It's only serving to ramp up all my nerves.

"Why are you going so slow?" I complain.

He laughs. "You're so used to everything so quickly, aren't you?" He shakes his head.

"You said it was late, and you wanted more time."

"I changed my mind. I'm going to take my time with you. I like to take my time opening presents, especially ones I really want."

My eyebrows lift. "That is a hell of a line."

"It's not a line." He gets my dress over my hips, exposing my seamless black underwear, and his mouth curves into a wide grin. His hands start to map the parts of my body again: legs, arms, stomach, breasts, hips.

He leans down to kiss me again, and in no time it is a frenzy of our mouths.

"Do you like to be touched here?" His fingers trail down to the band of my underwear.

"Yes," I sigh.

His finger slips inside, what feels like at a glacial pace, and gently caresses the bundle of nerves desperate for it.

I whimper. *Whimper. Jesus Christ.*

"Is that good?"

Bobblehead nod is back.

"Give me words." He nibbles at my earlobe. "I want to hear you."

"Yes, yes. Good," I manage to get out in what sounds like a strangled whisper.

"Do you like slow? Or a little faster?"

"I like ... I like slow. I like ..."

"Taking your time?"

"Yeah. It takes time." That just made me feel like an inconvenience. Too much and nobody patient enough to bother.

"I've got all the time you need." His smile is so damn perfect. Has he always been this hot? This seductive? This fucking amazing?

"Wait. What about you?"

"What about me?"

"Let me touch you, too."

He lets out a quiet groan. "Not yet. This is about you." He probably senses that I'm about to fight it, so he kisses me hard. "Let me."

And I can't do anything else but just let him.

His finger moves slowly, in soft circles, then he trails lower and dips one inside. I sink into the mattress, moaning in response, as he adds another finger, pushing in deeper.

"You feel amazing." His voice is rough against my skin, and goosebumps follow.

"Logan," I breathe out.

"Fuck, I love it when you say my name like that."

"Like what?"

"Like you're so desperate for me," he whispers. "Are you? Are you desperate for me like I am for you?"

Those words, his hands, all this feeling sets me on edge like never before. My answer is just a moan as his fingers pump into me, and his mouth meets mine again, his tongue matching the rhythm of his fingers. Our sounds are getting swallowed up by starving mouths.

"Are you going to come all over my hand?" He smiles.

"I think so." I nod, out of breath, in a frenzy. I can give him some hope, I can give myself some, too. But who knows if I'll get there.

"I hope so," he grins.

And I can't help it when I begin to move, my body aching for release. I should be embarrassed by how I ride his hand, relishing in this chase for my pleasure. But God if it doesn't feel amazing. And damn if he isn't encouraging and patient and so fucking hot as he's beside me bringing me to what feels like the edge of oblivion.

"Let go, Julie," he says in my ear, his teeth grazing along my throat, across my chest. "Let me take care of you."

My eyes are closed, head tilted upward, my body as tight as a wire. Something taut and ready to snap. But this is always the hard part: getting over that hump. Letting that wire snap. Letting everything go.

My mind races a mile a minute, my thoughts run free.

"Hey. Come back to me," Logan says above me, and my eyes open immediately. He's studying me intensely, head cocked to the side, those eyes burning into mine.

His eyes ... I don't look at them enough. We're too busy dancing temple to temple, but his eyes are the most perfect shade of brown.

"You're good with your hands, too," I blurt out and he smiles, something devious and heavenly in one.

"Am I?" He pushes in deeper, his thumb pressing down on my clit harder, and all I can do is cry out in response. "I'm also good with my mouth, if we're listing all my talents," he adds, smugly. And it doesn't have any right to be as hot as it is. "Can I kiss you here, too?"

"Fuck yes," I nod frantically, my body already reeling from every euphoric feeling it can manage. If he goes down on me, I don't know how long I will last. How foreign this feeling was to me just months ago.

His kisses trail down my body as he reaches for my underwear and pulls them off.

"Fuck."

I let my smile show that time.

"Lay back," he orders. His voice has lost some of the lightness, replaced with a tight, low tone.

I oblige immediately, watching him watch me, drinking me in like I'm all he's ever wanted. This feeling is nothing short of powerful.

"Fucking look at you, Julie. Who the hell wouldn't want to take their time with you?"

He places one sweet, perfect kiss on my inner thigh and then his mouth is on me, one thorough lick that has me falling right into this mattress and gasping for air. His fingers pump into me slowly, and his tongue is now exploring all of me expertly.

He *is* good with his mouth, too, and I'm reaping all the benefits. His head between my thighs feels like the most perfect thing. Everything—every new touch, new action, new step—continues to feel like the best thing. He grabs my hand and brings it to his hair, and all I can do is wrap my fingers around his messy strands and cry out for him. My legs are shaking, and this perfect feeling is reaching new levels, everything heightened.

He moves his fingers leaving me painfully empty and I whine in response. His laugh against my thigh is soft and sweet. "Can't get enough?"

His hands grab my thighs to pull me closer and wrap them around his head, one swift move that has me gasping at the action, almost wanting to pull away.

"Don't," he says. "Don't get shy with me, Julie." He bites the inside of my thigh, his eyes watching me intensely.

There's no reason to be shy here, I realize. Not when I can see how much he wants me, too. Not when I've spent so many years trapped in shame, aching to get out, to now be presented with him: somebody who is shamelessly devouring me in every sense of the word. And so, I relax my legs and wrap myself around him as much as I can, basking in this want. In this desire and lust and everything my body is craving.

His fingers find their way inside me again, and his mouth follows, something messy and damn near magical at once. Something sinful and delicious and every bit worth it. My legs tremble even more as I climb to new, practically undiscovered levels. The feeling inside me builds and builds. When I crash, it might destroy me, and it will all be worth it.

"You're doing so good, too," he says, then puts his mouth on me once more.

And that's it. Everything within me explodes. I let go and jump. My body shakes with immediate relief, and I cry out from the feeling of free falling as he watches my body writhe, ravenous. He doesn't pull away at first, staying put firmly between my legs, like it's the only place he wants to be. Once he does, I'm still breathing heavy, aftershocks coursing through me.

"*Fuck*," he says as he wipes his mouth with the back of his hand.

I agree. Because that was the most amazing orgasm I have ever had in my life.

Chapter Twenty-Four

Julieta

LOGAN'S LEG IS WRAPPED around mine when I wake up in the morning. His arm is draped across my stomach, a warm weight keeping me close. My body stirs, used to being up this early, even if I was up way too late last night. I'm in a post-orgasm stupor, some sort of bliss, when I look around the room and realize I'm still in the guest room. And then I notice he's awake, too, and he's smiling.

"I hate to be an asshole, but I've got to go."

"Oh God, of course. I'm so sorry you got stuck here." I try to sit up, but he pulls me in closer.

He laughs softly, raspy with sleep. "I didn't get stuck here. I'll be back soon, if you'll have me."

"Please." It's a quiet, embarrassing plea.

He leans over to kiss me gently, confessing, "I couldn't stay away from you if I fucking tried." Then he quietly slips out of bed, still dressed in last night's clothes, and goes out the door.

I spend the rest of the early morning not wanting to get up, letting myself enjoy the calm and quiet of a Sunday morning. I almost fall into a guilt trap with it, but there's nobody to tell me how ridiculous it is, except for maybe those voices that like to pop into my head once in a while.

I should spend the time catching up on my cases, the ones I've been practically neglecting. It takes too much effort, but I drag myself out of bed and get to work. Except my mind finds ways to sidestep the focus, to go back to Logan and the night before. A recurring memory, a lingering feeling, something I can't help but smile to myself about.

And then I fall into more worry, like what will happen to our partnership now that we've crossed a boundary? What about the lessons?

My mind finds another distraction with the loud sound of somebody harshly opening my door.

My brother stumbles in, dressed like he's headed out to go play soccer with his friends.

"Don't you knock?" I call out from my dining table surrounded by paperwork.

"Have I ever?"

Anybody else would probably be concerned by this, but the open-door policy between my family and me has led to always expecting guests. But suddenly I think about what would happen if he'd stumbled into my place with Logan here.

"Do you barge into Agostina's apartment like this?"

"Definitely not." He reaches for a LaCroix in my fridge, then grabs a glass and opens the freezer for ice. "Ooh,

Uncrustables." He reaches into the box and grabs one. "Mom asked if somebody could bring sandwiches de miga tonight."

"Okay, and?"

"And I'm going to play right now," he says like it's obvious.

"And I'm doing work." This is also obvious. "Call Delfi. Or Cecilia."

"They're all busy." He practically chugs his drink.

"You're not playing all day. Go to the store afterwards. What's the big deal?"

"Can I go to that other bakery near the park?" he asks.

"No, they aren't good. Go to Mariana's."

"Can you?"

I don't know what snaps—the way I'm tired of fixing everybody's problems, or tired of finding the solutions, or frustrated with how everybody else can do what they want but I'm expected not to. How my brother was raised to have everybody wait on him instead. But it pisses me off and I'm too tired to care.

"Are you joking? I am swamped with work. Look at this table. Look at this paperwork. Pick up the fucking phone and make an order if you need to. That way all you have to do is pick it up after your beloved soccer match. I don't care. But you are more than fucking capable of doing it, so *do it*."

His eyes widen slightly. "Alright, sorry. Fine. I can do

it."

Is this what setting a boundary feels like? Like I want to throw up everywhere? I hate it. "I'm sorry, too."

"I just thought—"

"I'm tired of doing all the work."

His face softens, and he nods. "Okay." Then he takes one more Uncrustable, says his goodbyes, and heads out the door.

I take one deep, shaky breath in and force myself back to work until it's time for dinner.

I step into my parents' house again without knocking. There's a certain irony in that, I realize, passing through the living room into the kitchen where I say hi to my mom.

"La ensalada," she says by way of response, pointing to the fridge where I find lettuce washed and ready to go. I grab it and find a small corner of the kitchen where I can chop some tomatoes, slice an avocado, and dress everything with olive oil and a squeeze of lemon juice. Everything is second nature and habit. The muscle memory of doing something enough times and it becomes a core action.

Like a strong arm wrapping around my waist, and a firm hand at my back, and the instant movement of feet. Steps to the front, ocho to the back.

Tía Cecilia puts on some soft music in the background, and I notice, almost secondhand, my feet moving in rhythm, another surprise in how my body has learned to respond. *In how it responded last night.*

"Arma la mesa, Julieta," my mother tells me, breaking the spell and taking me out of the fog. My feet obey quickly, moving to the dining room with plates and silverware in tow.

I start on my usual chore of setting the table. It's my favorite chore—the quiet, the repetition. T walks in and comes up next to me, a mild hurricane to my calm winds, grabbing some forks and helping.

"Hey, what's up?" I say.

"You know, sometimes it's a surprise how good of a lawyer you are cause you're a shit liar."

"What?" I ask, taken aback and looking at her.

"Javier came into the restaurant earlier today."

Fuck.

"And he told me all about how he ran into you the night before at the *milonga*. With *Logan*. The *tango instructor.*" She sets a fork down forcefully. "I fucking knew something else was up."

I sigh, and Delfina steps into the dining room just then, stopping short when she sees us. "'Kay, the vibe is weird in here."

"Javier told me that you danced two tandas with him." T says to me.

"Wait ... what?" Delfina chimes in.

"I just assumed you were just enjoying some sexcapades with him, but this confirms it."

"Sexcapades?" I ask, shocked, probably pale as a sheet.

"Two tandas?" Delfina adds.

I roll my eyes. "This is so ridiculous. We were just dancing." We *were*. Granted, right now I am lying through my teeth. Am I a shit liar? Can T tell? We are, in the end, still just partners. Yes, we were dancing at the milonga, but who knows if anybody caught our late-night activities in the parking lot afterward.

"Uh-huh. He knows the rules."

"How do *you* know the rules?" I ask.

"She was my grandmother too, asshole."

"Fucking Javier," I mutter.

T is smiling now, as is Delfina. Two wide grins pointed right at me.

"You *are* dancing!" Delfina says in a hiss.

"Keep your voices down." I look toward the kitchen where I hear my mom talking to tía Ana. "And keep your mouths shut."

"I won't say a word!" she says, with the same enthusiasm. "Though, honestly, I'm a little offended that I wasn't invited."

I don't know if it's the combination of feeling like I've upset them or excluded them. The thought that I've kept something for myself. Maybe it's all the guilt finally coming to a head, consuming me. Could be the feeling of the secret finally being exposed, at least only by the two of them for now. But all of it comes to the surface, and I do something I haven't done in front of them in a very, very long time. I start to cry.

"Shit," T mumbles, while Delfi looks at me wide-eyed.

"Hey Julie," Delfi says in a quiet, soothing voice as she comes over to me.

T walks over, too, wrapping her arms around me, her mouth a firm line.

"I'm sorry. This is so stupid," I say in frustration.

"No, no. It is not stupid." Delfi's voice is adamant, and a little louder now. She's shaking her head.

"I just wanted to do this thing for me. Give my life a little more excitement, a little more meaning, like you guys have done with yours."

"Shit, Julie," T says.

"I was only kidding about being invited. You deserve to do this for yourself. You know that, don't you?"

"Do I deserve to do it? Or am I wasting my precious time?" I look to the kitchen again. "Please don't tell them."

"Fuck them. Who cares what they think?" T asks abrasively.

"I do."

"And you shouldn't," she states.

"You know how my mom gets. And if she hears about what's been going on, she'll probably lose her shit."

"She's had a hard life," Delfi nods.

"It doesn't make her any less of a pain in the ass," T retorts.

"Abuela gave me the shoes. I thought maybe I should just go for it, I don't know," I try to reason.

"Yes! Of course, you should," Delfi agrees.

"I'm gonna need more details than that," T says.

I eye her, sighing in defeat. "Logan happened to be the instructor when I signed up for the classes. I met him before," I admit.

"Logan? Like Gavin's brother?" Delfi asks, looking between us and trying to catch up.

"Yes. That one." I sigh.

"Damn, how did I miss that?" she tells T.

"Anyway, it was getting tricky with work, but I didn't want to quit. So, I decided to do private lessons."

Delfi gasps, and T just laughs. "You tango *slut*, I love it!"

"Shut up," I say, wanting to be exasperated, but almost laughing it off instead.

"Okay, so now what?" T asks, egging me on.

"There's another milonga coming up in a couple of weeks. It's the end of the session and his partner is leaving."

"Are you taking over?" They look at me expectantly.

"No, no. Nothing like that. He wants to quit anyway, I think." At least he mentioned that last night. Where that takes us, I don't really know.

"Where is it?" T asks.

I roll my eyes.

"Where!" Delfina pushes.

"Can I ..." I search for the words. "Can I just have this?"

They both soften at that. "Of course you can." Delfi nods. But their disappointment is visible, palpable. Or maybe that's my guilt I'm feeling. It's been such a companion in my life, of course I should know what it feels like by now.

"Midnight Ballroom on Tenth. At seven," I concede. They would have found out anyway. T would have hounded Javier or probably even Gavin; Delfi would have scoured social media posts for any information.

"Oh. I think I've got work that night," T says.

"Oh, yeah," Delfi adds. "I think I've got another thing going on that night."

They're lying to give me this one thing. I want to thank them; I want to change my mind.

I take a deep breath in gratitude and pick up the knives to keep setting the table. But I should know better than to think they're going to let this go. Because that's what happens—once news gets out in this group, it doesn't float away. It ferments, it keeps growing, it takes on a life of its own.

"There's more," T says. She's watching me with a curious look, and I know better than to put anything past her.

"Dammit. Why are you so astute?"

"Don't deflect with fancy words."

I look to the kitchen again, making sure nobody can

hear. "I signed up to do a competition in San Diego."

They both meet me with shock, dumbstruck until T just says, "*Ho-ly shit.*"

"It's not a big deal." I wave it off, trying to calm my own nerves.

"The San Diego Tango Festival?" T presses. "I saw Abuela there."

"God, of course you did."

"*Julieta!* This is amazing," Delfi squeals, squeezing my arm, while T just unfurls a smile like this is the best thing she's heard all week.

I open my mouth to say more—whether it's to shrug it off or tell them to keep their mouths shut again—but tía Silvia makes her way in with a platter of food, and we quickly fall silent, getting back to our role of setting the table.

"Hola chicas," she says.

This time are some crispy milanesas, sprinkled with a squeeze of lemon juice, and potato salad Ana made. There's a platter of the sandwiches de miga that Dario was miraculously able to pick up. And there's the salad I quickly put together before setting the table.

The men walk in, making their way to their seats.

"Hola pa," I call out, kissing him on the cheek.

We take our usual seats, and I wait for most to fill their plates before I reach over and dig in.

"Bueno," my mother says, like this phrase is the equivalent of a green light, "a comer."

***

"Y CÓMO VA todo?" Cecilia asks me. She's trying to sound casual, but she's curious. I wouldn't be surprised if she ran into Javier, too. The night is winding down, and I'm sitting with her at the end of the table. She's nursing her glass of wine; my mother went to the kitchen to grab mate.

I shrug in response, but that answer probably isn't doing me any favors. "Bien," I reply half-heartedly. But, I realize, if there were one person to talk to in the middle of my own dilemmas, it would be her.

"How do you do it?" I ask her instead.

"Do it?"

"Do any of it. How did you create this perfect life? How did you break away from what everybody else wanted for you?"

"Mierda," she says, lifting her eyebrows in surprise. She takes a minute to answer, giving whatever she's about to say some thought. "You have to chip away at it slowly," she answers. "You have to learn to love the cracks, see the beauty in them. We learn something new every day. You should embrace it. It's so easy to fall into shame when it's that primal feeling you felt as a child. When too much was put on your shoulders," she touches my shoulder gently.

"When too much was expected of you and all you learned was to be good."

I swallow.

"Your mistakes don't define you, Julieta. Neither does your perfection. You are good." She points to my heart, driving her words home. "But still. It's a process to learn to do things for yourself. And it's a learning curve, a balance."

A balance. My whole life has felt like balance, never trying to fall too far in one direction, never wanting to tip the scales. "And how do I start then?"

"Well," she takes a breath. "You ask yourself what you want. That's a broad question, so you start small. What do I want right now?" She looks around the table. "What do I want to eat?"

"What do I want to eat? That's the life changing question?"

She laughs. "You come to this house every single Sunday, and you sit in that same chair, and you pick up that same plate, and your mother places serving upon serving of food on it, encouraging you to eat everything, and then sends you home with a ton of leftovers you may or may not want. What if you made your own plate without the imposition of others, what would *you* want to eat?"

I sit back, silent, unable to answer this one small question that, unlike my sassy remark, may very well be life-changing for me.

"And then you ask yourself, what do I want today?

And what do I want this week? And what do I want in the next six months? And then, what do I want in this life? But answering the question is one thing. Acting on it is another. Setting the boundary, teaching yourself not to care about what others think—that's the hard part." She lifts an eyebrow, eyeballing me like she knows the difficulty of it.

"You chip away at it," she repeats. "Little by little. You learn to slowly live life for yourself. And eventually, you build a life you love so much, that makes you so happy, that nothing else matters."

She finishes the last sip of her wine, and I sit a bit dazed.

Cecilia gets up to go into the kitchen and tells everybody she's got to go. "Me voy. Bye." She kisses everybody goodnight, gives me a wink, and then she's out the door.

There's a rustle next to me and I turn to see T sitting down beside me, eating a slice of cake.

"Where did that come from?"

"There's some in the kitchen. I dunno, I think she got it from Publix." She shrugs, taking a bite. "It's fine."

I snort in response as I pull out my phone to check messages and emails, something out of habit. But I realize as I do it, I don't care. I don't want to know what Barbara needs. I don't care about what tomorrow morning will look like. I can figure it out then. I click the phone off and put it back in my pocket.

"This is good," T nods, watching me closely. "I like it."

"What?"

"Your new hobby," she says around a mouthful of cake.

"Yeah?"

"Oh, yeah." She smiles like she's got a juicy secret, and I choose not to think too much of it. Instead, I lean on this newfound feeling of excitement and enjoyment. I lean on the relief of finally telling somebody else what's been going on.

"Keep going, Julie."

This feels like tumbling toward something in the best way, falling right into it and rolling downhill. That's how everything felt last night, like something unstoppable. Like when I caught sight of him at the Alley Cat that one night and wondered what destruction I could be barreling into. Except I misread it.

It's not destruction. It's pleasure in all its forms.

And I want it all.

"I think I'm going to go," I tell T.

"Me too."

"You going out tonight?"

"Nah." She finishes up the last bite of cake. "Tinder is trash."

"Love you, Agostina." I wrap my arm around her in a side hug, squeezing as I do.

"Yeah, yeah."

As I get to my car, my phone vibrates with an incoming call. I almost let it go to voicemail, but I look down and find Logan's name across the screen.

"Hi," I answer immediately. "This is a nice surprise."

"I was thinking ... maybe we should try and squeeze in an extra lesson this week?" I can't see his face, but I'm sure there's a smug grin attached to it.

"Sounds like a great idea," I agree. And then I think about chipping away at it. And asking myself what I want. And then I ask him. "How about tonight?"

Chapter Twenty-Five

Logan

She's the most confident I've seen her as she walks into my apartment, wearing one of those wrap dresses, smiling as she greets me and looks around my place. She's very much the lawyer now: standing tall, assessing, walking around confidently.

"I brought leftovers." She hands me a bag.

"Oooh." I peek inside, only to find a box from Mariana's Bakery filled with sandwiches. "Sandwiches de miga?" I asked, surprised. "You must really like me."

"They're not all for you." She laughs.

"Come here."

She smiles as she steps closer, and it's the perfect distance for me to lift her chin and kiss her. Just a quick kiss, but when I pull back, she leans in again. This kiss goes deeper, her tongue parting my lips. She's definitely the most confident now, and the dynamic is making me a little dizzy.

"How are you?" My fingers linger under her chin.

"I'm okay." She smiles. "How are you?"

"Better." I grin. "How was dinner?"

She breathes in deep. "I told my cousins about the dancing."

"Oh shit." That stops me. "How did that go?"

"Well, I was confronted. Because Javier has a big mouth and he told Agostina he ran into us at the milonga."

This gets a laugh out of me. "Javier does love to talk." But this is big news from somebody who wanted to keep everything under wraps. "Are you okay with this?"

She nods. "I think I am."

"What did they say?"

"They are very happy for me," she says, almost surprised.

I kiss her once more as I link my fingers with hers, walking us to the kitchen to put down the box of sandwiches. "So, this is the kitchen," I start with a tour.

I lead her out to the living room. "Here's our couch. Gavin has been watching a lot of Netflix documentaries here lately."

"How's he doing at the restaurant?"

"He loves it. Yeah, it's been good for him."

"That's good," she says softly.

We walk down the hallway, still hand in hand. "This is the bathroom. Always good to know."

She laughs as I bring her to the end of the hallway. "And our rooms. But ..." I lean down to whisper in her ear, "I really want a sandwich right now."

Her laugh is louder as she follows me back to the kitchen.

"Do you want one?"

"No, I ate plenty. My mom usually picks these up, but my brother did this time and grabbed a box of a hundred. Hence, the leftovers."

"I could eat a hundred of these by myself," I say, opening the box and taking out one of the thin sandwiches. I scarf one down quickly and grab another, taking a bite as she watches me with a smile, leaning against the counter. Comfortably like she's meant to be here. My eyes can't help but follow her body down, her dress that ends above her knee, her feet in casual sandals, her toes painted a dark red.

"What?" she asks curiously.

"I like you here."

Her smile gets wider, a light blush on her cheeks. "Thought we were dancing."

"Of course. Let's dance." I walk over to her and offer her my hand. She takes it without hesitation, this feeling like stepping into worn-in shoes.

We start slow, as I hum a song in her ear. A close embrace, the only one I ever want with her, temple to temple, heart to heart.

"This is nice," she says in mine.

"You're doing great, by the way."

"You might be obligated to say that." She chuckles.

We turn in rhythm and her moves look so polished, so effortless. "I'm still having fun dancing with you," I say.

"But you still want to quit?"

I falter. "We don't need to talk about that now."

We let the dancing do the talking instead, conversations with our legs and turns and movement. I keep humming, but the tempo has slowed significantly. With a side step and a giro, she turns and hooks her leg onto my thigh, executed beautifully.

"Is that how the enganche goes?" she whispers.

"Just like that."

My mouth hovers over hers as we continue to move slowly. But somewhere along the line, we lose the formality of it. My leg comes between hers and she straddles my thigh, swaying side to side as she does. I lean down and kiss her neck. Small kisses along her jaw, behind her ear. She sighs with each kiss I give her, and all I can do is hold her tighter.

Time. She likes time.

"What are you doing?" she whispers.

"Taking my time," I tell her, kissing her lips softly.

"You are trouble." She smiles.

"Am I?"

"You're going to get me used to all this luxury, and then what happens when the lessons are over?" She laughs softly when she asks this, like it's funny and maybe a little rhetorical, but it just feels like a punch in the gut to me.

"The lessons have nothing to do with you and me," I tell her, pulling back so she can see my face. "Whether I quit or not has nothing to do with you and me. In fact, you should stop paying me."

"Logan."

"No. You should stop paying me."

"I'm not going to stop paying you." She practically rolls her eyes.

"Is this relationship just about the lessons for you?" I ask incredulously.

She doesn't answer, studying my face and opting to stay quiet instead.

"This isn't some private-lessons-with-a-side-of-fucking. We're not going there. This is you and me."

"Is that what you want?" she asks quietly.

"*You're* what I want," I tell her adamantly.

Her eyes soften. "I like hearing you say that."

"I'll say it over and over again then." I bring her back to me, missing her body against mine. "What do *you* want?" My voice is low and shaky against her throat. My hands move slowly, around her waist to her back.

She swallows, before she answers. "You."

"Yeah?"

"All of you."

I kiss her hungrily. Her mouth is so sweet, I can't get enough of it. I tilt her head back to go deeper and bite her lip gently, coaxing a moan from her. I want to taste her all over. I bend down quickly to lift her up, and I set her down on the dining table, the closest surface to me.

She yelps in surprise. "This does not seem sturdy enough for whatever you're thinking."

I laugh against her neck, keeping my hands at her waist, pulling her closer to me.

"I'm not thinking anything," I say innocently. But even as I say it, I give myself away, as my hands move down to grip her thighs. She opens her legs wider, giving me more space to stand between them. I watch her movements, mesmerized.

Our bodies come closer, and the kissing intensifies. My mouth meets her throat, and I run a line down to her chest with my tongue, tasting the salt of her skin, hearing her sigh in response. My hands move up her thighs and my fingers find their way under her dress. Soft skin my mouth is craving. I want her so badly; I want to drown in every inch of her.

"Julie, fuck, I want you," I grit out.

"I want you, too," she says between kisses, gripping my shirt.

I kneel and lift her dress higher up to her waist. "God, you and these dresses."

"Convenient, huh?"

I laugh against her thigh as I kiss my way up, making my way to that perfect spot between her legs. Her hand flies to my hair and I want her to pull it harder. Right now, I want everything rough enough to sting.

My hands hastily grab at the sides of her underwear, pulling it off.

"Really? On the dining table?" She smirks.

"This wild streak of yours is out of control."

She laughs, running her fingers through my hair, making it messier. I want her messier, too.

My eyes meet her gaze as I laugh with her, but the look I see there stops me. It's intimate and vulnerable, something tender as her fingers weave through my hair slowly. This might be the happiest I've seen her, and this is definitely the happiest I've ever felt. As I watch her from below, I'm even more desperate to worship her. I'm at her feet, and it's just where I want to be.

I open her thighs wider, moving my fingers up to tease her lightly. She's soaked, and I moan with her in response. I bend to kiss the center of her then my tongue finds its way in, tasting every inch of her, drinking her in, inhaling her scent.

"Oh, God," she gasps, pulling at my hair. It sends a thrill down my spine.

I lean in closer, feasting on her like I can't get enough, and she falls back. Stretched out, dress bunched around her waist, her lips parted in pleasure.

"You laid out on this table is a visual I never knew I needed."

She laughs, that bright, happy laugh, and I bring my

mouth to her again, licking every inch of her with even more desperation. Her groan is louder as she pulls at the strands of my hair, and I've never been more turned on in my fucking life.

I don't stop. I can't stop. I wrap her legs around me, my fingers dig into her thighs, and my tongue devours her until I hear her begging. And then I go harder.

Her legs are trembling, body moving to meet my mouth. I press down on her hips to keep them steady.

"Logan, please, *please*, I'm going to—"

When she comes, I keep my mouth on her as she cries out, laid out and shaking on my dining table. I'll never fucking get over it.

I stand up quickly, the chair skidding behind me, as I pick her up and take her to my room. She's flushed, eyes hooded as she looks at me.

"Where are we going?"

"To a proper bed."

She giggles in my ear, and it's so sweet. So perfect like every other part of her.

I set her down gently and undo the bow of her dress. It opens up like a robe, leaving her half naked in the middle of my bed.

"Fuck. Look at you."

She lets the dress fall down her arms, tossing it to the side. Then she unhooks her bra and lets it fall in the same pile.

"Let me see you," she whispers like a plea, reaching for the band of my sweatpants.

I don't hesitate as I pull them off, along with my shirt, throwing them wherever. I step closer to her, and she watches me, eyes seemingly studying every inch of my body. The shift in the room is almost palpable, thick. There's that zing of awareness again, that feeling I get whenever I'm near her.

"Tell me what you want."

"I already did," she laughs.

"Tell me again." I kneel on the bed, hovering over her.

"I want you."

"Me?" I ask against her mouth.

"Yes. You." She runs her hands down my chest.

"I don't want to be your secret anymore," I suddenly confess.

She looks surprised when I say it, but I kiss her softly before she can say anything else. Still, she kisses me back and whispers, "Okay."

"I want to be inside you," I confess again.

"I want that, too," she says, clutching my shoulders, wrapping her legs around me.

I reach for my drawer to get a condom. She keeps her eyes on me as I rip it open and roll it on. And when I slide into her, it immediately feels like home. I'm drowning in how good she feels, just like this.

"Do you have any idea how incredible you feel?"

I lean down and take her nipple in my mouth, sucking and biting. Her hand flies to the back of my head, keeping me there.

"Fuck, Logan," she pants out, as I thrust into her.

My hands can't get enough of her skin and curves, her nipples between my fingers as she gives a soft sigh.

"You like that?"

"Yes," she hisses.

I thrust in again, slowly, taking my time with it, but it's too much and not enough. Starved for her, that's how I've felt, and the feel of being with her like this is bordering on fucking mindblowing.

"Tell me what else you like."

"You don't have to go so slow," she says, and it's all I hear before I thrust in harder, and her answering moan is louder. "What do you like?"

"I like whatever you like." I kiss her. "I like it when you're loud. I like it when you pull my hair." Every confession is another kiss, another thrust. "I like it when you're enjoying yourself and coming on my table. I want to fuck you on it again and again."

Her breaths are heavy as she whimpers underneath me, so damn sexy at my hands.

"I want to watch you ride me," I keep going. "I want to watch you take everything."

Her eyes zone in on mine, a heated gaze, and then she sets her palms on my chest, pushing me off her to roll over. She lowers herself onto me, warm skin and loose hair around her face, as she rocks back and forth slowly.

"I love this view," I tell her, grinning.

She sighs, letting out a delicate laugh that sounds like it's wrapped around pleasure. I thrust up, and she lets out another perfect moan.

"You can be louder for me, can't you?" My hands move up to pinch her nipples between my fingers, and she groans again, goosebumps following all over her body.

"Are you desperate for me like I am for you?" she gasps, repeating my own words back to me.

"You have no idea." Now I'm at her mercy. The confidence she walked in with is back, a hold on me like nothing else.

"Tell me."

"I'm desperate for you all the time. I want you here, with me, all the time."

"Oh yeah? Just like this?" she laughs.

"Just like this. And by my side. And dancing with me. I don't want anybody else; I don't want anything else." I can't help the words coming out. I'm under her spell.

"No?" She breathes out against my mouth, hovering above me, like she's something saintly and ethereal.

"This is it. I can't let you go." I kiss her frantically, like the words I've spoken have somehow revved everything up. She kisses me back and we are a hurricane between the sheets, our bodies moving in perfect rhythm, our sounds loud.

"You're so fucking perfect, sweetheart. You're so good."

Suddenly, her eyes widen, and she comes.

"Fuck, Julie. Look at you." My hand cradles her jaw, thumb at her chin, moving up to press into her bottom lip. "Look at how perfect you are, look at how perfect you come." Her eyes watch me religiously. I can't hold on much longer as I continue to talk her through it.

"It's so good, isn't it?" I grit out, watching her fall apart above me.

"So good," she says with a soft cry.

"Be selfish," I remind her. "Take everything. You fucking deserve all of it."

"Logan," she whimpers.

And then I come, a flood of relief, with her hands gripping my arms in a way that feels grounding, deliberate, and real.

Chapter Twenty-Six
Julieta

"Do you want something to drink? I'll go grab it." I'm standing by the bed, hair disheveled and haphazardly dressed, having just come from the bathroom.

"Sit down." He grins, grabbing my waist and pulling me back down into bed. "You don't need to do a thing." He says the words against my neck before he lightly bites it. "What would you like?"

"That seems like a loaded question."

He laughs in response, rolling me over to kiss me. My arms wrap around his back to bring him closer.

"I would love some water."

"Want some sandwiches, too? I've got a bunch."

I laugh. "No, I'm okay."

"I'll be right back," he says against my mouth, kissing me once more before he gets up and heads to the kitchen.

This feels indulgent. A warm bed, messy sheets, somebody else getting me water. In the realm of guilt, I should probably be right in the middle of it. I wait for it to hit me, but it doesn't. It just feels good for once.

I lay in bed for a moment, sprawled out, but then I get up and walk around his room. He has a bookshelf along one wall filled with books, and pictures, and some trophies. Medals are displayed on the wall. So many accolades, so many awards. What a wild life.

I look closer at the pictures: one with Gavin, some with Tara or other dancers, and then one in particular high up on the shelf like he holds this one in high regard.

Everything stops when I notice it. Logan, younger, a big bright smile with his arm around an older woman. One with a red lip, and a matching smile. One I know so well, because I've looked at it most of my life.

He walks in then holding two glasses of water and finds me frozen in front of the shelf.

"Ah, I love that picture," he says.

I can't respond. I can't do anything. I just keep staring, my heart starting to race.

"She is my favorite tango dancer," he says, almost triumphantly, showing her off. "Celestina Rossi."

I think I nod.

"What a name, right? Like she was born to be a powerful tango dancer." He smiles, like he's lost in a memory.

"You knew her," I say, but it's below a whisper. It's a miracle I even got the words out. My eyes are starting to burn.

"Yeah. You've heard of her, I take it?" He comes in closer, wrapping an arm around my waist, resting his chin on my shoulder. "Yeah, she's a pretty big deal. Well, was."

"You *knew* her," I repeat, taking a deep breath and leaning into the depth of this new information. I must sound stupid just repeating everything, but soon enough it all comes out. "I mean, it makes sense that you knew her. It makes sense that you would have even known *of* her, but maybe I didn't put two and two together. Maybe I didn't really think about it."

He turns to face me, a line between his brows. "Slow down."

"Maybe I didn't want to think about it," I continue. "How did you know her?"

"My mentor I always talk about? That was her."

He reaches up, and I feel him run his thumb along my cheek. Somewhere along the lines of this conversation I must have started crying. Feelings that snuck up on me, like everything else has.

"Are you alright?" he asks softly.

"She was my grandmother," I let out.

He stills. "What?" Logan looks between the picture and me, probably as confused and shocked as I am. "She was your grandmother?"

"Yeah," I sigh.

"Like, she was your tango-dancing grandmother?"

I nod, and he steps back, dropping his arms to his sides. Suddenly, I'm cold.

He runs a hand down his face. "Oh my God," he

sounds stunned. "Oh my *God*. Why didn't you say anything?"

"I don't know. I didn't think it was important," I answer, but maybe it was more than that. Maybe I just wanted to keep this for myself. I've been too busy keeping secrets from everybody, burying them down inside, never letting anybody in.

"Didn't think it was ... you didn't think mentioning one of the greatest tango dancers of the last century was *important?*" He puts his hands on his hips and starts pacing. Back and forth, back and forth. This wasn't the reaction I expected.

"Well, arguably. Not that I disagree ..."

"Holy shit." He starts laughing.

"It was complicated."

"Complicated." Now he's the one repeating words. "Your tango classes on a whim?"

I nod again, but the tears are slowly starting to fall. "How did you meet her?" I'm longing for more information, more of anything that will bring me new pieces of her.

"Years ago at a tango workshop. She really helped me. She gave me purpose. She was ... wonderful." He turns to look at me, and his eyes shine.

"I'm so sorry," I say, in between small sobs.

"Sorry? For what?"

"Seems like we both lost her, then."

His eyes soften at that, tilting his head to study me. He takes a step closer. "I did another workshop in Buenos Aires about five years ago. With Facundo, too. They were still so lively and electric."

I jump at the sound of my grandfather's name. Everything has suddenly become so entwined, and I don't know how to feel about it.

"She was still so captivating." He reminisces, and I get caught on that word. That one word that seemed to follow her everywhere.

I just smile as I listen to him talk about her, about the love he shared for her, too.

"I got her shoes."

His eyebrows lift. "Those were *hers*?"

"Yeah," I nod. I take steps to him, closing in the space between us, because now the distance feels like too much. This talk of my grandmother has worked as a bridge to get to him. "Turns out she left them to me."

"Holy shit." He looks at me wide-eyed, reaching out to caress my face. "She was so powerful and passionate. Now I see where you get it."

He wraps his other arm around my waist and pulls me in for a hug. The most comforting hug, something strong and solid, his hand rubbing my back slowly. And all it does is serve as a way to break the dam, letting all the tears flow for the first time in years. I cry loud, messy, embarrassing sobs, while he holds me tight. This is more crying than I've done in years, more than I allowed myself at dinner last night. This is months and months of pent-up frustration and sadness and grief. Years of holding everything in to appease those around me, to put others' feelings first.

Logan keeps his arms wrapped around me, rubbing circles on my back, holding me steady as I fall apart. I don't know how long we stay like that, but I eventually take a deep breath, the last of the tears subsiding. I feel lighter, but I still feel like I have a long way to go.

"I'm trying," I whisper into his shoulder, breathing in his scent.

He hugs me tighter, his arms around me like a life raft. Secure, lifesaving.

"This is so wild." He pulls back to look at me like he might be seeing me for the first time, his eyes roaming every inch of my face. I study him, too, soaking in this incredible moment of kismet.

"I don't know. I'm the one that's been parading around town in a dead lady's pair of shoes, so maybe I'm the crazy one."

He huffs out a laugh and shakes his head. "I can't believe I get to be here with you." And even though she's been the topic of conversation, I realize that statement has nothing to do with my connection to my grandmother and everything to do with his connection to me. One magnetic pull from the moment I met him. One slow moving train from the second that shoebox was placed on my lap.

"Maybe she set this in place for me to find you," I say out loud, my heart thudding with the weight of the emotions.

"Seems like something she would do." He laughs for a moment, his hands cradling my face, but then he quickly turns serious and he kisses me.

This kiss starts slow, delicate, but there's too much bursting at the seams, and it quickly turns greedy. He cradles the back of my neck as my hands find their way around him. We meet flush, kissing and kissing until we're out of breath. And then we pull back and do it again. Hands are traveling everywhere in messy chaotic movements. My kisses are uncoordinated in the best way: his neck, his ear, his forehead, his nose. Everywhere I can kiss him right now, I do. Everywhere I can shower him with affection, I do.

He reaches for my dress, unwrapping the knot in a quick move. I reach for his sweatpants, yanking them off. Once we've been rid of our clothes, we fall into bed, my legs wrapping around his waist. This feels like a dream: wanting, and wishful.

"Definitely not letting you go now," he says, as he gently settles over me.

I hold him close as he places the softest kiss on my neck, and reaches over for his drawer again. This time I take the condom from him, gently opening it and rolling it on. He watches me with that small smile as I guide him inside me.

He eases inside, and my legs shake from the sensation,

from the desire and the anticipation.

"Julieta," he says with wonder.

"Say it again."

He smiles and I trace it lightly with my fingers, wanting to commit this to memory. "Julieta."

I pull him to me and kiss him. Our bodies start to move and it's intoxicating how good it feels.

"Look at all of this passion," he whispers in awe. "Look at you."

"I don't want this to stop," I blurt out.

"It won't," he shakes his head. He grabs my wrists, pinning them above my head gently, pushing in slowly, making me crave it.

"You and me, Logan," I breathe out. "This is the best thing."

That tenderness is back, the look on his face that is saying too much for me to decipher. He thrusts in harder, and it feels so deliriously good, I don't want this to ever stop.

"I want all of this," I beg, in between moans. "I'm selfish for all of you."

"I'll give you all of me, sweetheart." He bites my neck, driving in harder. I wrap my legs around him tighter, crying out.

He lets go of my wrists and sits back on his heels, bringing his fingers between us to bring me over the edge. He watches me with that smug smile, one that's probably saying, *I'm good with my hands, remember?* as he keeps his fingers moving in tight circles. I didn't think I could come again, but now I'm so close I desperately want it.

"Right there," I gasp, a moan slipping past my lips.

"Yeah?" He keeps the pressure, he keeps thrusting harder, and then I'm pushed right over. He follows, crashing into me, shaking from his own release.

My mouth meets his and my fingers grip his hair and my body pushes against his. All these things that are saying *this is where you belong*.

I feel dizzy and disoriented in the best way.

"I'm ... *wrecked*," I say, breathing heavy.

"That good, huh?" He laughs, his own breaths coming in short spurts.

Quietly I realize that a word can take on a whole new meaning here, in the silence, in his arms, in being near him.

"I'm grateful for you," I tell him.

I don't expect a response, but he lifts up on his hands to look at me, and says seriously, "I'm never letting you go."

And maybe I'm wrecked in more ways than one.

Chapter Twenty-Seven

Logan

Julie is sprawled out on my chest, breathing softly. I'm slowly rubbing her back, my fingers trailing up and down. This feels like a bubble of calm, and everything leading up to it was overwhelmingly perfect.

I want to lay here forever; I want to jump up and dance with her.

"When I first walked into a dance studio," I say quietly, "I instantly felt like I was where I was meant to be. Like I was absolutely in the right place. You ever feel that?"

"Once," she answers. "I was eight. I watched her dance for the first time."

"That must have been wonderful to see."

"It was life-changing," she whispers.

"It doesn't happen often, at least not for me anyway. Life is always a series of too many questions, and never knowing the answer. 'Am I doing the right thing? Is this what I'm supposed to be doing?' You know?"

"I know." She nods.

"I feel it now, though," I tell her. "I feel it here. With

you."

Her heartbeat speeds up when I say it.

"There was another time," she swallows, looking at me. "When you blindfolded me. Remember that?"

"I do. Remember the very first time we danced? When I paired you up with Ethan?"

"I do," she laughs.

"I felt it then."

"Felt what?" she asks.

"A weird sort of calm. Like all my frustrating thoughts and complicated feelings about the dance sort of settled."

She doesn't say anything, just kisses me softly and snuggles closer.

Maybe this is working out just like it was meant to. A piece of my heart that had been healed by Celestina's mentorship and then broken when she passed has now come back to me.

And it's come back tenfold.

"Tell me about her," I say.

"Oh God, where do I even start? You could probably tell me more than I could."

"Why do you say that?"

"When my family decided to move here, she stayed behind and continued to compete and travel. I didn't see her much. I would talk to her on the phone occasionally, but a lot of times it was surface level stuff. She loved to dance. She was so good at it, too, you know. It's hard not to be completely mesmerized watching her."

Celestina Rossi was an idol when I got into dance, and the magic of her never faded, especially when I was in Buenos Aires in workshops and her name was spoken frequently in adoration.

"I miss her," she says. "Some days it feels like I let her down, like I didn't do enough. I didn't spend enough time or do enough with her. Or see her enough or talk to her enough. I didn't do *enough*. Maybe it would have never been enough."

I tuck her hair behind her ear, holding her close to me, listening.

"I'm just trying to be close to her again. I'm trying to make her proud."

"I think you're doing it, Julie. You're trying your best, and isn't that all anybody could ask for?"

"You haven't met my parents." She cocks an eyebrow.

"Not yet."

"No, not yet." She laughs for a moment, snuggling closer to me, then she lets out a sigh. "It was hard for everybody, but she had such a difficult time towards the end. She had severe arthritis; her body had been really struggling. The doctors would want to blame her instead of help her. They'd complain, 'you dancers mess up your bodies and then expect us to just fix you.' Nobody knew she struggled in the end, unable to do what she loved."

"That must have been so hard for her." I speak quietly,

my fingers lightly running up and down her arm.

"It was so, so hard. Tango was such a big part of her life. Imagine not being able to do it ever again, the one thing that was pivotal in your life. That was as necessary as breathing."

Faced with the thought of it now, I realize it would probably break me, too. Competing is one thing, but quitting dance altogether? Forever? I don't think I ever could.

"She had your grandfather, though."

"She did," she agrees.

"I think about that sometimes. When my body hurts, when I feel lonely. When all of this is gone, what do I have left?"

She reaches out to touch my cheek, and I lean into her palm, turning to kiss it softly.

"Do you know the story of how they met?" she asks.

"Tell me."

"They met at the tango clubs. She would sneak out to go dance, and when he saw her, it was love at first sight. They would dance together, but eventually he wanted to see her outside of it, too. He used to ride his bike ten miles just to see her."

"That's dedication," I smile.

"That's love," she clarifies.

With all this talk of Celestina, her plans make much more sense.

"So ... San Diego." I realize why she said it was personal

reasons.

"San Deigo," she repeats with a sigh.

"You don't know about what happened, do you?"

"What do you mean?"

"I went to San Diego last year. Tara and I fell apart, and we didn't even place."

She looks at me, quiet for a moment. "I had no idea."

"I figured you didn't. Anyway, I had been having a hard time. I was starting to look for other things then; I was feeling burnt out. And when we didn't even place, it definitely humbled me, but it also made me decide that I wasn't going to be doing it again. I was done competing, I was done with workshops. Tara and I talked it over shortly after—Silas was going to be heading into residency soon anyway—so we decided not to compete together anymore. We would teach locally, maybe host some milongas, but that was it." I breathe softly. "And then I met you."

"I feel like I've caused more trouble than I meant to."

"No." I move a piece of hair from her face, looking at her so she hears me. "You gave me back everything."

"I don't know what happens after this, Logan. I don't know what you want to do, but I want you to know that when all of this is done, you'll still have me," she confesses.

It's a bold promise, one that digs deep. One that tethers her to me, to my life. I want it desperately. "You'll have me, too," I say, clearly, definitively.

I grab her and bring her to me, kissing her deeply.

We make it to the kitchen sometime later, late enough that Gavin walks through the door and catches us eating sandwiches out of the box.

"Uh. Hi."

"Oh," Julie says, mid chew. "Hi."

I clear my throat, as we all look like deer in headlights. "This is Julie. You've met right?"

"Uh-huh." He smirks.

Thank God we're dressed. What time is it anyway?

"Nice to see you again." She waves, but she's blushing.

"We were just going back to my room," I say, grabbing the box of sandwiches.

"Not so fast." He comes over, reaches in, and pulls out a stack of them. "Thanks." And with that he walks to his room, some lightness in his step, and I think ... *whistling?*

"Shit, I lost track of time. Roommates." I roll my eyes.

She just laughs quietly, and says, "Come on. Let's go back to bed."

I follow her down the hall, mesmerized by her, and watch her climb into my bed. Comfortably taking up space here again. *Stay here forever,* I want to beg. *Don't ever go.*

"So, how long have you and Gavin lived together?" she asks.

"About five years. His previous job included a lot of travel and he felt like he was paying rent for nothing, so we moved in together."

"Makes sense."

"Does it? I can't even have you over without having to sidestep or figure out his schedule." I might sound frustrated, but maybe I'm just embarrassed.

She just takes it in stride, laughing like she doesn't have a care in the world.

"But really, since he got laid off, it has been kind of nice," I tell her.

"Yeah?"

"Our parents divorced when I was fourteen. It was hard on the both of us, and Gavin helped me get into dance to give me something to focus on. He saw how much I loved it, and so when I was sixteen and I had been priced out of the youth dance program, Gavin went to work full time to help me pay for it, while he went to school full time too. Imagine that."

"What a wonderful thing to do."

"It made fucking up in San Diego really hard. You and I didn't have the same childhood, no, but I understand wanting to do well for your family. I didn't want to let him down, either."

"Was he upset?"

I sigh. "No, he was so supportive."

"Just what you deserve."

"You deserve that, too."

"It feels like secrets have become the only way for me to get peace. As fucked as that sounds. When I was about fourteen, I joined my school volleyball team," she says quietly, lying next to me. "I loved it. I loved everything about it, and I couldn't wait to share with everybody else how much fun I was having, how much I was learning. And so, I did."

"I sense a but coming."

"*But* eventually it turned into a judgement. They would come to my games and watch me and offer unsolicited advice. I would get unnecessary comments. All I wanted was their approval, their support, but this one thing I had chosen for myself was being tarnished by everybody's input and opinions. In the end, my one happy thing became pressure and frustration until I eventually quit."

I can't imagine such a burden that I would opt to quit something I loved. But the opposite was parents that didn't care enough, and maybe that's its own burden to bear.

"And then I had to hear about how I was a quitter, too."

"So, they give you shit when you're doing it, and they give you shit when you stop. You ever think maybe they're gonna give you shit no matter what, so you should just do what you want anyway?"

"You make it sound so easy." She smirks.

"Healthy boundaries are a thing. Stop feeling guilty for setting them."

"Boundaries are the worst," she jokes.

"And now that your cousins know?"

"Now that they know, I worry about how long I can keep it from everybody else. And when it gets to everybody else, will they support it? Or will they tear it apart, too?"

"Sometimes, people surprise you," I say.

"And sometimes they respond just how you think they will."

I look at her for a moment, considering what I'm about to offer. "You should call Tara and go shopping for the milonga together."

"What?"

"I think you would like it. I think she would, too."

"She's not busy?"

I shrug. "Call her and find out. She'll be happy to hear from you."

"Why?" she asks, confused.

"Why will she be happy to hear from you?" I laugh. "She likes you."

"No. Why should I call her?" she clarifies.

"Because," I sigh. "I don't want you to get negative feelings about anything that we're doing here. Especially with the dance. I want you surrounded by supportive people that will root for you and whatever it is that you're doing."

She almost smiles, a small twist of her lips like she's fighting it. "Fine. I'll call her."

I kiss her forehead softly as her eyes start to close, and I

push down any more words that are prone to spilling out.
I've said enough tonight.

Chapter Twenty-Eight
Julieta

"You look ... different," Larissa tells me during our lunch hour. It's finally cool enough to truly enjoy the outdoor picnic tables.

"The hair cut?"

"That thing is old news. No, this is something else." She regards me.

I think about how I've kept her at arm's length, and how I don't know if I want to anymore. How hard it is when you're doing things alone, keeping secrets to keep the peace.

What peace is there when you're hiding everything?

"I've been doing ... something," I start.

"Something or *someone*?" she asks, eyebrows raised.

I'm sure my answering laugh gives me away, a sort of embarrassed chuckle that leads to a blush. "I guess both."

"Ah! Tell. Me. Everything," she squeals. Her smile is a mile wide as she dips a carrot stick in her ranch and takes a bite. I can't help but wince.

"Oh. Well. Remember that ballroom date you had?"

"Mr. Dancing with the Stars? Yeah."

"So, I sort of took that advice and decided to try my hand at tango."

Her jaw drops. "That is so great!"

"Is it?"

"What do you mean 'is it?' Of course, it is!" she says enthusiastically.

Of course, it is. She's right. It has been great. "Yeah, it's been fun." I smile.

"So, you met a guy in the class, and now you're doing the horizontal tango?" She leans in, waggling her eyebrows.

"You know, I knew there was a horizontal tango joke in there somewhere."

She cackles, picking at some cheese and crackers.

"Except, it's my instructor," I add in, almost apprehensively.

"Holy shit," she says with a gasp. "You go, Julie Martí. You fucking go."

"Yeah?" I can't help but smile.

"Yes," she says absolutely.

"Thanks, Larissa."

It's one thing for perpetually happy Larissa to notice something, it's another for Barbara to notice, too.

She hasn't said anything, but she's been asking for more from me, keeping an eye out over her reading glasses. She's sent some office-wide passive aggressive emails, her favorite thing to do. I've been focusing on my caseload just enough but opting not to stay too late at the office. Giving myself a break like the other associates give themselves, too.

And this evening after work, I've got plans to go shopping with Tara.

***

"So how are the lessons going?" Tara asks as she browses through different dresses.

"Great. They've been great."

Tara has taken me to Dancing Designs, a retail store for dancers. It's a large space filled with racks upon racks of dazzling, glittery dresses and matching suits. Salespeople are milling about, helping some customers with fittings.

"Uh-huh. I'm telling you, I wouldn't be surprised if he likes dancing with you more." She smiles. "It shows."

"Oh, no. That's—"

"It's okay, Julie. I promise. This is so good, I swear." She emphasizes those words with such genuine enthusiasm and kindness she's shown me from the very beginning, and it almost heals something in me. "I always caught him looking at that door like he was willing you to come through it. And then you would appear, and I swear to God, it was like watching one of those wilted flowers come back to life after you water it."

I don't know what to say to that, but I think of Logan waiting for me to walk into the dance studio and there's something about that visual that is so heartwarming.

"So, how did you get started in dance?"

"Irish parents," she laughs, but I'm not quite sure what she means. "They wanted me in dance since I could walk. I started with traditional Irish dances, believe it or not, but gravitated toward ballroom and then tango. I met Logan at another competition, and I kept running into him. We were friends at first, then we decided to partner up. Just friends by the way. Nothing between us."

"Oh, I didn't think ..." I trail off, shaking my head.

"People always wondered, which I guess is a sign of a good partnership. But, no, nothing there."

"You do look great together, though," I say.

"Yeah, but you two look better," she counters, smiling. "And what about you? Fancy lawyer. That's wonderful."

"Just pushy parents." I huff out a laugh, looking through a rack of blue dresses.

"Oh, I get that."

"Work is always hectic. I wanted something fun in my life, so I decided to sign up for dancing."

"Seems like you've been having fun."

"It's been amazing." I might be gushing, but Tara can see through all of it anyway. "How do you feel about leaving?"

"I'm ready," she nods. "Dancing will always be a part of

my life, but my competing and teaching days are behind me. I'm ready to get back to the fun of dancing, too."

She walks me over to a different section of the store.

"Alright, so for San Diego, you're going to want something that feels comfortable, that you can move with. But it needs to be presentable, too. Let's start over here."

"So, what happened in San Diego?"

"Oof. Did he tell you?"

"He said you didn't place."

"We didn't. When you get to be a bigger name in competitions, you're going to be looked at more. The judges are going to focus on you more. Logan had taken up a part time job with a theater, and he really loved it. Silas was going through med school, and I was itching to get back into school, too. And so, we were just losing the love for it. Losing the focus. It's hard, you know? We've been dancing since we were kids. It takes a toll."

"I'm sure."

"So, the judges panned us. Said not-so-nice things about our dancing and our routine. It wasn't fun, but it really hit Logan hard. He never took any of that to heart, but with that one, he really did. He felt like a failure, like he just needed to quit and forget about it."

"That must have been so hard," I say. I think about Logan's decades of dancing, tapering off with a bad competition. Little Logan finding solace in tango, and then losing that comforting feeling years later. That must have been heartbreaking.

"It was. It was a tough time. But we decided to keep teaching part time and slowly move away from it. No more competing, no more workshops. The travel is hard. Competing is hard, too. We were okay with our decision, but ..."

"But?"

"But now here we are, buying dresses." She laughs. It's not unkind, the statement or the laugh. There's almost an underlying joyful tone.

"I seem to have caused a bit of a shakeup."

"Only the best kind." She winks. "Ooh, this one is great." She pulls a dress from a rack and places it on a pile. "Hey, Marta. Can we get fitting rooms started, please?"

Marta gets two fitting rooms set up for us, placing our dresses inside.

Once we've made enough selections—enough being at least ten, according to Tara—we head to the dressing rooms to try everything on.

I opted for more jewel-toned colors, not too many sparkles, and plenty of sway. Tara went with everything bright and glittery.

I step out of the dressing room, hands in front of me like I don't know where to place them. I can't decide if I feel silly, or if I'm just nervous. Could be both.

But then I take a peek in the mirror, and it feels like that first milonga all over again. It feels like that black dress, but ten times better.

It's sleeveless, deep purple, with an open back. Form fitting mesh around the bodice, with a glittery flower design, one that's strategically placed around the chest. The dress drapes loosely around my hips, hitting below my knee, with a slit that goes up to my upper thigh. There's a smaller slit in the back, too, to allow for more leg movement.

This one makes me feel powerful.

Tara gasps behind me, jaw practically to the floor. "This is the one."

She's emerged from her own dressing room where she's tried on a red dress. Flowy and sparkly and bright. It really suits her.

"Yeah?" I ask.

"Oh yes. You look amazing."

"I feel amazing," I admit.

"And that's what it's all about." She grins, standing next to me in the mirror, eyes meeting mine in solidarity, in friendship. I can't help but smile back.

I sneak back into the dressing room and try on another one—one shoulder, rouged, deep wine red with some sparkles. This one has a slit up the back, too.

"Perfection," Tara calls out, now standing next to Marta who is nodding in agreement.

This feels like shopping for prom dresses, giddy and hopeful, with friends cheering you on. This feels like another piece of this new life is sliding into place.

"Take it," she commands. "And this one." She holds up the purple one with flowers triumphantly, "is for San Diego."

Chapter Twenty-Nine

Julieta

When I step into the ballroom, it's the most comfortable I've ever felt. It's the most sure. Logan is talking to the DJ, laughing, casually conversing. He looks so loose, so relaxed—that confidence that he wears so well. Effortlessly cool as always.

But there's something else. Some sort of calm I've noticed creep its way in the last couple of times we've seen each other. He turns and happens to catch my eyes, his widening as he excuses himself and walks over to me.

"Holy shit."

"I went shopping with Tara. How ridiculous do I look?" I step closer to him, hands stretched out to show the dress.

"Uh. You don't." His eyes scan my body, down and back up.

"No?" I run my palms down my dress to smooth the front.

"You look great." He clears his throat. "You look … really, really great."

"Thanks. You, too."

He's wearing a suit this time. Loose pants, tailored jacket. He steps in and gives me a kiss, a soft brushing of our lips, and the nerves want to bubble up to the surface. But he doesn't want to hide anymore, and being here in this beautiful space, with this joyous community, why would I even want to?

Tara walks in shortly after with Silas, greeting those around her. When she spots me, she smiles wide, moving in for a hug.

"Perfection," she declares, in reference to my dress. "Julie, this is Silas."

"Nice to meet you." I offer my hand in a handshake.

"She's a lawyer. Very formal." She winks in my direction.

"This place looks great," Silas offers, looking around at where they've added some extra balloons and a *Good Luck, We'll Miss You* banner.

"Aw, I love it!" Tara admires it gratefully.

Silas reaches down to kiss her hand, and they both excuse themselves to look around and talk to some more guests.

Logan and I find a small table by the stage, settling in. He moves his chair close to mine, draping his arm over my shoulders.

"There are a lot of people here," I say.

"Yeah, this is a great turnout. We invited everybody

from the class, and opened it up to the milonga regulars, too. They wanted to come give Tara a proper send off."

And then the couples flood the floor, the DJ welcoming all the guests, giving a special introduction to Tara, the guest of honor.

"Ready to dance?" He leans in to ask me in my ear.

This time I'm not nervous. I'm excited and eager to dance.

"Always."

And he leads me to the floor.

As we dance this tanda, I get lost in the feel of it. We're in our close embrace, eyes closed, completely succumbing to the music.

These shoes have had such a life, and now they've given me one, too. They've given me him. And I have to believe that even if abuela's not here, even if she can't see this, she approves of this. Of everything I've had the chance to do with her beautiful shoes.

Once I step off the dance floor, walking over to get some water, I spot them, staring back at me wide-eyed. Past me would have hidden behind guilt, but I just feel loved and supported when I see them. Familiar faces in what has become a familiar place.

"Oh my god, you were hiding *this* from us?" Delfina asks.

"He's practically falling at your feet," T says in awe.

"That's just the dancing." I try to wave off.

"Oh no, it isn't," they respond in unison.

"I thought you guys had things to do," I say.

"We lied," Delfi confesses.

"We absolutely lied," T agrees. "You expected us to miss *this*? And look at this fucking dress!"

"It's nice, right?"

"Nice is an understatement," Delfi responds, taking in the beauty of the dress.

Just then Logan walks up to us, waving. "Hey ladies, nice to see you again." He passes me a cup of water. "Thought you could use some."

"Thanks," I say.

They watch this exchange with wide grins, practically bursting at the seams.

"Why are you guys acting like you've never been out in public before? Go dance with somebody."

"I could introduce you to some people?" Logan offers.

"Sounds great." Delfina smiles.

"Oh no. I'm just going to park it right here and keep watching you. I am thoroughly entertained."

"Gavin might be here later," Logan adds, which only results in T scowling. But then her eyes snag on somebody nearby.

"Javier!" she calls out, and gives him a kiss in greeting when he comes over.

"Hola rubia, cómo estás?" He looks over and notices all of us, his eyes lighting up, his smile growing bigger. "En serio? Todos están acá? Qué bueno!"

"Sentáte," I say, offering him a seat.

Tara walks by our table and stops when she sees all of us sitting down, quickly joining in.

"Javier, hi!" she exclaims, then turns to Logan, "This is so great. Thanks for this." She looks over at the rest of the table and introduces herself. "Hi! I'm Tara."

"Oh, were you the partner?" Delfi asks, animated.

"Ah, yes. That's me. End of an era, you know?"

"But a new one is beginning," Javier adds, patting her hand.

I don't miss how everybody looks to me and Logan sitting side by side, his arm around the back of my chair.

"You know, they say tango skipped a generation," Javier says. He might be speaking to the table, but he's looking right at me. "Your grandmother did it, and loved it, but tango bands started to fall off after the fifties. And your parents' generation got into rock and roll instead. But now tango has come back around, and the younger kids are finding joy in it. I love it. It makes me happy to see it. It makes me happy to see you doing it."

"Oh, did your grandmother dance?" Tara asks me.

Now the table turns to look at her, a kind of heavy silence that almost feels hilarious.

"You don't know?" Javier asks. "She doesn't know?"

"Oh, no—" I start.

"Oh, shit," T laughs.

"Don't know what?" She looks around the table, confused.

Logan clears his throat, then says, "Celestina's granddaughter."

"What?" she asks in disbelief.

"Well, all of us, actually. But she's the one that got the shoes," Delfi adds, pointing at me.

Tara looks at me then to everybody at the table, her mouth agape. "Shut the fuck up." And then she starts to cry.

"Oh, no, mi amor." Javier reaches over to hug her.

But then I get up and wrap my arms around to hug her, too. This must be such an overwhelming night for her as it is. Soon enough, everybody at the table joins in for a hug.

"I loved your grandmother so much," she says through sniffles.

"Oh, Tara," I tell her. "We did, too."

And once we part, everybody getting back to dancing, to socializing, Agostina and Delfina stay by my side, looking at me with something that might be pride.

"Wow," Delfi whispers.

"Everybody still loves her. Everybody still talks so highly of her. I can't help but think that she wanted me here, too," I tell them.

"You wanted to create an exciting life for yourself, huh." T smiles. "You fucking did it, Julie."

Watching the crowds, the couples that move on the

dance floor like synchronized magic, and watching Logan walk back to me with his hand out ready to dance, I think I did it, too.

Delfi spends the night dancing with Javier, and a couple of other regulars. T dances once, and Gavin shows up later and just watches. I can't deny that I briefly wonder if Ethan will show up to this thing, but he doesn't. And I spend most of the time on the floor with Logan anyway. He and Tara have one tanda together, and it brings me back to the first time I saw them dance. The magic, the joy. How much I wanted to be her.

The DJ plays the last tanda around two in the morning, and then we wrap everything up. Delfi walks barefoot to her car, carrying shoes in her hand, with T at her side. The jubilation surrounds us, and I'm too happy to feel tired. I gratefully, excitedly, take Logan and my lovestruck heart home.

Everything was such a balancing act growing up, but here nothing needed balance. I wasn't too much of one thing, less than another. I was just me, and I fit into this space so beautifully. There is a seat at the table for me here, and there always will be.

Chapter Thirty

Julieta

THE COFFEE STAIN ON my blouse has somehow gotten bigger since I walked into the office. I never spill my coffee. I'm never without an extra blouse.

I have also learned to manage my time so well that I know the exact time to leave my apartment to avoid any of the early morning downtown traffic. I didn't manage my time this morning, though. I rushed out of my house, a frazzled mess, having spent the night with Logan instead. More specifically, the whole week. More specifically, in my bed.

The problem is, when you're living two lives and toeing the line between them, something is bound to slip.

"Julie. In my office, please." Barbara is at my door, eyeing me over her glasses, perfect posture as always. But this time it looks like she's about to rip me a new asshole.

"I'm sorry I'm late," I tell her. "Rough morning." I point to my obvious coffee stain.

"What's going on with the Lorenzo case?" She cuts me off.

"I'm working on it. Why?"

"Are you?" The question is accusatory. One quick jab to make sure I'm listening. "I have to say, you were always one of my most dedicated employees. I never had to worry about you, but these past couple of months have been concerning. Leaving early, not focused, no urgency in responding to any of my emails. You are not the associate you used to be."

Everything suddenly feels like quicksand. I'm sinking down, my life slipping out of my grasp, and I don't know how to pull myself out of it.

"Barbara, I can assure you I am dedicated to this job." My voice might be shaking.

She slams the file down on her desk and it makes me jump. "There's a request for production here. Did you see that? Did you realize there are thousands of documents to review and the deadline is *tomorrow?*"

I might be breaking out into a sweat-induced panic. *How* did I miss that?

"This Lorenzo case is an absolute disaster and not at all the work of somebody who is dedicated to this job. Or to being here."

I flinch at her words. A lump is forming in my throat. I've never been on the receiving end of her anger like this. I stay uncomfortably silent, a quiet so loud, it's only rivaled by her icy stare.

"*This* is the kind of work you put into this firm? *This* is what you have to show for it? This is *shameful*," she spits out. "So, if you want to still be here come tomorrow, I suggest you figure it out and *fix it*."

Fuck. *Fuck!*

This cannot be happening. The voice in my head starts screaming louder about how I should be focused on work. I could lose my job. I shouldn't be out so late on weekends. I shouldn't be sleeping in and pushing cases aside. I should be responsible.

I should be fucking grateful.

"It won't happen again," I tell Barbara, with as much conviction as I can muster.

I'm abruptly dismissed, and walk out of her office on shaky legs, straight to the employee bathroom where I let the tears run.

Once I've collected myself enough to make it back to my office, I call out, "Larissa, come to my office please."

"Of course." She stands quickly, with a worried look on her face, following me.

Once we're in my office, I shut the door and let it out.

"I fucked up. Like, royally. And I know that I'm an asshole for asking you to help me fix my mistakes. I shouldn't be asking for any of this, but I need you to help me figure this out."

"What do you need?" Larissa asks with no judgement.

"The Lorenzo case," I say. "There's a request for production. And the deadline is tomorrow." I run my hand down my face, frustrated.

"Okay." She nods, writing notes down on a legal pad quickly.

"We have to review so many documents," I say apologetically, pacing in front of my desk. "Thousands."

"Okay," she repeats, wide-eyed. "I can do that."

"Thank you," I answer shakily, taking a deep breath.

If she notices my red rimmed eyes and sniffly nose, she doesn't say anything. She just puts her head down and we get to work.

Larissa and I spend the rest of Thursday working on everything, and then I take the weekend to work some more from morning until night. I tell Logan I'm too busy, I silence my phone, I lock my door.

Now I'm at dinner, practically falling asleep at this table, ready to head to bed.

"Tired?" Cecilia asks.

"Very."

"Sabes quién me llamó?" my mom asks the table, probably about to get into some anecdote about an old friend that called her. "Javier."

Suddenly, I'm wide awake. T and Delfina look my way instantly.

"He said he was so proud of you, Julieta. He was so happy to see you out, and he said he'd never seen you look so happy, either."

Motherfucker. I take a big bite of an empanada.

"He said I must be so proud of you, too, taking after abuela and following in her steps."

The whole table turns to look at me, wide-eyed. But Cecilia's face slowly turns into a smile.

"And so I had to tell him that unfortunately my daughter hadn't told me anything. Guess I didn't deserve to know what was going on."

"Maria," my father says with a sigh.

"She doesn't have to tell you what she's doing," T adds, throwing fuel to the fire as always.

"No, she doesn't. But I don't like lies, either," my mother says, matter of fact.

"Nobody lied, ma," I say, exasperated.

"You just omitted information?"

"What does it matter?" I throw my hands up.

"Javier said he had never seen her look so happy and you completely bypass that to make it about you? En serio?" T says.

"Agostina," Ana says in warning.

"No. Honestly, this is so stupid. Who fucking cares what she's doing? She's a grown adult woman. But since you are all so interested in how she's been deceiving you, at least take a look for yourselves." She pulls out her phone, showing my mother a video she must have taken at the milonga. She watches it with almost no expression, mouth firm.

"Look at your daughter. Look at the joy. And the *tal-*

ent!"

"And what exactly are you going to do with this?" she asks me. She's referring to the dance, as if it should be some tangible good with a purpose. As if the joy of it alone isn't enough.

I guess this is the part where Future Julie has to own up to her mess. "I'm taking a weekend away."

"Dónde?"

"California," I say.

"You think that's a good idea?" she asks.

"I think so."

She shrugs, not saying anything else. But she doesn't have to, I know it by heart. *It's not a good idea. It's a bad one, in fact. You're pushing your responsibilities aside; you're wasting time on frivolous things. You should be grateful for your job. They're going to fire you and then what?*

"Abuela chose dance over her family. And that's what you're doing, too." And with that, she gets up and walks out of the dining room.

The accusation is a low blow, a real punch. It's meant to make me feel guilty and ashamed. It's meant to make me stop whatever I'm doing. And the worst part is that she knows me well enough to know that it would absolutely work.

I can't make the trip to San Diego. It was laughable to even think I could. To dream enough to actually book it.

I can't do any of this anymore.

She's right. My job will fire me and then what? I will have thrown away my years of studying and their sacrifices for my tuition on some dance classes?

I am so defeated. I am so full of guilt. An unbearable weight, a suffocating sadness. I feel like I've got no strength to even get out of this chair right now. The thought of driving home is overwhelming and exhausting.

This feels like everything is quicksand, slowly swallowing me up, surrounding me so I can't move. Naively, I never thought it would get to this. I never imagined it would come to a place where I am not allowed to feel joy. Where I am not allowed to do anything outside of the realm of what was decided for me. Not that law school was decided for me, but a solid career path was. And a focus on studies was always drilled into me.

I never let myself divert from any of it. Thirty four years of following a line, how could I possibly stray from it now?

I am so, so sad.

CHAPTER THIRTY-ONE

Julieta

I DON'T LEAVE WITH leftovers. I leave instead with pity looks from T and Delfi. Surprised looks from everybody else. And then a hug from Cecilia.

"Call me later," she whispers, worried. I nod solemnly, but we both know I probably won't.

I walk out quietly, not saying a word, and I drive to Logan's.

The thing about holding everything in for so long, for the sake of everybody else, is that sooner or later it's all going to come charging out.

"Hey, you okay?" he asks, concerned, when he answers the door.

"Can we talk?"

"Of course." There's a line between his brows.

I walk into his place and luckily Gavin is at work.

"Busy weekend?" he wonders.

"I had a lot of work to catch up on. I fucked up one of my cases." I take a deep breath, wounds still fresh. "I *never* fuck up cases."

He steps closer to me, and brushes a strand of hair from my face. I desperately want to lean into his palm, savor this before I destroy it.

"Were you able to catch up?" he asks.

I don't answer his question, I just keep pushing forward. "I've been spending too much time dancing. I've been too distracted."

"Okay ... should we cut back on some lessons, or ...?"

"I'm not going to San Diego." I come right out and say it.

He just stares for a moment. "What?"

"I can't go to San Diego." My heart is in my throat and I feel like I might choke on it.

"What happened at dinner?" His voice is low and calm, but still waters run deep.

I just shake my head. I want a clean break. I don't want this to get messy, but of course it's going to. It's about to be like the rest of the weekend—a disaster.

"Julie, this is *your* life," he says, reasoning. "You are allowed to live your life."

I stand still, unable to even move. His apartment feels familiar and cozy, and I wish I could allow myself the time to linger.

"Sit down. Let's talk about this. Please," he pleads.

"You don't understand. I can't just drop everything and do this."

"I don't—what is going on right now? What *hap-*

pened?"

"I was going to let you down eventually," I say quietly.

His arms drop to his sides quickly. "Don't fucking do that. Do not do that right now." The anger is starting to come out of him, too. Good.

"I know we had an agreement to do the competition—"

"An agreement?" he asks incredulously. "That's all this was? An *agreement*?" He has sucked all the joy out of his laughter. Instead, it sounds angry and strained.

"What else was this? You're the professional dancer. You can find anybody else you want to partner with."

"*What else was this?* Julie, are you listening to yourself right now? What are you even saying?" His voice is getting louder. "I don't want anybody else to partner with. *You* asked me to do this with you. And now you're going to leave me stranded, after everything I told you about San Diego?"

"I can't be the person you need me to be right now." I'm already drowning in shame and guilt, might as well dump more on top.

"Because you don't want to be."

"That's not true." I shake my head back and forth.

"You're walking away from this. Makes it pretty clear."

"What am I supposed to do? Quit my job and do this?" I throw back at him.

"I never said that, but I see where you stand."

"I can't let go, Logan," I say.

"Of your fancy lawyer job that you hate?"

"Well, that fancy lawyer job that I hate has been around longer than you or all of this!" My retort is full of spite and anger. It's full of blame and sadness, too. "I have pushed *all* my responsibilities aside for this dance, and it has fucked *everything* up."

"Nobody asked you to do that," he says.

"I don't want to play the blame game."

"You walked in here playing the blame game!" he yells. "Why are you doing this?"

"I can't go." I shake my head. I know it's not an answer, but I worry it's the only one I can give.

"Is this about your family?" he presses, seemingly desperate for anything to save this decision. "You're not responsible for their lives, Julie. And I know this might be hard to shake, but you don't owe them anything."

It's another punch to the gut, one I can't worry about tending to right now.

"I can't go," I repeat, but the words have lost their vigor.

"You *can*," he insists.

"*Why* are you pushing this so hard?" Now it's my turn to yell.

He looks broken, like he shouldn't have to tell me why he's pushing so hard. Like I should know because we used to be on the same team. But he answers me anyway. "Because this was saving me, too."

And I don't know how I keep it together.

"I'm so tired." I start to cry. "It's not my job to save you."

"Maybe I thought we were on the same page," he says softly. "I thought this was something we both wanted. I can see now that I was wrong."

I know I've let him down, and I don't think I can stand here much longer. I'm about to walk to the door, but he beats me to it: "Please leave."

And so, I do.

Chapter Thirty-Two

Logan

Maybe San Diego is just fucking cursed.

Maybe I only have myself to blame. For saying yes to private lessons, for saying yes to what she'd asked. For going back to teaching in the first place.

Come tomorrow morning, I'm going to call the dance studio and tell them I'm done. But in the meantime, I send some texts to other contacts. I get everything ready for the next step, because it sure as shit won't be dancing.

This time I'm done.

"Hey, can you talk?" I ask Tara when she picks up the phone.

"Yeah, what's up?" she says on the other line.

"You think San Diego is cursed?"

She huffs out a laugh. "What? What happened?"

"She bailed."

I can hear her sit up on the other line. "Who?"

"Julie, who else?" My anger is starting to show in my voice.

"What do you mean she bailed?" she asks, confused.

"Stop asking so many fucking questions." I don't mean it to come out so harsh, and I can't help but wince after the words are out of my mouth.

"Chill out for a second. I'm trying to figure out what happened."

"Sorry," I mutter. I huff out a breath, exasperated. "It doesn't matter."

"I think it does," she says softly.

I stay silent on the line. I don't know what else to say, not sure why I even called. But with Tara on the other line, I feel less lonely.

"Logan, talk to me," she pleads.

"What do you want me to say? She let the fear eat her up. She let them guilt trip her." I can't keep the bitterness out of my voice. She let them win. She didn't even fight.

"That's hard."

"Is it though? Or could she just ... tell them to fuck off?"

"It's so much easier when you're on the other side of it. When you're not deep in that guilt."

"Yeah, I don't know anything about that."

"You're not mad at me, Logan. I don't need the sarcasm," she warns.

"She said she messed up at work."

"Oh God, I can't imagine how she must be feeling. Like she really fucked it up. Can you imagine how terrible she must be feeling to quit everything?"

"She's an adult. She can make her own decisions." She told me about how she quit so many other things in her life, why did I think this would be any different?

"I think she was definitely trying, but it was years of living like that. People can't change overnight." Tara's words are full of kindness, like they always are.

"Remind me why I called you again."

"Oh sorry, were you looking to commiserate?"

"Guess not." I sigh. "I'm fucking done Tara. I can't do this again."

"I know." Her voice is gentle over the phone. "I'm so sorry about this. I'm sorry this is where you're at."

"I know you are." But I don't want an apology from her.

"Logan," she says slowly. "San Diego is not cursed. I think you look at it as your place of failure. You look at it as the place you fucked up because your heart wasn't in it. But that doesn't make you a failure. It makes you human. And it wasn't our first time there, either. It's like you blocked out how many times we went throughout the years, and how many times we won."

We went almost every year that we were partners.

"It's okay to step away from things, but you seem to be harboring the most guilt about it. Yes, Julie brought something back to you with dance. She livened you up, that's for sure. But that doesn't have anything to do with dance and whether you keep going or not. Even if you don't do San Diego, you've still got her, don't you?"

"I don't know." But I think about her words to me once, how it didn't matter what happened, I would still have her. How she didn't hold up her end of the bargain, and how I expected her to when I should have known better.

"Really?" She doesn't sound convinced. "I'd bet that she's scared and probably overwhelmed. But she's not looking to get rid of you. Give her a minute."

My sigh on the line must echo its annoyance.

"I know I said before I didn't want you to give it up, but maybe that was my own sadness talking. I don't know. I think ... you're allowed to let this go. Not that you need my approval anyway," she adds. "You can let this go. It was an era of your life and now it can be over."

Why have I held onto San Diego so much? I gave the bare minimum when I competed, and I assumed I would scrape by fine. But when I didn't, all it did was confirm that it was time for me to go. And maybe it felt like I was being pushed out.

But I pushed myself out.

"Let me know when you make it to Arizona, okay?"

She exhales loudly on the phone. "I will."

"Thanks, Tara," I mumble, and I can almost feel the smile on the other line. With that, I hang up.

***

"What are you still doing up?" Gavin asks when he gets in late from work and finds me on the couch with a mostly eaten pizza pie. Fuck, how the tables have turned.

"Julie bailed on San Diego."

"Oh, shit," he says, surprised. "You okay?" He drops his keys on the table and undoes his tie. The apartment immediately smells like a fryer, that distinct restaurant smell that somehow gets plastered onto his clothes, embedded in the fibers.

"Not really."

"You ... want to talk about it?" He shuffles closer to the couch.

"Not really."

"Want to watch a new documentary?"

"You know, I always felt like I had let you down. When I didn't even place last year, I thought, Gavin helped me with this. He made sure I could keep taking those classes and I failed him."

He furrows his brows. "Is that what you think?"

"You've always been my biggest fan. I know that. And that's always made fucking up harder with you around. And failing at something I was once so good at? That fucking sucked."

"But you know I was proud of you no matter what," he

reminds me.

"Doesn't make it any easier."

"I guess not," he says, eyes wide.

"I didn't want to face you for a while. Felt like I couldn't."

He nods, letting out a deep breath. "I felt like I was being a shitty brother, traveling so much for work. Never home, never around. Maybe we were both just walking around sidestepping the other."

"Maybe we should try to do better."

"I'm happy I got laid off, honestly. I get to be home more now. That job had turned into a fucking nightmare."

"And the restaurant business isn't a nightmare?" I laugh.

"Fuck, not like that job." He shakes his head. "So, what are you going to do about dancing then?"

"I'm quitting."

He blows a low whistle. "Okay."

"I should have quit it all back then, but I wanted to keep pushing forward. I didn't know if I could let such a big piece of my life go, but now I can." I hate this part of myself right now, full of betrayal and anger, the kind I've seen firsthand in the competitive world.

"What happened?" He slowly sits down next to me on the couch.

"Julie gave up dancing with me, too. Might as well call it quits for good now." That's the ugly, uncomfortable truth.

"I said yes when I should have said no. I threw myself back into dancing for her. And for what?"

Gavin just scratches his jaw, looking contemplative. "Is this about dancing? Because I feel like it hasn't been about dancing for a long time. Probably since the beginning."

"Maybe I just needed a partner." That sounds dismissive enough.

"Yeah. In life." He leans over to grab a cold slice of pizza from the box and takes a large bite. "You needed somebody to be your partner in life."

"And Julie was going to be the answer to that?" I laugh humorlessly.

"I think so."

"Well, she bailed," I say, resentful.

"On San Diego. Not on you." He rolls his eyes like he's just as frustrated with me as I am with everything else.

"Same thing."

"Really?" he asks, disbelieving. "Come on, get your head out of your ass, Logan."

I don't say anything in response. Everybody seems to think she's coming back, and if I hold out hope, I might just get crushed when she leaves me hanging again. Everything between us got too big, everything became too much. Like a bubble that got bigger and bigger until suddenly, it burst.

"Why do I keep getting the blame for this shit? *She* quit on *me*. She let this fucking go." My voice cracks, and my

eyes start to burn. "It was saving *me*, and she dropped it."
There's the truth.

He says nothing, silently watching me. But then he leans over and pulls me in for a hug, instead. A strong hug that feels nostalgic, stirring up memories of when we were kids. He holds me close for a while and I take a deep breath, feeling it center me, delivering a new sense of calm.

"Let's go to bed," he says. And just like last time, "We'll deal with this shit in the morning."

CHAPTER THIRTY-THREE

Julieta

"I stopped."

Larissa gapes at me. Somehow things have been flipped during our lunch hour, and now I'm the one with stories to share.

"Stopped?" she asks, dumbfounded. "Why the hell did you do that?"

The hard thing about letting people into the ins and outs of your life is when you inevitably have to tell them things didn't work out. When you have to tell them you quit, and you failed.

"It was affecting my work. The case. I don't know. Barbara let me have it."

"Fuck Barbara. She sucks." That aggressive crunch of the baby carrot seems somehow apropos here.

My eyes widen at her outburst.

"You know she sucks. It's okay to admit it. Don't think I haven't looked for other places to work."

"What's keeping you here?"

"Honestly, I don't know. The commute is nice. I like

the people I work with." She shrugs.

What's keeping me here?

"You know I messed up the Lorenzo case. I really fucked it up. He was counting on me, and I let him down. I prioritized myself instead of my job. Instead of helping those that need it."

"Both things can be true. Both things can be done. It's just a matter of balance."

"I don't know what that word means," I say tersely.

"It takes practice. I know you know that one," she counters. But her tone is kind and compassionate. Larissa herself is compassionate and warm, friendly and thoughtful. A team player I have been so lucky to have on mine.

"Thank you for helping me last week."

"You told me thank you a million times. It's my job. Thank you for asking for help. That's what I'm here for."

I smile at her response. "It meant a lot."

"Anytime," she beams.

Our lunch hour is over, but I don't want to rush to get back into the office. I just want to enjoy this nice outdoor weather a little bit longer.

"So, how are you and that instructor then?" she asks.

"Not good," I shake my head. That's certainly an understatement. "I royally fucked up that, too."

The only good thing. The *best* thing. And I gave it up because I thought I didn't deserve it.

"My life feels like a bunch of falling dominoes lately," I

lament.

"Well," she says, snacking on her last piece of cheese. "With dominoes, soon enough they'll stop falling, and you can pick them all back up again."

Some days, perpetually optimistic Larissa is just who I need.

Once I drive home, late at night, I fall back into the same routine. Like somehow it knew I would be back, and it didn't let me forget.

I go up the elevator alone and walk into my apartment. I take a shower, slip into pajamas, and bring my case to the table, working quietly.

T barges into my apartment without knocking shortly after, the usual.

"What are you doing?" she demands.

"Working," I state from behind my laptop, not looking up at her. I'm sure I know why she's here.

"Gavin said you bailed on Logan." There it is.

"I swear to God, the way news travels around all of you." I huff in annoyance.

"What the hell are you doing?"

The question, probably meant with good intention, feels like a punch to my very injured heart.

"What everybody always expects me to do."

"What does that even mean?" She throws her hands up like she's tired of my shit, too.

I slam the laptop shut and stand up to walk to her.

"It means that I should have known better than to make any plans or try to change any trajectory of my life. My whole life has been consumed by guilt, dictated by guilt. It's always been about the next person I need to appease."

"You don't need to appease anybody."

"Of course I fucking do," I retort. "Were we not at the same dinner? Did you not listen to the shit I got?"

She just rolls her eyes like that dinner was so minuscule, such an unimportant thing. "What do you want to do?"

"I don't even know! I have no idea what I want to do. Everything has always been about what other people wanted for me."

"You wanted to dance, didn't you? You made that plan by yourself; you went in there alone."

"Did I? Or was I influenced by those shoes? Those fucking shoes." The words spill out of me in a bitter tone, and I hate it. "Shit. You don't even know what that guilt feels like."

"I don't? Really?" She rears back like she's been hurt, and her voice gets louder. "That's a hell of a thing to say. I know guilt, too. I've seen guilt and I've lived it, and you know what I did? I took the other fucking turn. I didn't let that dictate my life. I chose to live my life. This was your choice."

"No, it wasn't." I shake my head, my eyes starting to burn from the tears I'm fighting against.

"Sooner or later, you're going to need to stop playing

the victim and start taking responsibility for your actions. It is all a choice." Her words are delivered with bitterness, too, loud and raw, but she means it.

"You don't understand." I might be pleading, my voice rising in volume to match hers, but who knows for what.

"Don't fucking condescend me, Julie. Talk like that to your work peers if you want to, but don't you dare fucking say that to me. I'm in this family, too. I've lived this life, too. We have seen all these problems firsthand and together. We just chose different ways to handle them. And I'm living. What the *fuck* are you doing?"

The knockout punch.

"You're a bitch," I spit out.

"No, Julie. I'm a realist."

"You're. A. *Bitch!*"

We've reached screaming levels.

"You know what the fuck you want, and you need to go out there and do it. Just *do it*. What the hell is stopping you? Don't answer that because I already know. But do you know the answer? It's you. It is *you*." She points her finger straight at me, aiming for her shot, and hitting.

And then I cry. Loud, angry sobs that would feel cathartic if I wasn't so pissed off.

She exhales sharply, falling onto the couch. "I'm sorry."

"Are you?" I yell through tears, accusatory.

"Yes, I am. I'm sorry, Julie. I love you and I'm just so tired of watching you let life pass you by. I'm so tired of watching you make these stupid decisions that I know are making you miserable, but you're willing to appease your family no matter what it takes. And for what? It's not their life. It's yours."

I crash down on the couch next to her, drawing in my own ragged breath.

"I was so excited when I found out about all this shit you were doing," T says. "When you went to the Alley Cat, when you came out after work. When I found out you were dancing, and you wanted to go to San Diego? I mean ... *Julie*. You were fucking doing it just like she would have wanted."

"You think so?" I ask, still crying.

"*Yes*. Fuck."

"Sorry, sorry." I cross my arms in front of me, making myself smaller as the tears start to slow.

"You're a shit liar and an unconfident lawyer," she teases.

I can't help but laugh, snot in my nose. "You're an asshole."

"I know." She smiles. But she isn't. And she knows that, too.

"I let him down."

"You didn't let him down, Julie. You let yourself down."

And fuck, if she isn't right.

"I just thought maybe it could be as easy as doing one

thing every day that scares me," I explain.

"Yes, but it sounds like you took on several days at once."

I huff out a laugh. "Beginner's mistake, I guess."

"You'll learn," she says, with a smile.

And then I wrap my arms around her in a truce. "Love you, T."

She hugs me back, squeezing. "I know."

Later on, sometime after T leaves and I eat my feelings in the form of an Uncrustable, I grab the empty shoebox that I had stowed away in my closet. I don't know what makes me do it. Maybe I think about putting the shoes back, hiding them away so I don't have to look at my failures. As I grab them, I find another pair of shoes in my closet. The ones I wore as I child when we moved here. White Mary Janes with worn soles and a now rusty buckle. My mother held onto them then gave them to me in a box of my baby things when I bought this place. I think about that confused little girl, that scared girl that was taken out of her comfort zone and brought to a new place. I think about how I loved those shoes and wore them out. About the parallels between those and the ones that were gifted to me. Both of them working as a means to a new life.

There must be some sort of symbolism here with all the shoes I'm hoarding.

I grab the empty shoebox, opening it out of habit, and I come face to face with the card she'd left with them. The simple, but direct instruction written on it: *Para Julieta.*

For me.

The paper is thick cardstock, heavy as I rub it between my fingers, feeling the indent of her handwriting on it. Except as I rub it between my fingers it moves, something that slips and slides. Because this isn't just a piece of cardstock, I realize, but a card, folded over, that must have, in the years it sat in the closet under the shoes, gotten stuck closed. And when I peel it open, I come face to face with more of her writing: *Te mereces la alegría del tango.*

You deserve the joy of dancing.

And it takes everything in me to hold it together. But everything in me is not enough, and still, I fall apart.

There was one other time—one of the last times I saw her, one of the last shows she competed in. I was out of law school by then, working for another law firm, and I left early to go watch her compete. And at the end of it during an open dance, she'd invited me to dance with her. I celebrated her win, danced my heart out with her. The wild abandon I'd searched for buried deep within me and reaching for the light. Reaching for the music, for her hand. She taught me some moves, but I remembered some basics I'd picked up from watching her for so many years.

"No te olvides de esto, Julieta," she was almost pleading. Don't forget about this. "Tango will always be in your heart."

She saw what I feared: that I loved this dance. That I

wanted it to be a part of my life. That I worried about taking the wrong step, upsetting those who made this life possible for me.

How quickly I forgot all of it.

How quickly I continued to keep myself within comfortable parameters.

I gave up my joy for the comfort of others. I can't do it anymore.

Chapter Thirty-Four

Julieta

I WALK INTO MY parents' house without knocking as usual, but it feels strange today. It feels nerve wracking. Who knows what awaits me past the door?

I know my mother's upset with me, but I know, or maybe I hope, I'm still welcome here.

"Hola ma," I say, tentatively.

"Hola." She's sitting at the table sipping mate.

I pull out a chair, slowly taking a seat next to her. This is going to be a hard, but necessary, talk.

There's a box of pastries in the middle of the table from Mariana's, and I pick out a croissant. It gives me something to do with my hands.

"I'm sorry I didn't tell you about what I was doing," I start, looking down at the pastry.

She sips her mate, then pours more water from the thermos, avoiding any eye contact with me.

I breathe in deep, expel everything, and then it hits me: this is an exhausting way to live. This is walking on eggshells, passive aggressive, too much pressure and it's *exhausting.* Maybe this is why I'm so tired.

"You can't wish a better life for us and then resent us for it afterward," I come out and say. "You can't give us a guilt trip about everything that we do. Yes, we have been afforded so many privileges by moving here and being raised here. You wanted better for us, and you got it. We don't forget where we came from, and we don't want to. But we can also acknowledge where we are—in this country, and in this generation that allows us much more freedom than you grew up with. I'm sorry your childhood was hard, and I thank you for the life you gave us."

"I don't need a thank you."

"But it's still nice to hear, isn't it? You gave us everything we could ever need, but we're adults now. I am an adult now. And I will make choices you may not like."

"I know that," she says with a defeated sigh. "Didn't hurt to try, though."

Except it did hurt.

She looks at me, across the table from her. This may be the most intimidating staring contest I've ever been a part of.

"I remember when she bought those shoes," she says, reminiscing. "She always thought I would follow in her footsteps, but I couldn't. I didn't want it. I chose another life for myself—one with your father. And with you and Dario. And this country. I don't regret it one bit, but sometimes I wish things had been different. It was hard.

It was hard for her, too, I know that."

"I'm sorry you feel like she chose dance over family."

She shakes her head as she tells me, "Don't listen to me."

"Your feelings *are* valid, ma."

"I was angry with her as a child, but I know she loved us. We're the ones that moved away. Maybe we chose this country over her." Her eyes are wet with tears, I notice. "Thirty years ago, imagine that. I wanted so much more for the both of you, but could be that I wanted all the time away from her to have been worth it, too."

When we hit a wall with our immigration troubles, falling into traps with scammy lawyers, getting overwhelmed with all the paperwork, my mother felt stuck. Stuck between two places: the country she'd come to build a new life, and the country of her birth. And tied up in the legalities of everything, she didn't really belong to either one, stuck in a heartbreaking limbo. She didn't have a place to call home.

My mother was made to be strong. She was the oldest, too; she fell into that role of being a caretaker for everyone. She was set in survival mode from the beginning and learned to never let anything make her flinch. She jumped into this new adventure, providing for her family, learning a new language, raising her children in a new world. My parents even picked up extra jobs to help pay for our college. They did it all without complaint, without second thought.

But in turn, she raised her daughter to be soft. To not have to deal with the hardships she did. To not have to deal with the roughness of life. To, unfortunately, unknowingly, make her afraid.

"You were so brave," I say in admiration.

"I think there's bravery in what you did, too."

I shake my head. "Not like you."

She places her hand over mine, squeezing it lightly.

"I miss her," I admit.

"Yo también. But seeing you dance in that video was … magic." She smiles softly when she says this, something that looks gentle and kind. "It made me miss her even more, but in a good way. Like she's still here, and she's with you, with us. Like she's cheering you on. She knew what she was doing. She always did."

This feels like support and approval. And maybe I'll never be able to entirely break free from my desire to make my parents proud. But maybe I can reframe what that looks like for me.

"I will always love you. I will always acknowledge everything you did for us. But if you wanted a better life for us, if you want a successful life for me, it starts with letting me make my own decisions free of judgement and guilt. And it starts with letting me be happy. And I'm not happy at my job, ma. I'm really not. This can't be the life you wished for me."

"You're right," she says with a nod.

I rear back in surprise at her response, blinking slowly as I repeat the words in my head. "I'm not going to run off and start competing all over the world," I tell her. "I'm just dancing. I'm dancing socially and I'm having fun and," I pause, "I met someone." Where that stands right now, who knows. But it's out there at least.

Her eyebrow lifts, but there's that smile again. "Bueno," she says. And then, "Te quiero muchísimo, Julieta."

And somehow, it was like all I wanted to hear.

***

MY NERVES HAVE MOSTLY subsided by the time I park my car, but as I walk into the office building, they ramp up again. If I don't fight it hard enough, I could let the nerves win. I could change my mind and not do this and walk out just as disappointed in myself as I've been all week.

But I challenge myself to do the hard thing today. It might feel like an impulse, the kind of decision I'd learned to make within the past couple of months, the one that brought me so many good things, but this one has been secretly brewing for months.

"Good morning, Barbara. Can we talk?"

She looks up at me from her desk. "Sure."

I close the door behind me, the click reverberating throughout these walls. I turn to face her, back straightened, steady, with a deep breath in.

"I am officially handing in my two weeks' notice."

When I leave her office, I hope to feel lighter, but I'm mostly just shaky. The guilt is still a companion, but I'm learning to give it less of my time.

I don't have another job lined up, which is both terrifying and ridiculously unlike me, but who's to say what's unlike me any more anyway?

I walk past Larissa at her desk and knock on her door briefly. "Hey, can we talk in my office for a moment?"

She looks a bit concerned, but stands and follows. "Of course."

Once she's in my office, door closed, I break the news to her, too.

"I put in my notice."

Her jaw goes slack as she stares.

"I just wanted you to hear it from me first."

"Congratulations." She sounds impressed.

"What?" I ask, perplexed.

"You're getting out." Now she sounds almost wistful.

"Yeah, I guess I am."

"I want out, too," she states.

"Larissa." I put my hand up. "I'm not trying to piss off Barbara any more than I already have."

"What did she say?" she asks.

"Nothing, really. She was cordial about it. She thanked me for my time here. I'll have an exit interview soon."

"Alright." She nods. And then walks out of my office, leaving me confused.

When she comes back some time later, she proudly declares, "I'm leaving, too."

"Oh God, no."

"Yes," she says adamantly. "And I'll go where you go, if that's okay. I will work with you and do my best, Julie."

Larissa has been a support in this office from the start, and I feel like an asshole for not giving her any more of my companionship than was necessary. These past months were a slow start to making amends, and maybe it can continue.

I throw my hands out in resignation. "How about we go celebrate tonight then? Drinks on me."

She gasps. "Absolutely."

Larissa and I leave work early enough for once and meet at the restaurant shortly after.

"Oh, The Ivy," she says. "This place is fun."

"My cousin works here. I come here sometimes," I explain, and then I realize I sound too indifferent when in fact, "I like it here, too."

The bar is busy for happy hour, and T and Gavin are working together again.

"Hey, what are you doing here on a weekday?" Delfina is here, too. We find unoccupied stools next to her and squeeze in.

"This is Larissa, my paralegal," I say to the group, and she waves. "These are my cousins Agostina and Delfina."

Manny walks by and kisses my cheek in greeting. And then, because it's as a good a time as any, I blurt out, "We just quit."

The four of them stare at me, speechless.

"And so, we would love some drinks."

They don't move.

"Larissa, what would you like?" I ask.

"Oh!" She sits up straight. "Well, maybe just a glass of red?"

"Great. A glass of red. And I'll do my usual."

"I'm sorry. Did you say you quit?" T asks, wide eyed.

"Yes. Mmhmm. We did." It shockingly doesn't feel as nerve wracking to tell them this. Well, it may be a little stressful, but not like I imagined.

"Like, *your job*?" Delfi asks, stunned.

"Yes, our terrible job!" Larissa chimes in with a joyous voice.

Suddenly T, Manny, and Delfi break out in celebration, dancing and shrieking in place, shouting out all sorts of well-wishes and congratulations, while Gavin gives me a high-five.

"Julieta. I am so proud of you," T says with a big smile on her face.

"One step at a time," I sigh.

"Does the next step involve dancing?" Manny boldly asks.

"Seriously?" I look at T. "Does everybody in here know?"

"There's no guilt like Hispanic mom guilt," Manny mutters, shaking his head.

"That's the truth," T agrees.

Gavin shrugs. "I can't relate."

"Nobody asked you," she retorts, with a scowl.

"This is so great, Julie," Delfi adds, squeezing my arm.

But the question lingering is the one I've been thinking about, too. I clear my throat, then admit, "I didn't cancel the plane tickets."

Delfi might have gasped, but I'm focused on Agostina in front of me. She's listening intently to what I'm saying, probably already planning what her next move will be.

"When do you leave?" she asks.

"Well, it would have been tomorrow at five."

"And when's the competition?"

"Friday night," I answer.

She whips her phone out, typing away.

Manny chimes in, "I'll see if Alexis can take your Friday night."

"I'll take your bar shift," Gavin adds.

"Wait. What are you doing?" I ask.

"I'm so in," Delfi says, practically vibrating from the excitement.

"What?" I look around, confused. There's a whirlwind of plans being made around me, and I feel like the eye of the hurricane, surprisingly calm, the chaos swirling around me.

"We're going," T answers quickly. "Larissa, you want in?"

I start to protest, like I've even got it in me anymore, but T stops me.

"No. *No.* I don't want to hear a thing from you. We are going. We're going to support you because that's how this works and that's what you need." She lifts her phone. "Besides, I got a great deal, so yeah, we're going."

I soften at that, but reality quickly hits. "Wait a second. I haven't even talked to Logan yet. He could very well tell me to fuck off. Or he could have found my replacement by now."

"So, go talk to him," she says casually, like we didn't just make some flight plans involving him *without* him.

"Now?" I ask, my voice high-pitched.

Trevor appears from the kitchen, dropping off plates of food, and when he notices all of us, he comes to say hi.

I almost miss Larissa's double-take, but I don't miss the smile and the soft-spoken "Hi."

"I'll give you his number later," T winks. "Julie, get your head out of your ass and go talk to him."

"No better time than the present." Manny shrugs.

"You can do this, Julie," Larissa adds, cheering me on.

"Go get my brother, I guess," Gavin says with a smirk.

And with that, a bar full of friends new and old, my bold, loving cousins, and a newfound sense of self, I grab my bag and run out to my car, headed straight to Logan.

I think grief pushes on the accelerator. Makes you move quicker. Makes you realize that life is short, that it is fragile, and what are you even doing if you're not enjoying it?

Grief pushes on that accelerator. But, I very quickly realize, so does love.

Chapter Thirty-Five

Logan

WHEN I HEAR THE knock on the door, I run over to grab it. But standing in front of me is Julie, and that is unexpected. I catch her bouncy haircut, her sad eyes. She's wearing a dress again, something that looks so soft, so Julie.

She's *here*.

"I thought you were the pizza guy," I manage to say.

"Oh." Her face falls. "Shit."

But fuck, I want to blurt out. *I'm so happy that it's not.* I almost tumble into her with relief and scoop her into my arms.

"Did you see the pizza guy?" *I don't even care.*

"Um. No, no, I haven't seen the pizza guy. And I've been sitting in my car for a minute. So ..." She turns to face the parking lot, like she's ready to leave, but I don't want her to go.

"How long have you been here?"

"I don't know. I ran out of The Ivy, probably ran some red lights to get here. Wild streak, I guess," she adds jokingly but it falls flat.

"Why?" My voice is below a whisper.

She swallows before she answers, "Because I fucked up."

My throat is dry even as I clear it, not saying anything in response.

"Because I let everybody else dictate all of this between us, and I shouldn't have. I made this decision myself from the beginning, and I should have followed through. I shouldn't have abandoned it. I shouldn't have abandoned you."

"And what's supposed to happen now?" I lean against my doorframe. My feelings are back and forth at worst, upset and hurt and so happy to see her.

"I didn't cancel the plane tickets," she says quietly. It sounds more like a question than anything else. It sounds like a plea. And it takes me by surprise.

"And I know that it's unfair to ask you to brush everything off and hop on a plane with me like nothing happened. You didn't deserve for me to let some outside events make decisions for me, or for us," she says with such emotion that it sounds deeply remorseful. It sounds like her heart is cracking as we talk. I don't think I can handle it. "It won't happen again." She shakes her head adamantly.

"You don't know that," I tell her.

For a minute, she just stares back, maybe unsure of what to say. I shouldn't feel like an asshole right now, and yet, I do. I don't know what to do with all these mixed feelings. A jumble of nerves running through my body, a racing heartbeat working overtime.

"You're right, I don't." And with that, she takes a deep breath and starts to cry.

"What do you want, Julie?" I ask her softly. My own heart is cracking, too, quietly begging *please say me* as it tries to stop itself from crumbling.

"I can't do this without you. I don't *want* to do any of this without you. I never did. Ever."

I stay quiet, but inside, I feel like I'm drowning. I desperately want to hold her.

"This saved me, too," she says then. And I melt a little bit more, reaching over to brush a tear away. She leans into my palm, her wide eyes watching me, and I can't keep this up any longer. I can't act like I wasn't the happiest to see her when I opened my door.

"'These shoes have brought me here," she says, her hand tentatively reaching up to hold mine. It feels so good to touch her, to be touched in return. "They carried me from the start, that very first step I took into the dance studio and now to here. They brought me back home. And I'll be damned if I don't get to dance with you in San Diego."

There was never a doubt in my mind that she wasn't strong and passionate, deeply caring of everybody around her. But it's a different thing when it's aimed toward you.

"You are my home," she says, standing in front of me,

vulnerable and honest. "And I'm not doing this without you. I have loved every second of dancing with you, Logan. This was never just some agreement and I'm sorry I ever said that. This was always you and me. The best thing."

The best thing.

And that's the final blow to my hardened shell. My heart jumps into my throat as I move my hand from her cheek and offer it to her, palm up, a silent plea for her to take it. For her to dance. She looks at it in surprise, then places her hand in mine.

We fall into step together, like we've been doing this for all our lives. Temple to temple, chest to chest. My arm around her back, her hand at my shoulder. Like maybe in some other lifetime we were partners, too. Like Celestina is here, smiling as she says, *"Guess what, Logan? I found you a partner."*

"Logan," she says, almost like a question, but I just keep dancing with her. How much I missed this even if it's only been days.

An ocho, a giro, everything familiar. A close embrace, eyes closed. She's right, this feels so much like home it hurts.

What am I doing, thinking I could give this up? Thinking I could walk away from the community, from the craft, from this one thing that has been part of my life for so many years? And I can't do this without her either.

"I love this dance," I whisper, opening my eyes to look

at her. She looks at me, too. Suddenly, the feeling is a bright burst of light, something so clear it's inescapable. "And I love you."

She gasps, a soft intake of breath, before she smiles through her tears and whispers, "I love you, too."

That does me in. My hand cradles her jaw, holding her like she's the most special thing, and I kiss her.

"I think I fell in love with you when you ran into me," I tell her. "You were looking for a way out, and you ran right into my chest, like you kick-started my heart."

I don't let her say anything else, I just kiss her and kiss her until I can't breathe. Long, lingering, passionate kisses at my door. I hold her, and I touch her, and I smile. I missed her soft skin, her smile, the way my hand molds to hers perfectly. Her perfume, and her voice, and the way she makes me feel.

"Whatever happens after this, I still have you?" My heart is in my throat, my hope is hanging on for life.

"Yes, a million times yes."

I lean my forehead against hers. "Whatever happens, we're a team."

"I know," she nods.

"You came back," I say as I hold her close, feeling her heartbeat against me.

Her eyes soften at that, maybe a touch of sadness lingering, as she whispers, "I never left. I promise you I never left." I know what she means by it, what everybody else clearly saw. She just needed a minute to come back.

"I love you," I say with a smile, with all the newfound joy radiating from me. "Let's go win you a competition."

Chapter Thirty-Six
Julieta

"Nervous?"

"Oh, I'm a mess." I chuckle. "Are you?"

"Nah." He shakes his head. "You're going to do great."

We're in the hotel room, warming up and getting ready. The doors open at six thirty, and the ProAm portion starts a little after seven. There's a soft knock on the door and when we open it, Tara walks in.

"Tara?" I ask, shocked.

"Hi!"

"What are you doing here?"

"I wouldn't miss this. Are you kidding? Besides, I'm here to help." She sits down next to me, throwing her carry-on on the bed.

"How was your flight?" Logan asks.

"Not bad! Arizona isn't too far." She smiles.

"Tara," I repeat, elated. "This is such a nice surprise."

She reaches over to hug me. "I'm going to do your hair and makeup, okay?"

I look to Logan then back to her. "Are you sure?"

"Julie. I got on a plane to come here." She laughs. "Yes, I promise I'm sure. This is what I'm here for. I'm going to make you look amazing." She smiles like she thrives in this environment. She's used to it, of course, but maybe she's living through us this time around.

"I'm going to go walk around downstairs for a bit," Logan says, then gives me a kiss on the forehead.

"Okay," I oblige, and I let go and let her take over.

Once it's time, I take one longer look in the mirror. Deep purple dress with a high slit, glittery flowers. Lush, red lips, my hair pulled back into some sort of intricate low bun that Tara styled. And the shoes. I can't *not* feel powerful like this.

"Ready?" Logan calls out as he walks back into the room. He's dressed in a suit. Fitted jacket, loose pants, the definition of handsome. But when he sees me, he stops short.

"How did I do?" I ask shyly.

"You look incredible." His eyes roam across every inch of my body, from my feet to my exposed thigh, up to my face and my hair. He comes closer, holding my face in his hands, kissing my cheek lightly.

"Thank you for doing this with me," I whisper, spilling my immense gratitude for this into my words.

He just smiles, as he says, "I'm so proud of you."

I wasn't expecting that. I wasn't expecting to feel any more elated, now I wonder if I might possibly burst.

"You can't say these things to me before we have to go on stage and dance."

He just laughs, kissing me on the cheek again, and below my ear, and along my jaw.

"Oh, I brought you a snack." He holds out a bag of mixed nuts. "I'm sure you haven't eaten, and you need something."

I just sigh in gratitude as I take the bag from him.

"Vamos a bailar." He winks, linking his hand with mine as he leads me downstairs to the ballroom.

It's the most magical thing I could have imagined. And I'm in it. I was worried it would be overwhelming, or intimidating, but in this ProAm part of it, everybody has been welcoming and kind.

This feels like being eight all over again, except this time I'm on the other side of it. And I'm with Logan, too.

"Maybe afterward, we can go celebrate," he whispers.

"Oh?" My eyebrows lift.

"You and me. Somewhere quiet, somewhere nice. Relaxing."

"Sounds like you're describing my bed." I smirk.

"Maybe I am," he waggles his eyebrows and I laugh in response. He leans in to kiss me, out in the open, and this feels even more freeing than the dance has. This feels even more comfortable, even more familiar, even more like home.

We find Tara, Delfi, and T sitting at a table, waving

excitedly, blowing kisses, taking pictures on their phones.

What started as a secret, something I found joy in behind everybody's back, has become something to be shared. Joy that could no longer be contained, that found an outlet and support in everybody here right now.

In showing up for myself, they showed up for me, too, and that has been the best gift.

The announcers speak into the microphone, introducing the ProAm singles dance.

This is it.

I faintly hear the applause, the loud cheers from the friend table, because it's drowned out by my own nerves. But then, a wave of calm. Like whatever happens after this, it doesn't matter, because I've already won.

I squeeze Logan's hand, moving in close to him. "I can't believe I get to be here with you," I say, a repeat of his words, and his gaze meets mine like he feels it too.

"From Florida, Number 110, Julieta Martí and Logan Beck," the announcer calls out.

And as we walk out to the floor, I feel my grandmother with me for the first time. I feel her presence, a solid weight right beside me, like my very own approval.

We're out on the floor with seven other couples, each of us spaced out enough to allow room for dancing. Logan gives me one quick smile, that small one that I've claimed as mine, and then the music begins.

Walking to Logan, ready to dance in these shoes, to this

beautiful music: this is exactly where I was meant to be. This is somebody and something that was meant just for me.

His arm comes around me to settle in the middle of my back. Mine finds a place around his shoulders. Our palms meet, and he squeezes my hand just once, like a reminder that he's here. That it's just us.

And then we start to dance.

***

THE AWARDS ARE LUCKILY handed out right after the dancing portion, moving the night along. Logan and I are standing on the stage with the other couples, awaiting news for first, second, and third place.

Third place goes to a couple from Texas, and they rush to grab their trophy, joyously cheering along the way.

"Second place goes to Number 110 from Florida, Julieta Martí and Logan Beck."

There is polite applause, and then there's our table, which has erupted in cheers. When I turn to look at Logan with wide eyes, he looks back in shock, and elation.

Second place. *Second place!*

We walk up to claim our trophy, and congratulate the other winners, too. When we walk off the stage, Logan wraps his arm around my waist, bringing me in for a tight hug, lifting me off the floor.

"You fucking did it!" His smile is the biggest I've ever seen, but mine must be mirroring it. One huge grin from ear to ear. My heart's racing from what we did, from everything we've done, this wild journey from the beginning.

"That was amazing," I gush.

"That *was* amazing," I hear Tara say.

Agostina and Delfi come in for a big hug, too, squeezing me so tight. "We are so proud of you!"

"Ready for the next one?" Tara asks with a smirk.

"Oh, I think I got it out of my system."

Logan laughs loudly, those eyes crinkling at the corners again. "So, this was it?"

"This was perfect." I kiss him because I can't help it, because I want to. "Thank you for this."

"Thank *you*," he says. And he kisses me back, proudly, passionately, in front of everybody.

The very last time I saw my grandmother was on a family trip to Buenos Aires. I got to watch her dance there, and I felt so close and attuned to my culture and my family. I felt so understood, so complete. And I hadn't felt that since. Not until Logan blindfolded me, and everything shifted. Before that everything had been, maybe naively, just something to do. Just something on a list, just a way to use the shoes. But that night it became bigger than everything else. It became bigger than me. The ghosts of everything before me led me to that very moment. They converged to build inside of me, overwhelming and terrifying.

And liberating.

It was like limbs that had fallen asleep, but bit by bit woke up. The tingling feeling sparkled throughout my body, bringing everything back to life. And I look around now and wonder, so fervently, how I ever could have slept through all this.

Those shoes, dropped on my lap, carried me to the studio, to the milonga, to Logan. To here.

My grandmother always said tango gave her the love of her life, but it seems for me, it gave me everything.

Julieta, One Year Later

When you spend enough time in Buenos Aires, your schedule gets tossed upside down.

Like how it's ten thirty at night and we're just now headed to dinner because that's when our reservation is. They didn't open until eight thirty, anyway.

Like how we spent some time having a siesta in the hotel because that's what everybody does, and frankly it's the only way to make it through the night.

We're headed to Bar Sur, a small tango bar that hosts dinner shows nightly. A place my grandparents visited maybe a handful of times.

We were looking for something quieter, something more intimate. As he guides me down the cobblestone streets of the more historical parts of Buenos Aires, we hold hands, and I walk at his side happily, reminding myself that this is indeed my life.

After we went to San Diego and placed second—the most thrilling surprise—we spent a couple more days there, riding that high. We visited touristy attractions, and reveled in delicious food and the glorious sun.

Once we got back home, I got to work applying for new jobs—something that I thought would be both terrifying and daunting, but soon after found a great match at a boutique firm. I even got to bring Larissa with me, making for an almost seamless move. I learned what work-life balance really looked like, and I spent it in an office that appreciated me.

After San Diego, Logan decided to work as a choreographer with a local dance program. He couldn't give up dancing entirely, just step back from it a little. Crawl up from the depths of it where he had become too entwined. And we still dance socially at milongas, basking in the warmth of the community there. That I could never give up. I love it too much, too.

He decided to move into my place about six months ago, leaving Gavin to his own space. We spent the past year enjoying each other. Doing new things together just for fun, just for the hell of it. There were some weekend trips, plus one week long adventure where I got to use my beloved paid time off. We spent mornings sleeping in, lazy Sundays sipping coffee, wrapped around each other.

Logan opens the door for me now, letting me walk into the bar. This place is romantic, really intimate and charming. Sure, it's full of tourists, but still, it's nostalgic.

The tango show at Bar Sur is dazzling as the dancers move across the checkered floor to the sounds of the live band. Our small table is lit by candlelight, and I'm enthralled watching the show. I catch Logan watching me from the corner of my eye, and I reach out to squeeze his hand.

"Watch the show," I whisper, but he just smiles.

Once we leave, stumbling out into the street, we walk slowly down the sidewalk. Every so often he stops to kiss me, smiling as he does.

"I love you," he says, hand cupping my face. "I never want to let you go, you know that, right?"

And then he gets down on one knee.

"What are you doing?" I ask, wide-eyed.

"What do you think?"

"Here?" I might be panicking.

"No better place, I think," he grins.

His smile is the same loving one I've always seen on him, but his hands are shaking as he pulls something out of his pocket. Mine shake too, as I reach over to hold his, suddenly bursting with joy and laughter and happy tears.

"You changed my life," he says softly, his own eyes shining back at me. "You gave me back hope, and this dance, and a happiness I never thought I'd feel again."

"You changed my life, too," I say, shakily.

"Want to be my partner forever?" he whispers, small smile tucked into the corner of his mouth.

There's no answer but yes. I nod quickly, frantically, as I pull him up to kiss him. This has been the best year, a whirlwind that started when those shoes were placed on my lap. When my grandmother gave me the smallest little push and it lead me back home.

The night sky is covered in stars, and one is brighter than the rest, twinkling. Like my grandmother is winking down at us, mischievously. And lovingly.

Tomorrow morning T and Delfi fly in, joining us to spend some time in our beautiful country. But for now, for tonight, it's just us.

"You and me," I say, in between kisses, smiling so much it hurts. "The best thing."

Acknowledgements

This book required a lot of research and conversations and I am so grateful and thankful to have people in my life who were willing and happy to help. Very, very heartfelt THANK YOUs go out to:

Cecilia (my own cousin!) and Adjani who kindly chatted with me and shared stories about their childhoods and their upbringing.

Jeremias Fors of the Miami Tango Show, who graciously took time out of his busy schedule to talk with me about tango culture and dance. If you ever have the chance to see one of their shows, please go!

Brian (Esquire), who enthusiastically answered all of my lawyer-related questions and taught me the term "appellate briefs." Can't guarantee I won't text you if I get sued, though.

Kelsey Painter (fellow indie author and ProAm dancer!), who kindly answered all of my random questions about ProAm competitions and ballroom dance.

Friends who excitedly read my drafts, love them even

if they're garbage, and are the best cheerleaders: Nicole, Stefani, Sara, Jane, Brian, Nick, Jackie, Megan, and Jenn. And anybody else I'm forgetting!

To family who give me so much love and support.

Kristen and Kelsey, who kindly and generously took time to beta read and give me such wonderful feedback.

Allie Samberts for editing and guiding me to help make this book the best it could be.

Lucy for being a delight to work with and again making the cover of my dreams.

To the romance book community and indie author community, those who have let me squeeze in. Who have commiserated and shown support, always up for answering questions and willing to chat. To indie bookstores championing and making space for indie authors. You are amazing.

To YOU, reader, for picking up this book. Thank you for taking a chance on my words. It means so much!

And most importantly, always, Brad (and the kids!), for tolerating my time behind a laptop and loving me anyway. For the long hours, nights, days, etc. I know it sucks sometimes, but I'm so grateful for it.

About the author

Natalia Williams writes contemporary romance featuring characters in their thirties and all their emotional baggage. Born in Argentina, now residing in Florida, she spent over a decade in the culinary field, but now spends her days wrangling kids and writing love stories. She loves a good cheeseburger, dogs, and has a freezer full of ice cream.

Find her on Instagram @nw.writes